# WHAT OTHERS ARE SAYING

The plot, characters, and landscape of this story related closely to the historical time when Ireland was indeed made up of different kingdoms. The settings of the forest, the hills, and the open moorland are well described, and the contrast of darkness and light representing good and evil infuses the atmosphere of the countryside, fortresses and villages.

Through the tone of the novel and its changing scenarios, the book's short sentences which are very clear and direct, the longer ones carefully constructed to give a sense of continuity, I wondered what was going to happen next as the novel progressed.

The themes of the story fuse together the culture of a nation divided with the struggle for power and control, protectionism, contradictions of belief within families, villages and kingdoms. These *themes* of hate and love, despair and hope, trust and mistrust, courage and cowardice, good and evil are very distinctive as binary opposites to shape this novel, as the direction of the main plot and sub-plots progress and integrate.

The variety of characters from villains, kings, princes, princesses (mother and daughter) servants, holy men (contrast of monks and Druids), foreign invaders like the crusaders, military personnel of all ranks became real as each one was introduced into the story. Their feelings, actions and words fused together to make them believable within their station - royalty or service, rich or poor and what behaviours were expected of them. The drama of choice and the making of wise decisions is evident throughout. A thoroughly engrossing read.

**June Meyer, Retired professor from the University College of the Fraser Valley BC in the field of Early Childhood Education**

This sequel, "Beyond Evansing", focuses on the trust & solidarity between Evansing and its allied kingdoms as well as on the endeavor of Edwin in developing right relationships with those in his life. Magic, dreams, illusion and visions are infused into this epic adventure towards a royal united and proud Ireland. The sacred, passionate bond in lifelong intimate marriage is pronounced between Edwin & Greer expanding them as best and trusted friends into intimate expressive lovers. What a dazzling prince and princess they've become! Edwin has ultimate trust and solidarity with Joan of Arc, especially after her proclamation that Evansing must resume its divinely ordained mission of uniting Ireland. Edwin and King Erith must be sensitive and strategic in every consultation with allied kingdoms in order for this mission to be accomplished. Edwin's inner strength and wisdom temper the gallant warrior within him as he shows his assertive skills and abilities in convincing others that there is more to come and to live lives that count. Belief in their noble cause makes it feel right!!! What a captivating book filled with redeeming right relationships of honor, courage & character. I was drawn again into a universe rich with wonder, genius wisdom, devoted faith and hearts full of hope. Boldness and righteous authority fuel the "noblest pursuit". A fine read!!!!!!

**Arnie Chamberlain, Chaplain, Carewest**.

"The quest continues! I was very happy to read the sequel, Beyond Evansing. I loved the first book and this one did not disappoint either! Glen picked up where the first book left off and carefully weaved a masterful story with twists and turns that kept me glued to the pages again! The only thing left to do now is to make it into a movie!"

**Russ Dantu, Professional Speaker**

Glen Klassen has finally broken the suspense he has kept his readers in for almost four years! The sequel to his fiction novel, Evansing – Heart of the Irish Kingdom has been released! His tale of the quest for a united Irish kingdom continues in this second episode, Beyond Evansing – Courage of the Irish Kingdom.

Glen spares no time in getting us underway again on the mission for which King Erith first brought Edwin to Evansing. True to the form of his first book in this series, he steers us through many twists and turns, incorporating the relationship between the physical and spiritual realms, the battle of good versus evil, and the elation of victory intertwined with seeming defeat. The courage of Edwin continues to grow amidst warfare, kidnappings, spiritual battles, time travel and heartbreak. He also continues to grow in wisdom and discernment as a true Crown Prince of the kingdom. Glen has a unique way of using imagery and conversation to bring out demonstrable truths, both relational and spiritual, to help cement a higher road for all of us to ponder.

This sequel will not disappoint the reader who was captured and has been held spell bound after experiencing the first adventures of Edwin, Greer, King Erith and Percival in 11th Century Ireland through the pages of Evansing – Heart of the Irish Kingdom.

**Ruth Yesmaniski, Author, Editor, Book Shepherd**

# BEYOND EVANSING

## COURAGE OF THE IRISH KINGDOM

Glen Klassen

Beyond Evansing  -  Courage of the Irish Kingdom

By Glen Klassen
www.gleneklassen.com

Published by Evansing Publishing
Copyright © 2017 by Glen Klassen
All rights reserved.

Printed in Canada
ISBN: 978-0-9948740-1-6

# Dedication

This book is dedicated to

Noah, Josephine, Bennett and Nathan,

my four delightful and highly valued grandchildren

# Prologue

Previously, in *Evansing – Heart of the Irish Kingdom* (the first book of this series), the story unfolded in the 11th century quest for Irish unity that moved a young man from meager beginnings to becoming a Crown Prince. The Quest required the hero's personal transformation as he collaborated with the supernormal in war and statesmanship. The tale involved extraordinary interventions to facilitate assassinations, rescues, winning battles and successful diplomacy. Romance was not failing in this novel as our hero was introduced to what true love is through meeting and eventually marrying the King's daughter.

The adventure was primarily driven by four main characters with the hero Edwin, playing the leading role. The plot involved developing an effective and mutually agreeable plan of bringing together the numerous small Irish kingdoms into one united Ireland. Extensive dialogue filled with inspirational life lessons and wisdom about leadership, relationships and personal wholeness rounded out the enticing story which now resumes.

# Chapter 1

Two years have passed since the Quest for uniting Ireland had come to a distressing halt. Erith, the King of Evansing did his best to stay in good spirits. He worked diligently at strengthening the gains made by working closely with the Kingdoms of Aldred, Tara, Dagarath and Randar. Prince Edwin and his wife, Princess Greer, played vital roles in building and maintaining those relationships. Progress had been made, but not as much as had been hoped for. There had been no indication the Quest was about to resume, until one night, Joan of Arc reappeared in a dream to Edwin. In the dream Joan communicated the time of resuming the Quest had arrived.

Edwin woke with a start. He considered what Joan had announced. Mulling over the dream, he wondered if it was simply his wishful thinking. Then Joan appeared in his bedchamber in full armor riding a war horse. She glared at him with a fierce look and disappeared. Now he knew the time to recommence the Quest had come.

He was too excited to sleep and lay in bed pondering all the implications of resuming the Quest. He acknowledged that it would not be easy to shift back into that gear. A certain comfort level had been attained with just managing things as they were. Other than the occasional skirmish with the Kingdom of Nerland, now the lackey of Merethath, there had been a state of peace. This proved to be quite enjoyable and a source of prosperity for Evansing and her allies. Greer enjoyed having her husband by her side and being able to accompany him on visits to their allies. She would be disappointed, to say the least, at discovering this would change.

In the morning, Edwin tenderly gazed at his wife rousing out of her sleep. She reached for her husband and held him close, feeling rather amorous. Edwin normally of course would have been delighted at this initiation by his wife. However, this morning his mind and emotions were caught up with the Quest and he found it impossible to shift into something light and delightful like making love. He gently disengaged to the chagrin of his mate.

"Greer, I need to talk to you about something very important."

"What can be so important as to spoil our fun?"

"The Quest. Joan of Arc appeared to me in a dream and showed up in our bedchamber in full military array with her war horse. That tells me it's very important."

"You are saying she showed up unannounced? In our bedchamber?"

"Yes, with her horse."

"Isn't that a lack of protocol? It doesn't seem proper for her to do that, no matter how important her message."

"Perhaps, but she doesn't do this on her own. I felt uncertain as to whether the dream truly meant I was to resume the Quest or was it my wishful thinking. Then she showed up in our bedchamber. That left no doubt and it means it's time to get on the move."

"I don't want you to go to war again. I like our life just the way it is."

"I like our life too, but it's not what we were created for." "Edwin, I don't know if I can do that, keeping a brave face and not worrying when you go to war. I don't know what I would do if you died."

"His Grace will keep us both strong and able to handle whatever we must face. Remember your original determination to not worry about what would happen to me. We both are committed to living lives that transcend merely being concerned with everyday comforts and desires. We want to live lives that count for generations yet to come. I know you will be the courageous Princess you are. Now I need to go see Erith and let him know what has happened. I'm sure he will be excited to get started."

"This may be just what he needs to get into a happier way of being. He certainly hasn't been very cheerful the past few months. He looks like he's lacking purpose and finding it hard to maintain the present routine. His personality requires something more."

"More has come. I will see you later."

# Chapter 2

"**S**ire, Edwin wishes to meet with you."

"So early? It must be urgent. Send him in."

"Good morning, Sire. I have a pressing matter to discuss with you. The time has come to resume the Quest." Edwin then went on to relate his encounters with Joan of Arc.

When he finished Erith looked quizzically, not quite certain how to respond.

After a moment of silence, he replied, "Previously I would have been ecstatic at this news. Now I find myself more concerned about all the costs and losses associated with it. Yet I have been less than happy with not pursuing it. There you have it. A conundrum, I am neither glad about resuming it nor am I happy about not resuming it. What a wretched place to be."

Edwin was tempted to speak but then stopped himself to see what Erith would say next.

After several moments of silence, Erith looked up at Edwin and said, "Well, what do you say to that?"

"It is not an option. It is a command."

"Yes, you are correct about that. Knowing it isn't simply my decision helps me to deal with the costs and losses that are part of this call. First thing we must do is call a meeting of the Evansing Council in order to get the members aware of what has transpired. At the same time we will need to discuss how to resolve Nerland. That will be the first order of business for the resumption of the Quest. Then we will want to establish a plan on how to approach our allies with the news and our initial intentions concerning Nerland."

The next morning the members of the Evansing Council were buzzing with curiosity as to the reason for calling the meeting on such short notice.

Erith called the meeting to order.

"Fellow council members, this meeting is to advise you that the time has come to resume the Quest to unite Ireland into one glorious Kingdom. It will require stout hearts and a need to order our affairs accordingly. This is a divinely ordained mission intended to create a flourishing Irish society for many generations to come. A noble pursuit, of which we can all be proud."

The next several hours were spent hammering out the stratagem to restore Nerland to the fold of allies. The Council decided that plans for attacking Merethath would be determined after Nerland had been fully secured. After a short break, the meeting resumed to determine how the news and Nerland plan should be shared with its allies. The biggest hindrance would be the same as what Evansing had to face, namely, contentment with the status quo.

An evaluation of each ally was done as follows:

Tara - King Clarendon is still considered an ally but certainly not a strong one. He seems to be much influenced by how he feels at any particular moment. A key would be to try and get a sense for where he is presently. What would be better is to discover the source of his mercurial temperament and remove it once and for all. Edwin and Percival are to search for a solution.

Dagarath – King Jillian has increasingly warmed up to the possibilities of his kingdom benefiting from a united Ireland. At this early stage Dagarath would enjoy status as part of the initial insider group with Evansing. It may be fairly easy to prod them into action. Edwin accompanied by his good friend and fellow officer, Eamon, are to pay them a visit.

Aldred – King Barris of course is closely aligned to the interests of Evansing. His daughter Chandra is married to King Erith's nephew, Carson. As well, Barris increasingly sees the advantages of resuming the Quest as a means of expanding his kingdom's influence throughout Ireland. This was both gratifying and troubling to Erith. He did not know if Barris is maintaining a noble ambition for the good of all Ireland. Or is it now tainted with selfishness? He would personally visit Barris and reiterate the true objective of the Quest.

Randar – King Chafen had recently expressed that for him to participate in any future Quest ventures he must receive substantial compensation. This came as a complete surprise as previously he appeared to be very compliant to the wishes of Evansing. To comply with his request would create a dangerous precedent. It would make Randar more of a mercenary than an ally. The Council postponed further discussion on how to deal with Randar.

Obstacles needed to be overcome with their own allies before proceeding any further. This did not faze Erith. He knew anything great could not be accomplished without opposition. He and his fellow Council members would together see these obstacles removed. Once again a coherent alliance would be formed to continue the Quest.

# Chapter 3

"Percival, I have an idea on how to discover what makes Clarendon so susceptible to swings in his support of the Quest," said Edwin.

"What is it?"

"Why don't we simply ask him?"

"You aren't serious?"

"Yes, I am serious. We have tried befriending, cajoling and persuading him to be our ally. As well, Greer has spent time mentoring and befriending his daughter Kendy. You've indicated that going into his dreams like you did with Carson is not an option. Please explain again to me why you can't."

"It has all to do with authority. I had authority from Erith to intervene in the dreams of Carson. Erith does not have adequate authority over Clarendon."

Edwin replied, "Therefore we now have the duty to get Clarendon solidly in line with the Quest. We cannot afford to have a wobbly ally. Either he is totally for us or else firmer measures need to be taken."

"What you are proposing is serious. It could backfire and cause us the loss of a valued ally."

"I appreciate the risk. However we can't afford to have an uncommitted ally. I would prefer to go to war against Clarendon than find out he won't support us when we need him."

"Let's go and share this with Erith."

As the two men walked to see the King, Percival reflected on how mature Edwin had become during the past two years. Edwin had developed a tremendous inner strength and wisdom. This gave him the confidence to hold his own with Percival.

The King was available and they were ushered into his presence.

"Welcome, Percival. Welcome, Edwin. What would you like to discuss?"

Edwin replied, "I have considered our problem with Clarendon and have decided it is imperative for the long-term success of the Quest to ensure his absolute loyalty. Even to the point of going to war if necessary. Pain now will spare us much pain later."

Silence.

After several moments the King answered, "That, as you know, is a very extreme response. But, I believe you are right. I want you and Percival to go and inform him of the need of a firm commitment for troops and supplies in our initial war with Nerland. If he does not appear to be solidly in alignment with that then we must first give him an opportunity to reconsider his position before commencing action against him. Of course, if he outright refuses, then we will issue an ultimatum prior to attack, giving him time to change his mind."

"I will send a message to Clarendon today requesting that he meet with you and Percival within a fortnight."

"I would like to bring Greer as well."

"No, I would prefer you didn't. This mission is potentially too dangerous for her."

"But she has great influence with him."

"Yes, but what about when she is not there? No, Clarendon has to be with us because he firmly believes in the Quest, not because Greer sways him for a time."

"Yes, Sire."

Edwin and Percival left the King's quarters and walked back to Percival's place. They would discuss the upcoming trip and how to make it most worthwhile.

"I was surprised at Erith's response to my request to bring Greer. He must be sensing that Clarendon may respond sharply even to the request for help. Why couldn't

Clarendon be a simple, easy to figure out kind of person? But no, we have all these intrigues with no clear sense of where he is at from one time to the next. I now see Erith's wisdom in not bringing Greer. It would only provide a temporary fix which would disappear as soon as Greer left his presence."

"Yes, Edwin... people are often complex. This experience with Clarendon is an opportunity for us to grow in our wisdom in dealing with such complexities."

"My head says you are right, but my heart is just plain frustrated."

"Yes, I'm sure you are frustrated. Let us now devote our time to planning our approach to be successful in obtaining a firm commitment."

"How can any planning help with such a personality? We may sway him with our clever reasoning only to see him change his mind later."

"Nevertheless, we must try," replied Percival.

"Where do we begin?"

"I have decided the reason for Clarendon's wavering is a lack of faith in Evansing and its allies' ability to protect him and his kingdom. He needs to feel protected or in other words he needs to feel safe. I came to this conclusion because when someone is wholeheartedly focused on a particular objective, they no longer concern themselves about personal safety but rather the attainment of the objective."

"That's a plausible insight. How do we convince him that we can protect him? After all we can't guarantee his safety."

"I know. But then safety is often mainly a perception. If we can move him to perceive Tara being protected and safe then that will be enough."

"What magic are you going to use to accomplish that?"

"No magic. I will create an illusion in his mind indiscernible from his present illusion."

"Oh, what illusion does he have now?"

"The one that makes him feel unsafe."

"I thought you said you didn't have authority to do a major intervention in his dreams like you did with Carson?"

"I don't. This will be done by other means which are totally benign and legal for me to do."

"Great! What is it?"

"I am asking for two angels to continually speak soothing messages into his spirit. These messages contain thoughts of feeling safe and protected. When I called it an illusion I was actually just saying it for effect. Belief would be a better word. If Clarendon believes he is safe then he will feel safe. Once he feels safe he will be more open to taking the kinds of risks necessary for him to be a valuable ally in the Quest."

"When do the two angels start? Do we still need to go to Tara?"

"They start today and will continue non-stop for a fortnight. Then we go to Tara to check out Clarendon first hand. We will send a messenger next week requesting a meeting for a date as close as possible after the fortnight is completed."

"Is it guaranteed that he will respond to the angel messages?"

"No, he still has free will. If his spirit is so muddled that he can't respond positively to the messages then he may well be indifferent to them. However I am expecting him to respond well."

"What if he doesn't respond well?"

"If there is no change then I turn the next step over to you."

"If there is some change then I say we ask the angels to do it again."

"How are we going to check him out the second time?"

"Erith could invite him to Evansing. If Clarendon says he can't or won't come then I would say he's not going to change his mind the way we need him to. Our next communication would be the ultimatum."

Edwin replied, "I feel tingly at the thought of Erith issuing the ultimatum."

"Yes, I'm sure you do. The warrior in you wants to get back into action, even when it's not the best option. You will need to work on that inclination so it's only activated when absolutely necessary. Now let's start drafting our letter to Clarendon."

# Chapter 4

On an unusually bright sunny day, Edwin and Percival set out for Tara, accompanied by a hundred soldiers on horseback. Clarendon had said yes to the visit. Both men expected to achieve an agreement of his wholehearted participation in the Quest.

After several hours of riding they decided to take a brief rest. At that moment an arrow came out of the forest and penetrated Percival's chest. He groaned and slumped off his horse hitting the ground hard. Edwin looked in disbelief at what had just happened. He almost got into a frenzied panic but managed to calm himself. He shouted for the men to dismount and position themselves for defense against the invisible enemy. Edwin took hold of Percival's head and upper body. He could see that the arrow went deep and blood was streaming from the wound. He called for the physician to come to his aid.

The physician arrived at his side and looked grimly at what he saw. To pull the arrow out required great care or else much damage could be done to Percival's internal organs. At the same time the bleeding had to be stanched. This would be difficult with the arrow still in place. The physician did the only thing he could do and that was to first place a salve made of herbs on the wound to help slow the bleeding. Then he got on with the delicate task of removing the arrow. Percival, in a state of semi-consciousness became fully conscious when he felt the pain of the arrow being drawn from his body. He screamed loud and long. Then he fainted. The physician continued. He looked almost as white as Percival. He grunted in anguish every time the arrow caught something inside Percival's body. The physician felt most unsatisfied when he pulled the arrow completely out. At this point Percival's breathing was much labored. He did not look good.

In the meantime the rest of the troop was waiting for the attack. But nothing happened. The forest from where the arrow flew was completely silent with no sign of movement.

Edwin motioned to several men at his right to stay low and venture with him into the nearest part of the forest. One by one they followed Edwin, not knowing if an arrow would strike. None did. The silence continued. Edwin stealthily led the way through the bush toward the area that he estimated the arrow must have come from. After half an hour he noticed a piece of scarlet cloth caught on a branch. It was a very fine cloth. Something a nobleman would wear. He placed it in his pocket. There had still been no further action from the unseen force. Or could it have been a single assassin with one intent, to kill Percival? There was no sign that a large army had been in the area. Yes, it could very well be that only one man was involved. Edwin swore he would get him. He turned to the men accompanying him and indicated they should go back and rejoin the others.

When Edwin and his men got back to where they had left the rest of the troop, they were dismayed and confused. No one was there. At first they thought they must have gotten lost. But each one of them agreed they were in the right place. If so, then where were the almost 100 men they had left behind? And where were their horses?

Edwin took stock for a moment trying to determine what to do next. It was difficult for he had never been in such a situation before. "How does an entire troop of men and a severely wounded Percival just disappear?" He decided to ask his men for their input. There were four of them with Edwin. Three of them shook their heads in disbelief. One did not. His name was Leif, a bright young man with very intent eyes. He always had a way about him as if he clearly knew who he was.

"This is the work of the Donegal Dwarf."

Edwin answered, "I have never heard of such a being. How can you be sure?"

"My grandfather on my mother's side would tell me stories of his childhood in Donegal. Several of them related to a mysterious dwarf sighted just before or just after disappearances of large groups of people. It was during that time they gave him the name Donegal Dwarf. Nobody knows what he calls himself, but that was our name for him."

"Supposing you are right, what do we do now?"

"We have to get a Druid priest to draw him out of his cave."

"A Druid priest? Are you serious?"

"Yes I am. I know where we can find one."

"What is a Donegal Dwarf doing so far south?"

"I don't know, but it's the only answer I have."

"When you say 'his cave' are you referring to his cave in Donegal or are you saying somewhere nearby?"

"It could be either, but I think we should first look nearby."

"How does a mere dwarf disappear with so many people? What does he do with them?"

"I don't know. But the Druid I have in mind may well know. He is just over three miles back the way we came."

The five men returned on foot back to where a little cottage stood just off to the right side of the road. There was smoke coming from the chimney and they noticed movement inside. Leif went to the door and knocked.

A man answered the door. He looked rather peculiar. He certainly appeared the part of being a Druid.

Leif spoke, "Hello, sir, we have need of your services."

"What services could you be speaking of?"

"I believe there is a Donegal Dwarf in the area and we need you to draw him out of his cave."

"What makes you believe I am someone who does such a thing?"

"Because you are a Druid and know such things."

The man looked alarmed and then quickly calmed his demeanor, hoping nobody noticed his reaction. Then he replied, "You have the wrong man. I am not a Druid."

"Then what is this?" said Leif as he pointed to a Druid cape and hat in a dark corner of the cottage. "Look, we don't have time to waste. You have nothing to fear from us. We will not harm you. Now come and help us."

"Why would you think I could help you with such a matter? Different Druids may well do what you ask but others may not. How do you know I am one who can help you?"

"Fifteen years ago you drew a Donegal Dwarf out of his cave in Donegal."

"That could have been anybody. You don't know that was me."

"Roll up your left arm."

"What does that have to do with anything?"

"You have a green snake tattooed on your right arm. Now roll up, or do we do it for you?"

"You are right. I am the one. Take me to where you believe the dwarf was last located."

Returning to the scene of the attack, Leif pointed to the open area where almost one hundred men and their horses had simply disappeared.

The Druid began to survey the scene. He walked around looking intently for clues. Finally he stopped and seemed to have come up with an insight. However he also looked rather puzzled.

Edwin asked him, "What have you found?"

"I have found a clue, but it also means something which is the opposite of what the Donegal Dwarf would normally do."

"Please explain."

"The only clue I have found is some traces of his hair. From his hair I can tell that he is living nearby and has been there for some time."

"The traces of hair have elements of a diet found in this area. This means that he has moved from Donegal for some significant time, at least a few months. This is very unusual for the Donegal Dwarf. Something very scary must have caused him to move all this way."

"I don't care about that. What I want to know is where he is and what has he done with my men."

"There may be a connection. He may need your men as a bargaining chip to regain his old territory."

"Why couldn't he have simply taken men from Donegal and saved the trouble of transporting them all the way from here to there? How does he do that? I mean even if he's fairly big, how does he pick up and move that many men and horses?"

"He uses dwarf magic."

"What exactly does he do?"

"Shrink each man and horse to a tiny fraction of their normal size and place them in a cage especially prepared for them. Then he picks it up and takes it away."

Edwin considered what he had just heard, not fully knowing whether to believe it.

"How do we avoid getting shrunk by him ourselves?"

"That is why you have me. I too have magical arts to work with."

"What do you plan to do?"

"I plan to lead you right to him, but before I do I will use an incantation that is sure to shield all of us from the Dwarf's magic."

"Wait a minute, how do we know you won't put us under some harmful spell?"

At this moment, Leif spoke up, "Sir, I know this man by reputation. Even though he is a Druid he is an honorable man."

Edwin struggled within himself as to whether he should delve further into using the Druid's assistance. He knew that allowing himself to be willingly placed under a Druid incantation was the last thing Percival would have wanted. Yet what was he to do? His dear friend Percival may still be alive, and of course the missing men were his valued friends and fellow warriors. Surely the circumstances justified him foregoing his normal standards of avoiding any dark side magic.

With a sigh he said, "All right let's do it."

The Druid started muttering in an unintelligible tongue. After a few minutes he stopped.

"Now we are ready to face the Dwarf."

Edwin looked at his men and thought to himself, "Nobody looks different and I don't feel different. Yet now we are going to entrust that we are protected. This is crazy."

The five men followed the Druid up a winding trail into the woods. After five or six miles he stopped abruptly and motioned for everyone to be very quiet.

The Druid got down and started crawling, with Edwin and his men following. After crawling almost 30 yards they could see the entrance to a cave, a rather large cave. The Druid pulled out a slingshot and placed into it a peculiar looking black rock. He stood up, swinging the slingshot and began whistling. Then he slowly walked toward the mouth of the cave. As he got closer and closer everyone expected the Dwarf to come out. But he didn't. The Dwarf wasn't there. The Druid started looking around the outside of the cave and discovered a trail leading to the other side of the forest. His Druid senses could detect where the Dwarf had walked. He could also tell that he had left not more than two hours ago. Nothing had been left in the cave.

At this point Edwin began to wonder if they were all victims of a Druid ruse.

"Is there any sign that he has our men?"

"No sign, but I know the Dwarf was here. And I know he is quite capable of taking your men and horses."

"Lead us onward to find the Dwarf."

# Chapter 5

Visibility became poor as nightfall came. This most frustrating day had finally come to an end. It was time to find shelter in the woods and start a fire. Fortunately the warm spring weather helped ease their emotional pain.

All six men glumly ate their rations. As they did so, Edwin reflected on the fact that they were headed toward Tara. "Hopefully Clarendon will give us men to help track down the Dwarf."

Suddenly, Edwin started feeling very strange, like he was falling, even though his feet were on the ground. He began thinking he was hallucinating as his surroundings got very large, while he felt very small. Abruptly he felt something very large grab him and put him inside a cage.

Inside the cage, Edwin felt someone come up to him. It was one of the soldiers that had been part of the original force taken captive. Then more of the soldiers came until he became fully aware that he was in the same cage his men had been placed into. He noticed the horses were also there. At this point he felt strange and unsure of himself. He struggled with maintaining his composure in front of his men. He determined to do so even though every part of him wanted to panic and flee. This new situation certainly made the urge understandable. He noted that he and his men were all about four inches tall. Their weapons, clothes and horses had all shrunk down but all were in the same proportion as before.

One of the men said to him, "Sir, we are so glad you found us. We knew you would come looking for us."

Edwin replied, "Yes, I did. But you can see that I am in the same predicament that you are. Where is Percival?"

"Come we will take you to him."

Edwin came upon a very weak Percival. "Oh, my dear friend." He held Percival close to him and started weeping. It was at that very moment he realized he should be able to use his healing power. He placed his hand on Percival's head expecting him to quickly recover. He waited and waited and still did not notice any change in Percival's condition. Instead his wounded friend's breathing got ever more labored. Then it stopped altogether, as he gasped like a man drowning and wheezed his last breath.

Edwin stared in disbelief.

"This cannot be. This is not supposed to happen. Percival cannot die."

He grabbed Percival and shouted, "Wake up, you can't die, wake up!"

No response.

Edwin sat there, as wave after wave of shock came over him. The trauma of all that had happened in less than twenty-four hours overwhelmed his senses and he went totally numb. For the next three hours he sat next to his fallen friend, in silence.

Then, as though he had stirred from a dream, he looked around noticing his men. They too were all in a state of shock. Edwin was stupefied, the only thing he could do was go to sleep, for there was no strength left in him to think or do anything.

The morning light was stark and gray. Edwin and his men all awoke with what felt like the worst hangover they had ever experienced. He lay there trying to comprehend what had happened.

"Percival is gone. It is now all up to me. But what to do?" Edwin thought. "I could ask for Prospero or Joan or Patrick or maybe all of them. Why didn't I ask for their help yesterday?"

At this point the Dwarf opened the lid, reached his hand inside, grabbed five horses, and slammed the lid shut. Then to all the men's horror, they saw the Dwarf swallow each horse one by one.

The name Dwarf was a misnomer for he stood seven feet tall with broad shoulders. His skin complexion was bumpy and bluish in color. The Dwarf's eyes were bloodshot and too close together. His face didn't look mean but rather, stoic, as if to say this was his life and this is the way he needed to live it.

Edwin decided to call for Joan. Nothing happened. Then he called for Prospero. Again nothing happened. Finally he called for Patrick. All he got was silence. This surprised and alarmed Edwin. Then he determined that help would come just in the nick of time, he hoped.

"I need to stay calm and trust that all is well."

He looked outside the cage and noticed the sign indicating the Tara boundary with Evansing. "How can I communicate with Clarendon?"

After his meal, the Dwarf picked up the cage and began travelling the back trails, undoubtedly to avoid people. Occasionally they would cross paths with someone, but people gave him a wide berth.

Edwin wondered where the Druid had gone. In all the confusion no one noticed whether he had fought with the Dwarf or had just fled. Or perhaps he had collaborated with the Dwarf. Edwin was angry with himself for having agreed to be helped by a Druid and especially for allowing the incantation to be spoken over him and his men.

Erith would have no reason to be alarmed as he would not expect to hear news for at least a couple more days. Clarendon should sound an alarm if Edwin did not arrive within a day or so of what had been planned. By that time they may well be through Tara and getting close to Donegal.

Edwin decided to ask for a dream.

The first dream was seeing himself with Greer and they were heavily engaged in lovemaking. He woke with a start. Then he fell back to sleep and this time he was flying but not with Percival. This was a white eagle with very shiny light in its eyes. Edwin was hanging onto its neck and they were soaring ever higher. Down below he could see all of Ireland and much of what is now known as Great Britain. The dream stopped abruptly. He woke shortly after and pondered what he had just seen and experienced in the dream. He recalled a sense of joy and a sense of going somewhere of great importance. However he had no idea as to where he was going or why he felt joyful. He felt encouraged, even though nothing in his circumstances looked encouraging. As a result he now experienced a surge of motivation and sense of duty to start planning an escape.

First he needed to connect with each man and instill a sense of hope. He stood up and looked around. It was still dark, but he noticed a number of men huddled together. He walked over to them. Their faces brightened at the sight of their commander. He looked more like himself than the seeming broken shell he was the day before.

"Greetings, gentlemen. It is time to consider the best way to get out of this cage and get back home."

The men brightened at the words spoken but appeared puzzled as to how there could be any way out. One of them did ask, "How do you intend to make that happen? It looks so hopeless."

Edwin replied, "Yes, I know, but we will find a way." He proceeded to shake the hands of each man and tell them he knew he could depend on them to do whatever was required.

He then looked around for other men starting to awake and did likewise with them as well.

Now he needed a course of action, but nothing was readily forthcoming. This disturbed Edwin as he normally came up with ideas when needed. Of course, he often did get supernatural assistance which at the moment had not yet materialized.

A wave of grief came over him as he thought about the loss of Percival. Not only was he a valued friend, but he always had an answer or at least gave strong assurances that an answer was forthcoming. He now realized what a source of confidence and comfort Percival had been these past few years. "Even so, I need to keep calm and exude confidence. My leadership role demands it."

As he looked in the distance he caught a glimpse of something familiar. He stared for a moment to make sure his eyes were focused and that he was clearly seeing what he thought he was seeing. No mistake, there flying slightly above the horizon was a white eagle. The thought came to him, "I have a plan for you." Upon receipt of that thought, his body and soul felt very calm.

He knew now that the undertaking would unfold. He just needed to keep expecting it. The biggest challenge would be to keep his men expectant and assure them that he would have a winning plan of escape. Not knowing what awaited them in Donegal meant that certainly they would want to escape sooner than later. However, the white eagle must know. He would intervene at the most apropos time. Edwin debated as to whether to share his dream and sighting with his men, but he decided that too many of them would be unable to take it seriously. Best to keep it to himself.

The lid opened and a bluish bumpy hand reached in for five horses. It grabbed them and proceeded to take them out. Then it hesitated. His other hand came down and took hold of one of the men. The man screamed in terror. In horror the men watched as the Dwarf swallowed the five horses and then with a wicked gleam in his eye while looking right at the men in the cage, he swallowed their comrade.

A shudder of horror rolled through the men as they considered what they had just witnessed. Edwin realized time was now of the essence and something had to be done quickly. The greatest concern had been not knowing exactly what the Dwarf's intentions were. When he ate their friend, it became rather apparent that they may all end up being a quick snack. Edwin thought, "The white eagle may permit some of us to die, but he won't let us all die. He has a plan and it will unfold."

Edwin called all his men together. It was important to get them to settle down, stay calm and stay expectant. They all needed to be in a good mental state to take advantage of an opportunity when it arose.

"Men, there is no reason to believe that he is going to eat all of us or even some more of us. I believe it was simply a tactic to keep us in a place of fear so we won't try to escape. I'm expecting a plan to come or an opportunity to present itself. So be alert, be aware, because you may see something we can use to make our escape."

The men perked up a little with the encouraging words, but many also looked askance at the suggestion that anything could be done except to wait to die.

"Men, let's live our victory not our circumstances. We have family counting on us getting back home. Stir yourselves up to expect success. You are gallant warriors. I handpicked you because I know you are all skilled and courageous. Now is the time to be both."

As Edwin finished, a piercing scream was heard from the forest. The Dwarf was so startled he dropped the cage.

# Chapter 6

The Dwarf pulled out his sword and peered into the forest. Everything went quiet.

A clucking sound could be heard up ahead and a chicken could be seen walking towards them. The Dwarf smiled and licked his lips. As the chicken got within reach he grabbed for the chicken's neck, but the chicken evaded him and started running past him. The Dwarf snarled in anger and ran after it.

The men in the cage all strained to see what was going on. Then they could see a rope go taut across the path and the Dwarf tripped and fell hard. Nobody expected what happened next. The Dwarf doubled in size as he raged at being tripped. He ran into the forest looking for who tripped him. Unbeknownst to him the cage was being spirited away while he was distracted. The men knew they were moving low along the ground, but they could not see who or what was moving them. They were being taken into the forest. Many of them started shivering, some because the forest was very cool. However, some were afraid, even though it looked like they had escaped the Dwarf. They feared the unknown for they didn't know who had them now.

What they did know was that whatever was carrying them was very low to the ground and moving very fast. They came out of the forest on the other side into a clearing. There they saw a wide open white tent. A blue pennant on the tent fluttered in the breeze. They moved steadily towards the tent. Nobody was seen in the tent. It appeared empty. Nobody was in the clearing, it also appeared empty. The men were both excited and terrified. Those who saw it as an adventure actually enjoyed it. They were taken right inside the tent and left there without seeing who or what had brought them.

The men waited. Everything was quiet around them. Then a man, shimmering in white came into the tent. He looked at the men in the cage with a bemused look. "So you have yourselves a wee problem. What shall we do to resolve this? I could totally release you and restore you to normal size. While that may seem very attractive to you, I am not sure if it is likewise for me. There are certain advantages in leaving you the same size. One is that I would truly get to see what kind of men you are. The other is that I want to make certain types of gadgetry that require very small hands to do properly. I could train you to do that work. I would provide you with a comfortable working area, properly secured, of course."

The Evansing men felt shivers go down their back as they wrestled with the prospect of remaining their present size. They collectively contemplated, "Is this man our savior or just another rogue like the Dwarf?"

"Edwin, I have a proposal for you." Being known by his name didn't surprise Edwin as this person undeniably had special powers and knowledge. "I want to give you and half of your men a special assignment. The other half I will keep with me and put to work on my gadgetry. I will leave it to you to choose the men you want to take. The assignment is the assassination of Clarendon. I will make that objective easier for you to accomplish when I tell you that it is he who is the reason why you and your men were captured by the Dwarf. Clarendon has been playing you for the fool. He is a lot cleverer and more devious than he appears."

"Sir, given your obvious powers why wouldn't you simply do it yourself?"

"Protocol prevents me from doing this. Besides it is an opportunity for you to truly prove what stuff you are made of. When you succeed, I will return all of you to your normal size, including the ones left behind. You will all be free to go home. As well I have other special rewards to make it worth your while."

"What resources are you giving us to accomplish such a task?"

"Resources? What makes you think I am giving you anything? I will allow you each to bring your own resources, a horse to ride on and your weapons."

"What you are assigning would be difficult if we were of normal size. Given our present size it would be something impossible without some special help."

"Nevertheless, this is what I offer you."

Edwin realized that imploring further would be to no avail. He decided to start selecting his force. The first twenty-two were quite easy as they were all accomplished warriors with exceptional character under pressure.

Choosing the next twenty-seven would be more difficult as he knew all the remaining men were excellent warriors. The key factors would be their staying power in a seemingly hopeless situation. He needed men who would trust his command and stay focused on the task, no matter how overwhelming the obstacles. As he named the last man, there was a groan of disappointment among the men not chosen.

Edwin said, "I know you are all good men, however, I am making a choice based on the right men for this assignment. On some other assignment you would be chosen."

Edwin looked up at the person in white, "I have chosen my men. When do we leave?"

"Now!" He proceeded to unlock a side door at ground level so the men could walk out, each one leading a horse. As they did so they bid their companions that were left behind an emotional farewell.

Once on the ground outside of the cage, the men felt the fear of being unprotected from whatever creatures may be out in the forest.

Edwin asked the person in white, "In which direction is Clarendon's palace and how far is it?"

The person in white pointed almost due south and said, "It's about twenty miles from here."

Edwin and his men started riding south. They stayed along the edge of the forest. Each one wrestled with a tremendous sense of inadequacy. At the same time a thought came to Edwin, "The person in white must believe that we can do it." This quite startled him. He knew this thought didn't come from him. As he mulled it over and over in his mind, a change started taking place in his soul. The thought came that they may have a chance. He knew he better believe they had a chance or else his men certainly wouldn't believe they had a chance. This new expectancy greatly encouraged Edwin. His spirit lifted as he felt more prepared for this assignment, less afraid and with greater boldness.

He stopped his horse in dread when he saw in the shadows a red fox loping towards them with its tongue lolling out of its mouth. It looked hungry and it was about to leap into the middle of them.

# Chapter 7

The fox was in midair when it seemingly hit an invisible barrier. It just stopped and slumped to the ground, momentarily stunned from the force of running into something unseen. It looked frightened, turned around and ran away.

Edwin decided they had to have a response in the event of that happening again. He gathered his men around. "Men, we just saw a miraculous escape from certain death. We don't know what or who helped us, but certainly it's encouraging to know we are not alone. However, I believe it prudent that we devise a defense in the event of this happening again." Edwin and his men then discussed the best defense they could prepare in the event of another attack. They decided to ride in tight bunches of four abreast so they could quickly join their swords to create a credible resistance to any predator.

Now they all felt a little more secure and confident to face whatever dangers awaited them.

Shortly thereafter, they could hear voices of people nearby. They all stopped, got off their horses and hid behind whatever shrubbery was available. They could hear the voices getting louder. One was of a woman and the other sounded like a young boy. Edwin thought it strange they would be out here alone unless they lived quite close nearby. Then they heard a man's voice coming up from behind them. "Where do you think you are going? You can't leave me. I bought you both, you are my property."

The woman replied, "Yes, we can. You bought us illegally. We are going back to Tara Town."

"No, I won't allow it; I will kill you both if you don't turn around and come back to me right now."

"We'd both rather die than be your slaves."

"Well then my conscience is clear for what I am about to do."

The man came within ten feet of where the men were hiding. They couldn't stand by and let the lady and her son be murdered so they all pulled out their bows, aimed at his right ankle and let their arrows fly. The man yelped in agony for it was as though he had been struck by porcupine quills. The pain was intense and he started to bleed. He sat down and gingerly started pulling out the arrows. At the same time he wondered who or what had shot him full of arrows. In the meantime the woman and her son hurried down the path to freedom. As the man dealt with the arrows and attempted to stop the bleeding, Edwin and his comrades continued their journey south.

Edwin mused to himself as they rode along the edge of the forest how different this journey was when one is only four inches tall. His senses were extremely aware of his surroundings. "Understandable when one is vulnerable to so many things around him."

The night was rapidly approaching when Irish predators such as owls, stoats, martens, badgers and foxes would be hunting. Edwin indicated to his men it was time to find a secure place to hide. They were also keen to light a fire as the evening was getting cool. Nearby they noticed a clump of larger rocks creating a protective covering. The entrance was somewhat restricted but would not totally keep out a determined hunter. By posting a watch with weapons poised it would provide a degree of safety. Total security was not possible unless whoever or whatever had intervened with the fox continued to watch over them.

Edwin and his men sat around their fire, munching on the last of the provisions they had brought from Evansing. Now they would be faced with foraging or hunting for food. One source of meat would be earthworms. They would be relatively easy for them to kill. At this size even mice were a challenge, especially since they were so quick. Even they could inflict a deadly bite. Insects were also on the menu. Certainly a different type of hunting was required. They of course could also be adventurous in choosing to eat whatever plant life was available on the forest floor.The men commented amongst themselves how they felt no disdain for these new sources of food. It was what was necessary to survive. They joked amongst themselves how when they got home they would prefer earthworm to venison.

Edwin started to nod off; his final thoughts were of his most beloved Greer. He was starting to enjoy a most delightful encounter with her when he abruptly awoke to see a dark clawed paw reaching around him and his men. The watchmen cried out warning and stabbed repeatedly at the intruder. Edwin reached for his sword and stabbed the paw. It was quickly withdrawn but not before it mortally struck two of Edwin's men. Other men raced to the entrance of their refuge and fired arrows at what turned out to be a stoat. The creature was crying in pain and distressed by this most unusual defense. It turned around and fled into the darkness.

Edwin went to the side of his two fallen men. He was deeply saddened at their loss. What a way to die, killed by something which in their normal size they wouldn't have given a second thought. The men were shaken by the experience. It sharpened their sense of vulnerability.And yet there was a growing determination that they would get home. Each man had tremendous faith in his companions, and a mystical sense of Someone watching over them in spite of the tragic loss of one of their comrades to the Dwarf and now two to their encounter with the stoat. Edwin assigned four additional men to stand watch. In some ways it seemed laughable to think that four men would make a noticeable difference. However, he felt it had an important symbolic significance in giving a concrete response to the attack that had occurred.

Since dawn was only an hour or so away, Edwin decided to stay awake and plan their next day's travel. Planning was difficult since their small size created an entirely different set of challenges and the route was unknown to them.

As he considered the situation, Leif walked up and asked if he could talk to him. Edwin nodded his assent. Leif began to share how sorry he was to have trusted the Druid who apparently led them into a trap. "Leif, I am responsible for agreeing to use his services. It went against my morals to engage a Druid to help us. I felt desperate and was willing to try anything. Unfortunately it has led us into greater desperation. Let go of the need to be hard on yourself. Instead you can be a help to me in planning today's travel."

At dawn everyone sleeping awoke to prepare a quick meal made from leftover earthworm and sliced rootlets. Then they mounted and resumed their journey south, continuing to stay along the edge of the forest. The day started unusually bright and sunny and even felt warm. This helped to cheer the hearts of the men who were in want of encouragement.

By noon they had travelled unimpeded an estimated half mile.

They could hear horses coming along the trail from the south. Everyone stopped to watch what was coming. Three men came along, each one dressed like nobility. Edwin recognized one of them being a cousin to Clarendon. He thought to himself, "What are Tara's nobles up to?"

The nobles kept riding north. "Strange," Edwin thought, "that they didn't have a guard escort."

The men resumed their riding. At mid-afternoon they started to consider where they would stop for the night. An hour later they came upon an ideal location. It consisted of a clump of tightly knit bushes near a small stream. Not more than 20 feet away came a boy of about 12 years of age. He looked down and saw one of the men walking alone along the stream. The boy's eyes lit up in excitement as he bent over and picked up the man. "I'm going to take you home and show you to my mother and father." Edwin faced a difficult decision. He needed to stop the boy, but he didn't want to hurt him. However, stopping the boy was more important. As the boy walked away, he commanded his men to shoot their arrows into the back of the boy's left calf.

Forty or so arrows found their mark, causing the boy to almost drop the prize he was holding. But instead of stopping the boy started running with a limp. Then he disappeared into the forest.

# Chapter 6

Now Edwin had a real dilemma. If they stayed, chances were the boy would bring back his parents and others to come looking for them. He gave the order to pack up and get moving. After an hour they could hear people talking in the area they had left in haste. They kept moving. In case dogs were used, each man had smeared himself and his horse with dead leaves to disguise their scent. After three hours the horses were getting exhausted. A place was found, not nearly as suitable as the one they had left but somewhat acceptable.

Edwin pondered the fate of the man picked up. He finally shrugged his shoulders and decided the man was on his own. It was an important lesson for the others. The missing man had broken the rule of never venturing away alone from the group. Sometimes breaking rules has consequences. This one certainly did.

Now they were down to forty-seven men after only two days. This attrition had to stop or they would have a serious logistics problem in achieving their objective. The men felt glum about their situation. Once again Edwin had to rouse their spirits and encourage them to stay in hope. This time it was harder for him because he had niggling fears that threatened his own hope.

The night passed without incident. Everyone felt relieved the morning had arrived and they had all survived.

Edwin tried summoning Joan. Nothing happened. Then he tried St. Patrick. Again, nothing. Then he tried Prospero. Two gigantic feet appeared before him. That's all, just feet. A familiar voice could be heard. "Yes, Edwin, how can I help you?"

"You could start by transforming us back into our normal size"

"That's not within my authority limit."

"Then what can you do to help us?"

"The best I can do right now is move you five miles down the road."

"That is a bit disappointing. I hoped for something much greater, but if that is your best we will take it."

A moment later they had been translocated down the road. At least it saved them almost a week's travel.

The unusual move energized the men as they had experienced tangible assistance from the supernatural. It restored their hope and heightened  their anticipation of something more in the future.

Shortly after they resumed riding they sighted a badger. The men dismounted and held their horses very still. The badger was sniffing and looking over in their direction. He started ambling towards them. When he was within ten feet, the three nobles sighted earlier came riding on the path. This startled the badger and it ran in the opposite direction. The three men stopped twenty yards past where Edwin and his men were hiding. They dismounted and decided to share some food and drink.

Edwin excitedly led his men on foot, hidden by bushes and trees, to get within 15 or so yards in order to better hear the nobles' conversation.

"Prince Eric's promise of help should be all that we need to overthrow my dear cousin. Now to secure the loyalty of one more Tara commander and we can settle on a date."

"Yes, it's almost ready."

The men then mounted their horses and resumed riding south.

Edwin considered what he had heard. "If Clarendon is killed by others before we do, how will that affect the arrangement we have made? We have to move a lot quicker in order to make sure we don't lose out. If we do lose out, we may stay this size forever."

Edwin called his men to come around him. "Gentlemen, we have a problem. As we heard, those men are planning to overthrow Clarendon. The implication is that if they do succeed, we may not be able to fulfill our assignment so as to return home in our natural size. Therefore we need to move quickly and we need special help. I want each of you, even if you don't have a strong faith, to start crying out to the Divine Creator to help us."

The men started to implore the Creator to send help. After several minutes, they stopped. They then resumed riding, albeit at a quicker pace than before. They had to balance the desire to move quickly with realizing their horses could only maintain a quicker pace for so long before they risked damage. This was the quandary they faced. With their own resources, their prospects looked bleak. They needed supernatural intervention or they would fail. It was as simple as that.

Rain started to fall and added to the bleakness of the moment. Rain drops made a much bigger impact on their bodies now that they were only four inches tall. In short order they were thoroughly soaked and feeling quite miserable and cold. They needed to get cover and light a fire to dry off and warm up. They noticed a small shed less than twenty yards ahead. Nobody appeared to be in it, as the door was open and all was still. The shed was a welcome relief from the forest even if it was pretty rough. Water dripped down into one corner of it, but most of it had kept dry. Scraps of wood chips and shavings were inside, which would be useful for starting a fire.

The men huddled together for warmth and as they started to feel comfortable a rather peculiar light began glowing in the corner from where the water was dripping inside. The light got more intense and the men began to feel concerned that it may be dangerous. Edwin told them to relax as he felt this would be an answer to the prayers they prayed earlier.

A voice spoke from the center of the light: "Men of Evansing, everything is good, keep believing your Creator is good and faithful. He will help you." Then it disappeared. The men waited and waited in anticipation of something more, something spectacular. But nothing further happened. All was quiet except their beating hearts.

The experience was both good and bad. Good that it happened in a very supernatural way. Bad that they were no further ahead, except they did have a promise.

The men moaned in amazement and disappointment. The supernatural had visited them, no one could deny that. But they had hoped that now was their time of deliverance. They settled in for the night, grateful at least for the visitation and shelter from the rain, which continued to pour on to the roof.

In the morning they surveyed the sea of mud and water puddles lying before them. It would be a hard slow slog of riding today. Nobody felt eager to get going, but Edwin knew they had to do their part and trust their Divine Protector to do His part. The rain had stopped a short time earlier to at least give them a more comfortable start.

Progress was treacherous because at their size they faced the potential of a horse and rider sliding into a puddle and drowning. Therefore they took care to give all puddles as wide a berth as possible. By mid-morning the sun came out and life seemed better. So did a fox and he was coming straight for them. The call went for everyone to run to the nearest bush, dismount and get their bows ready. As the fox came up, the men released a volley of forty or so arrows right into his face. Blinded in one eye and squealing in pain it turned around, running and scratching at his face at the same time.

An experience like that left them drained for ten or so minutes. In their diminutive state to be attacked by a huge fox transcended the experiences of normal warfare. Perhaps they would get used to it. Although they hoped they wouldn't experience it again.

Once more they struck out south towards Tara Town. Everyone wondered when they would see some great deliverance from their quandary. None appeared. Yet somehow they believed the promise given of help to come.

"Stay in courage, men. All is well," said Edwin.

As he finished, a shadow could be seen passing over them, quickly followed by a scream as a horse and rider were picked up by a hawk and carried away.

Edwin looked into the sky in utter disbelief and disgust all mixed together. "How could it be the very next day after our divine promise we would lose another man. Creator! Who are you? What are you doing?"

Men were assigned to keep a lookout for hawks and Edwin pondered the best way to counter a future attack. The speed of an attacking hawk would be a difficult thing to defend against. However, it needed to be done. The idea with most merit involved each man first creating a holster for each side of their horse. A long sharpened stick would be inserted into each holster. A hawk would risk impaling itself in its attempt to capture a man and his horse. This seemed a simple and yet effective solution. It would be cumbersome but doable.

He told the men to stop. He then informed them of his idea.

The men agreed that it seemed like a sensible approach and they proceeded to start making the holsters and fashioning sharpened sticks.

Upon completion of their assigned tasks the men resumed riding south.

There didn't seem like much of anything was happening until who should show up ahead but the Dwarf. He was walking rapidly towards them. Edwin and his men melted deeper into the forest, scattering in several different directions and then tried their best to hide their horses and themselves under whatever cover was available. They waited.

When the Dwarf arrived at the spot in the trail where the men had been, he stopped. He sniffed around and smiled. He looked into the forest and began walking into it. A horse neighed giving away the location of two of the riders. The Dwarf stooped down and moved away some brush from where he had heard the horse. At that point an axe, wielded by an invisible being lopped off his head. The head and body dropped with a thud, narrowly missing the two riders and their horses. Then the axe disappeared and all went silent.

Encouraged by the unexpected intervention, the men once again resumed their journey, eager to get away from the massive corpse.

The men travelled until just before dusk at which time they found an ideal shelter of rocks piled up by the side of the road. The men settled in for the night, hoping it would stay quiet.

Then they heard an animal rustling around in the area. It must be something fairly large, probably a badger. They kept quiet. Everyone stayed awake, tense with apprehension of a possible attack.

# Chapter 9

All went quiet until the badger began pulling against one of the stones in an effort to gain access to their little sanctuary. All the men arose with their bows poised to release a volley. Badgers were tough and large. This would be a challenge. As soon as he tore away the stone they shot numerous arrows into his eyes completely blinding him. The animal howled in pain and extreme distress. It dove into their hideaway grabbing three horses before another volley caused it to turn around and flee. The camp was in an uproar, as again they were allowed to be attacked after their promise of divine help. Edwin pointed out to them that only horses and no men were lost. Perhaps this meant they now were receiving increased protection.

Nobody felt calm enough to fall asleep and yet some attempt had to be made. Being attacked by a creature much larger than yourself is a most terrifying experience. Their bodies and souls reverberated with the trauma of what had just happened.

In the morning they could hear birds singing. The sound had a most soothing but also irritating effect on them. The melody had a cheeriness about it, but it was much too early after too few hours of sleep. Nevertheless, the men arose and got prepared for another day.

Edwin awoke with an unusually bright expectancy. He found it strange given the nature of their circumstances which had little to naturally feel expectant about. However he did recall his statement to the men about only losing three horses and no men. He decided it must be the belief of their now being on an upward rise in their fortunes. His spirit placed more weight on the divine promise than on the circumstances. As they started riding in a gentle morning mist, Edwin realized he felt happy. He thought to himself how ludicrous to feel happy. He pondered his reality, four inches tall, facing an impossible task and the real possibility of instant extinction at the paws of a fox or other animal. Nevertheless, he felt happy.

The men travelled for only a few hours when they came upon a sign pointing to Tara Town. The sign shocked them because it indicated the distance as being only one mile to the town. By their calculations they should by well over ten miles away from Tara Town, and yet this sign indicated one. The men huddled together to discuss the phenomenon of covering so much ground in such a short time. They concluded it must be the divine help they were expecting. Now they faced the more imminent prospect of devising a plan to assassinate Clarendon. Just getting to the castle without being spotted by townspeople or attacked by cats and dogs would be an accomplishment. Then when they get to the castle they must sneak by the guards, attendants and cats and dogs and deliver a death blow to someone many times larger than themselves. This would be interesting. The only thing they could do and of course must do was trust. There was no point in being afraid and focusing on the obstacles. They decided to expect help when and how they needed it. They chose to believe they would be safe and successful.

With this new confidence the men continued to ride towards their destination. Greater traffic as a result of being so close to Tara Town necessitated them staying further inside the forest that bordered the road. They expected help sooner rather than later, but experience had also told them that dangers still could be allowed to kill or injure them. They knew they played a role in their safety by being prudent.

Edwin wracked his brain for how they would achieve their objective, however no idea came to him that made sense. Their size required a total shift in the types of strategies and tactics necessary for such an undertaking. The unfamiliarity of how to do life at four inches made it exceedingly difficult. He decided to quit wrestling with it and allow the solution to come to him. After all it was quite literally beyond him and his men to accomplish such a task. They clearly needed help or it wouldn't happen.

At the end of the day they were about a half mile from Clarendon's castle. They managed to find an abandoned hut in the forest near the road. It had a dirt floor and no door but it did have at least a partial roof and walls which provided adequate shelter from the elements. As well it had a protective configuration, making it easier to defend.

Edwin said, "Men, I have no concrete plan so I am open to ideas."

No one spoke up. They were surprised that Edwin was stumped because he always had ideas. This would require a greater leaning on whoever was helping them. It most assuredly was out of their hands and ability to pull it off themselves.

Edwin and ten of his men were riding on the back of eleven over-sized jays and landed right inside an unoccupied room in close proximity to Clarendon's private living quarters. They were all armed with bow and arrows and swords. After the men dismounted, the birds flew away. There they were a lot closer but still needing to get by the guards and deliver the coup de grace.

When Edwin awoke, he considered the dream. He knew it indicated the next step. He also decided it would be best to stay in the hut and await the jays' arrival. He realized that choice meant a lot of leaning on the accuracy of his dream. "Oh to have Percival to talk to."

In the morning Edwin shared his dream and his conviction that it was accurate and would happen. However, he didn't know when. The men sat in silence a moment before one spoke up, "It sounds like it's your wishful thinking, Edwin. How preposterous for us to be transported by jays. I don't think it's going to be that easy. I believe we need to continue our journey to Tara Town and not delay."

Edwin sat slightly stunned after being talked to so bluntly by one of his own men. This was a new experience. His feelings were a mixture of anger and sadness. He struggled momentarily to keep his calm and respond in a manner that was agreeable. "That's an interesting view. Anyone else want to share their thoughts?"

A man called Jarrett shared, "I believe Edwin's dream is possible. My perspective on what is possible has changed since I became four inches tall. We have all witnessed and experienced remarkable, seemingly impossible examples of intervention. What to do now? I think we should continue on if after three days we have not been whisked away by the jays."

Edwin thought to himself, "Sensible response."

"Anyone else have comments?"

Leif answered, "Jarrett has given us a wise response. It makes sense to believe some sort of supernatural intervention is going to happen. We've been given a promise and some basis for believing it. I say let's stay here for three days and then move on if nothing happens. This place is as comfortable and safe as any we are going to find. The closer we get to town the more people will be around and increase the likelihood of our being spotted."

The combination of Jarrett and Leif finally produced a general affirmative response to staying for three days.

Edwin responded, "Thank you for your input. I decided the extraordinary nature of our circumstances required me to discuss this with you and get at least a majority agreeing on a course of action. Now who would like to volunteer to accompany me on this adventure? I need ten men."

All the men put up their hand. "I expected as much. You are all brave warriors. I will consider each of you as to which ten will be most suitable for this particular type of mission. I will decide in the next day or two. For now we need to gather some provision, so we need to have 20 or so men venture out to gather what is available."

The 20 men who decided to go hunting first stopped to consider the most prudent approach. Should they split in two forces of 10 or stay together as 20? After a brief discussion they decided it would be safer to stay together.

Shortly after they had started, the forest got very quiet. This alarmed the men for they knew there had to be a reason. Everyone stopped in their tracks and waited. A stray farm cat came bounding into the middle of them, crushing a rider and his horse, and injured two others and their horses. The men's reactions were immediate. They unleashed a volley of arrows at the cat, several of which blinded his right eye. The cat squealed in pain and started scratching at its blinded eye and other areas of injury on its body. It came after the men again, but this time before it could do any further damage it appeared to be picked up and thrown 15 yards away. When it landed it just kept running.

One of the men started screaming obscenities at the heavens. The rest just stood still in shock except for a few who attended the injured. After they had shaken themselves out of their stupor, they gathered some available plant pieces they knew were safe to eat. Then they returned to their home base.

Edwin heard the ruckus with the cat and had prepared himself for bad news. When he saw his men carrying the body of one and helping two others, his heart fluttered with dismay. To the best of his knowledge his men had done everything in a prudent manner, and yet still they were vulnerable.

The men gathered around Edwin, disappointed at the losses. Once again he assured them that given what had happened it still indicated protection and intervention, as they could have lost many more.

Two days later, early in the morning, Edwin awoke with the sound of beating wings. He leaped up and looked outside. There he saw 11 large jays about to land. Each one was just the right size to carry a four inch person. Edwin had earlier completed his selection of the men and had ordered them to be ready to leave on a moment's notice. Therefore all 10 men were ready with their weapons a moment or so after Edwin sighted the jays. The men had a nervous anticipation. Before them lay a mission unlike any other they had ever experienced.

Each man got on and grabbed the neck of their bird. Edwin sat on the lead bird. "Go." The birds lifted off, slower than they would without someone on their back. The gentle ascent avoided jerking the men and the possibility of dismounting them. These men were picked especially for their bent toward daredevil antics. Consequently they enjoyed this most unusual ride. Edwin recalled a similar experience when he had been picked up by a huge bird. That flight led to a most fortuitous end. He trusted that this one would do likewise.

The sun had not fully risen so there were still shadows and partial cover of darkness. It only took a few minutes to cover the half mile to Clarendon's castle. The jays dropped each man off inside a room of the castle. There they all considered the next move. The question was raised as to why they were brought to the castle in the morning instead of the night. Edwin looked at the questioner and said "I don't know except this is when the jays came. That is all I can tell you.

It would be best for us to now determine how we are going to get out of this room as the door is closed. Let's get over by the door and expect it to open for us. After all the Divine Being who is helping us didn't go to the trouble of flying us here just to leave us trapped."

The men waited by the door for several hours. Then the door opened and a servant walked in with a chair. While the door remained open the men slipped out into the hallway. In the distance they could see two guards standing in front of a double door. They surmised it must be Clarendon's private quarters.

All the men squeezed against the wall and kept low. They faced a decision as to whether to wait where they were and see what would happen or would they advance and see what would happen? Edwin decided they would advance. He had confidence they would see another intervention. As they crept along, two dogs walked right by them. None of them breathed. To them it was totally unbelievable that the dogs didn't notice them. What they didn't know was they had been cloaked by an angel so as to now be invisible to the dogs and to the guards. Being unnoticed by the dogs emboldened the men to continue to advance closer and closer to their objective. They crept right up to the doors and then waited. Shortly after midday, Clarendon came to his quarters. As it turned out he normally took a nap at this time. The jays had had impeccable timing. At this time of day no family members would normally be in the quarters with Clarendon.

How to get into those quarters? Whether it was there all along or whether it just appeared now, one of the men noticed a hole in the wall, large enough for them to crawl through.

One by one they pressed into the hole, squeezed through and carefully stepped out into the King's quarters. They could hear Clarendon's breathing and occasional snoring as he napped. The men were slightly awed at finally seeing their prey within striking distance. Because of the size difference, they would have to choose a method resulting in quick death. They chose a strike to the temple. The men climbed up the bed and crept toward Clarendon's head. They connected three spears to form one large spear that would be driven home by three men. Those men were positioning themselves for their attack when Clarendon suddenly turned over to his right side. Now they faced a quandary of how to get access to his temple. As well it seemed like he was starting to wake up. Something had to be done quickly. Edwin shouted, "Look up." Clarendon turned his head back and immediately the three men drove their spear into his temple. He groaned but the blow was sharp and hard enough to achieve the objective. It killed Clarendon.

The men all held their breath. They got down the bed and walked back to the hole they had used to enter the room. Then back into the hallway and down to the door of the room they had originally landed in. It had been left slightly ajar and they were able to re-enter the room. Once in the room the big question was, how do they get out of the castle? No plans had been unveiled as to that part of the mission. Edwin believed that a way was being made for them. They achieved the objective and therefore some provision must have been made for their successful escape.

Within an hour of their killing the King, they heard an uproar upon the discovery of his murder. Two guards entered their room and after giving a quick look around left to continue their search for the assassins elsewhere. The men waited and waited several hours. Fortunately they had brought some provisions to eat and still had something to sustain them for part of another day. As the sun went down, still no sign of the jays or anything else that would create a way of escape. They settled down to an uneasy sleep. Two or three sentries at a time were awake to keep watch. They rotated every two hours.

The next day they awoke as the darkness began to surrender to the dawn. The men encouraged themselves by saying it wouldn't be long before they were back at the camp and then soon in Evansing at their normal size.

With the first rays of the morning sun, each man experienced a rather extraordinary transformation. Feathers started to sprout from their bodies, their arms changed into wings and within the hour they no longer needed the jays to come back, for they had become jays themselves. The process was interesting. It would have been scary, but a serenity stayed with them the whole time. When the change to birds had been completed, they all flew out the window to meet up with their companions. Upon landing near the hut they had adopted as their shelter, they experienced a rapid change back to their human form.

Most of the men left behind were present to view the bizarre sight of birds turning into men. The changed men stood still, exhausted, several of them sunk to their knees and stayed there. The other men came over to help them into the hut and gave them some food and water.

After an hour or so the men felt revived and restored enough to begin the journey back to reconnect with their friends left behind.

# *Chapter 10*

Ironically, in some ways going back felt harder than the initial trip to assassinate Clarendon. Partly it was the sheer exhaustion of living at four inches tall. It entailed a constant pressure of being on the lookout for something that wanted to kill you. As well they felt the psychological pain of going back to where they had been, which led them further away from Evansing. Going back of course must be done. They were still the same size, which meant they had to get back to meet the man dressed in white. They needed him to change them back. Given the powers they had seen he certainly could have changed them now, but for whatever reason he chose not to.

Edwin thought, "This man in white appears to be both good and not so good. I must believe he is all good and there is a purpose for this."

The day dragged on relentlessly. Everyone had the malaise about going back. Then one of the men exclaimed, "Hey we are going to be changed back to who we were. Every step brings us closer. Let's be excited." Some of the men gave half-hearted responses of agreement, but most stayed silent. What he said was true. However the men couldn't engage it. Even though this should be a happy time it took all they could muster to keep going. Edwin thought, "There must be a way to encourage them."

The next moment a brilliant flash of light appeared on the road before them. There stood an angel at least eight feet tall. He spoke, "Men, I have been sent to speed your journey. Edwin, hold my hand and someone grab his hand and so on until you are all one unbroken chain." When they were all connected everything around them looked blurred, and then after only a moment or two it became clear again.

There before them was the clearing with the white tent. Standing beside it was the man shimmering in white.

"Welcome back, Edwin, and well done! You have achieved your restoration and freedom."

Each man started to feel very peculiar as now they experienced the reversal of being shrunk. Every man felt himself expanding and getting taller and taller. Soon they were back to their previous size.

Coming from the forest a couple hundred yards away were their friends, already changed back to their previous size. The two parties ran to meet in the middle and grabbed each other in celebration and gratitude for being given back their lives. When they stopped celebrating their reunion and looked toward the white tent, it was gone and so was the man shimmering in white.

They unanimously agreed to start travelling back to Evansing, but they would take a route leading them further away from Tara Town. There was bound to be trouble there with Clarendon dead and his family members vying for the throne. They didn't want to get embroiled in Tara's troubles right now. There would undoubtedly be a need to deal with it later.

Now when the men started on the road back home they were greatly encouraged. Their transformation gave them a brand-new outlook on life. They kept riding even after dark. Nobody wanted to stop. When the time approached midnight, Edwin decided it would be prudent to stop and rest the horses. The men didn't need rest, they were still so high from all that had happened and the anticipation of being back home.

In the morning as the sun came up over the horizon the men were already packed and ready to go. Nothing could hold them back. All they could talk about and think about was getting home and being normal again. There was however, a disruption to their joy. One of their youngest members, a nineteen-year old, woke up bleeding from his mouth and nose. Soon after he convulsed and struggled to breathe. The men became somber at what had transpired. It didn't seem right to them for the young man or themselves to have such a turn of events. Not after what they had all experienced and been delivered from. Edwin placed his hands on the young man and spoke words of healing over him. Momentarily the youth responded, his features looked more normal and then he had a sudden convulsion and died. Edwin stared in dismay at the dead man.

Everyone stayed silent and grieved at this most unexpected loss. The youth had several kin in the group and they grabbed him and howled in pain while holding him. After an hour or so, Edwin decided it was important to move on. They buried the young man under a tree and resumed their journey.

Overhead a large flock of ravens flew in the same direction they were headed. Edwin and some of the men who had accompanied him on that fateful trip to Aldred had an eerily familiar feeling. Further confirmation came when the temperature dropped causing them to feel chilled.

Edwin stopped his horse and turned it around to address his men. "We have a situation developing ahead. Those ravens are not normal ravens. They are a sign of something dark unfolding in the very direction we are going. We have several options. We can continue in the same direction and be prepared to encounter some sort of difficulty. Other options are to go left of our present path or go right of our present path. The latter takes us closer to Tara Town, which for the reasons we all know is not desirable. Therefore I recommend we go left."

The men, a bit impatient with having to take a detour, voiced their agreement. They'd had enough dark magic and would rather ride longer and safer.

As they rode, Edwin pondered the direction the ravens were headed. He thought, "If they continue straight and go far enough they will end up in Evansing. Surely there can't be an attack on Evansing. But then why not? If the Druids know of the plans to resume the Quest, they may well do whatever they can to stop it. Could Erith and Greer be susceptible to such an attack? Had they been sufficiently diligent in taking the Eucharist to ensure they had the virtue necessary to be protected?"

The route the men were taking would actually take them through a corner of Aldred. Edwin briefly considered diverting their journey to go and visit King Barris and Crown Prince Kerris. He quickly reconsidered as he knew he would not be popular with his men.

About a mile down the road and several hundred yards to their right, they noted thick black smoke. Edwin contemplated going straight and ignoring it or investigating to see if someone needed their help. "What if it was part of the struggle for the Tara throne?" He did not want to involve himself with their internal affairs at this time.

As Edwin and his men rode alongside the billowing smoke they could also hear screams and saw several women running naked. Behind them were a dozen or so men wearing the insignia of Tara's army. Edwin couldn't bear to ignore what he saw and he ordered his men to confront them. This they gladly did for they were of the same heart as their commander. When the Tara troops saw they were severely outnumbered they turned around and retreated into the forest. Edwin and his men stopped to gather the women's clothes. They rode after the women who were terrified and didn't know what to expect of these strangers. Edwin led the way to soothe the women and brought them their clothes. "We won't harm you. My men and I will turn our backs while you get dressed." After the women dressed they told the men they could turn around. One of the four women shared how the Tara troops decided on some sport. They first burned their house and sheds. Then they forced the women to undress and told them to run. Whoever got a woman could do with her as he saw fit. They also shared how they were all childless widows who had banded together to survive. Now they were homeless. This placed Edwin and his men in a dilemma. If they stayed much longer the Tara soldiers could bring back a much larger force. If they left the women they would be outside in the cool Irish spring with a high chance of dying from exposure. As well the Tara army would most likely return and finish what they started. Edwin offered the one chance they had for survival. If they like, they could come with him and his men. The women discussed the offer amongst themselves and decided to take it. Even though it was scary for them, they decided it was the best option available.

Edwin decided it would be best to take the most direct route to Aldred which they did. In a matter of hours they arrived in Aldred. Shortly after they crossed the border they were greeted by a platoon of Aldred soldiers out on patrol. They enquired of the Evansing group's business. They also advised them of alarming reports from Evansing. Apparently a minor rebellion had occurred in the area adjacent to the Aldred border. They cautioned them that there may still be rebel activity in the very area they were planning on passing through.

The news alarmed and surprised Edwin and his men who couldn't fathom anyone in Evansing wanting to rebel against King Erith. Edwin discussed with his men the strong possibility that dark spirits must be at work in Evansing.

"Those ravens we saw most likely were reinforcing whatever was already at work. We need to get to a priest and have him serve us the Eucharist in order to increase our level of protection."

They enquired of the Aldred troops where they could find the nearest church. As it turned out it was another mile or so down the road they were about to travel. Upon their arrival at the church, the priest came out having heard the sound of horses. He looked rather intimidated at having such a large number of rough looking men come to his tiny parish church.

"Father, we mean no harm. We are all God fearing men who would like to receive the host and the wine before we continue our journey."

"Thank you for your assurances. I will require some time to prepare. Wait here."

After fifteen minutes the priest had not yet come back. Edwin motioned to Leif to go inside and see when the priest would be ready. After several minutes he came back and said the priest could not be found.

Edwin considered this a moment then ordered Leif and one other man to go inside and find the host and the wine. They looked at him with some trepidation. The idea of anyone other than a priest authorizing such an act caused them discomfort. However they had been ordered to do so and they went inside the church. A short time later they came out with the bread and the wine. Edwin dismounted as did all his men and the women. He took the bread and wine and indicated that everyone should line up and partake just like they did at church. Edwin took his portion when all had been served.

"Ladies and gentlemen, we have now been given at least some protection against the dark spirits we are about to encounter. However at least some of us may still have susceptibility to being attacked. Be aware of your thoughts and feeling. Take special note if you start thinking or feeling different than normal without any apparent cause. Also we should all be aware if we notice someone acting different for no apparent reason. These can be so subtle, seemingly reasonable thoughts and feelings that the person experiencing them is not even aware something is amiss. On the other hand (with a bit of a chuckle) I don't want everyone paranoid about their companions."

The party mounted their horses and continued on toward Evansing.

# Chapter 11

The trip to the Evansing border was filled with a mixture of joyful anticipation and angst about what they would encounter given the reports of rebellion. Edwin and those of his men who had previously gone to Aldred sensed an uncomfortable familiarity when they crossed over the border.

Next they would need to get to a place suitable for camping as it was already dusk. Suitability required it to be somewhat defensible as well as providing some measure of shelter. Within half an hour they found a spot on top of a small hill that also had trees for some protection from the elements. They would not light any fires so as to avoid drawing unwanted attention.

Edwin was back in France meeting Joan. She had an important message for him. "Edwin, you are about to embark on a most difficult journey. All the ones you thought were nearest and dearest to you will have turned on you. You are being declared a wanted outlaw. Your men are being pardoned providing they turn you over to the new ruler of Evansing."

Edwin awoke feeling troubled. "Was that a real message from Joan or just a nightmare of no consequence? If it is real what do I do with it? Who do I trust?"

In the morning, Edwin looked at his travel companions with a new appreciation that if the dream was true some of them may well betray him. These were men he would die for. People he entrusted with his life. Yet the wrong kind of influence or right amount of pressure could turn them against him. For now he would continue as planned.

Everything remained quiet on the trail. Even the first village they encountered, normally a pleasant bustling little settlement had virtually no one outside. The men warily looked around to see any sign of life but saw none. Then came a volley of arrows striking four of the men and one of the women. The men and women dismounted and tried to find shelter behind whatever they could. Edwin and his men identified the source of the arrows as being from behind a wall. They encircled it coming up behind it. No one was there. Another volley of arrows and two more men went down. This time they could see the clutch of men shooting from the grass. Those men, perhaps seven or eight, turned and fled into the nearby forest. Edwin posted some guards to stay watch while he attended to those struck. The two latest casualties were both dead. He then went to see the other five. Three of the men were still alive. Edwin tried his healing power once again. This time two of them recovered immediately. The third showed some improvement but remained badly injured. They couldn't leave him behind but forcing him to ride may be fatal. It must be done so they securely strapped him to the back of his closest friend. His friend loved him dearly and welcomed the opportunity to support his wounded comrade.

The three remaining women grieved the loss of their friend who had been struck probably in error, but nevertheless she lay dead. Edwin too keenly felt their loss. It seemed so unjust to him that this lady would be killed after being rescued from gross indignities and privation.

After burying their dead and pronouncing over them a few words, they resumed their journey.

The air was cool as the temperature had suddenly dropped. Not a good sign as it didn't seem a natural cool. Sure enough the behavior of some of the men started to change. They got rather loud and complaining. They complained about a number of things, but the most disturbing thing they complained about related to Edwin's leadership. He could have had them executed on the spot. However instead he reminded them that they were being impacted by spiritual influences and they should do their best to resist. This created a mixed response as some got even more belligerent. Fortunately most of the party was unaffected and responded by trying to quiet the loud ones. Seeing they were outnumbered, most of those affected started to settle down. Except for a man named Niall who got even more contentious and pulled out his sword. The man closest to him, named Iosua, reined his horse back a few feet and drew out his sword as well. For a moment they just stared at each other. Then the anger mixed with bad influences pushed Niall to attack Iosua. He came directly at Iosua, swearing and swinging his sword. Iosua got his sword up to fend off the blows. At first Iosua maintained a defensive posture as he did not want to hurt his fellow soldier. However the attacks from Niall grew in intensity for he obviously was fighting to kill Iosua. To slow him down, Iosua struck Niall on his sword arm hard enough to knock the sword out of his hand but not so hard as to cause severe damage. Instead of giving up and being grateful, Niall pulled out his dagger and with his other hand came after Iosua. But this time another soldier grabbed his arm and wrested away the knife. Still Niall would not quit so the soldier who had grabbed the knife, punched him on the side of the head knocking him unconscious. Another soldier quickly grabbed Niall to prevent him from falling from his horse. Iosua gently lifted him off his horse and lay him down.

Edwin felt pride at how his men had responded. It gave him reassurances of their nobility and loyalty. His men needed to get more Eucharist. The next church was only a few miles further along the road. Hopefully they could hang on awhile longer.

The physician treated Niall's arm. Two soldiers tied up his hands, placed him on a horse, and secured him behind the rider. Niall remained groggy and in a lot of pain.

The party resumed its travels. However they did not go far before they encountered another challenge. In the foggy mist, a half mile or so ahead of them they sighted a troop of what appeared to be at least two hundred Evansing soldiers. What to do? Given Edwin's dream he had no way of knowing whether they would be friend or foe. His men, unaware of any possible treachery kept riding towards what they expected were their fellow soldiers in the Evansing army. Edwin reminded them of the possibility of the approaching soldiers being rebels. Everyone had their arms at the ready in the event this would be the case. The tension built as the two forces got closer and closer. When they were within about 100 yards of each other, both sides stopped. The leader of the approaching army asked them the nature of their business and their identity.

Edwin replied, "I am Prince Edwin and these are my remaining men from the mission to Tara. What is the nature of your business?"

"We are on patrol looking for rebels. Come closer so we can clearly identify you."

Edwin briefly considered whether this would be wise or whether they should consider another alternative. "Let the leader of each side ride into the middle and resolve this matter."

The other leader hesitated and then said he agreed. Edwin and his counterpart started to ride toward each other. As they got closer Edwin identified the officer as a man named Liam. The officer also recognized Edwin and his face expressed pleasure at seeing his commanding officer.

"Edwin, it is so good to see you again. Reports from Tara indicated you and your men had disappeared. Then we got reports of Clarendon's assassination and of a civil war in Tara. There has been a most peculiar change in the atmosphere over Evansing. Everyone has been on edge, not simply because of your disappearance but also as a result of new tensions in relationships. People have been squabbling over the most petty of issues. Confusion, misunderstanding and fear have been rampant. Then there arose a rebellion here in the northern part. It now appears to have been quashed without too much bloodshed."

Edwin's mind did not perceive anything amiss. However his heart felt uneasy. "Should he trust Liam?" Then he looked into Liam's eyes. He had to control his response. Liam's face and words were all friendly, but his eyes reflected pure hatred. "What to do? If I say I need to go back to my troops he will wonder why." He decided to continue on with a little bit of light banter until Liam told him to tell Edwin's troops to come. The tone of command was unseemly for a subordinate to say to his superior. Edwin replied, "Soldier, you do realize who you are talking to?"

Liam blushed momentarily realizing his insubordination. "I beg your pardon, sir; I guess I am a little on edge." The words were correct but the tone had a pronounced surliness about it. The hatred in his eyes spread to his face.

Edwin commanded the officer to accompany him back to the contingent from Tara. The officer hesitated and then realized he was in danger of directly disobeying a superior officer. He kicked his horse to get going and both rode back to Edwin's troop. When they arrived, Edwin immediately ordered Liam to surrender his weapons quietly and in a manner that didn't arouse the suspicions of Liam's troops. Liam did as ordered without protest for he knew by Edwin's tone he would be killed on the spot if he resisted.

"Liam, what true intentions do you have with us?"

"What do you mean, sir."

"You know what I mean."

"No, I don't. Please explain."

"Your words are inconsistent with the hatred and disdain I see in your eyes and hear in your voice. Something is amiss."

A surge of evil came upon Liam and he leapt from his horse onto Edwin.

Liam had drawn out a dagger from a concealed compartment in his uniform. Edwin grabbed Liam's arm holding the dagger and while maintaining balance on his horse drew his own dagger and jammed it deep into Liam's chest. The assailant fell down to the ground and lay there motionless. Upon seeing what had transpired, the Evansing troops accompanying Liam started to charge toward them. Edwin ordered his men to retreat to the top of a small nearby hill where they could more readily defend themselves against a force greater than twice their size.

Edwin, his men, and the women raced ahead of their opponents for over a mile before reaching the top of the hill. With much sorrow they started to shoot arrows into the ranks of the oncoming force. The sorrow they felt was intense for they knew they were killing their fellow countrymen, many of whom they recognized. However their survival instinct rose stronger than their sorrow and they took deadly aim to kill as many as possible. This they did with great skill. The army coming against them had an obvious disadvantage in being exposed and needing to ride uphill. When halfway up the hill the withering fire of arrows stopped their opponents' upward progress. Many of them used fallen horses as a shelter of protection. After half an hour or so, the beleaguered force retreated from the hail of arrows.

No cheer of victory by Edwin and his men. Rather they felt relief at having survived. Given the nature of the battle no one truly won. Now they faced the prospect of staying on the hill and likely battling a much larger force the next day. Edwin decided to take his force down the opposite side from where the fighting occurred. They then continued deeper into the forest and selected a small ravine as a place of shelter for the night.

Around the fire Edwin chatted with Leif and Iosua. He asked Leif what ideas he may have as to what their next course of action would be. "I say we keep riding toward Evansing Town and expect we will meet friendly forces."

"How will we know who is friendly?"

"I say just keep expecting to meet friendly forces. It will be alright."

"Your optimism is to be commended; however in this case it could also lead to our demise."

64

"Iosua, what do you think should be our next step?"

# Chapter 12

Back in Evansing Castle Greer and Erith had become greatly distressed at the long overdue absence of Edwin and his men. As well they heard stories that Edwin had persuaded his men to become bandits, guilty of all kinds of heinous crimes against helpless women and children. This made no sense at all to Greer and Erith and neither one of them could believe Edwin to be guilty of such a turnaround in his character. But then there were stories from different sources all repeating more or less the same facts. This started to cause some wavering in them as to what to believe. In the meantime there had been a gradual shift in the atmosphere over all of the Kingdom of Evansing. Being so gradual it inclined the people to be more relaxed about their spiritual disciplines. This resulted in Greer and Erith taking the Eucharist less and less frequently. Erith became more and more inclined to believe Edwin had turned bandit.

Since Edwin could no longer to be trusted, his position of lead military officer had to be filled. Erith pondered who would be competent and loyal. Given the growing sense of paranoia in the Kingdom, his suspicions resonated with all the prospective candidates. This confused the King for it was not that long ago he would have trusted any one of them. Now he trusted no one.

Greer did her best to stay calm and maintain hope against hope in the belief Edwin was innocent. She struggled with wavering between that hope and the growing number of reports against that hope. To complicate things she realized shortly after Edwin had left, she was now pregnant with their first child. Morning sickness combined with all the uncertainties of distressing times made this a most wretched time for Greer.

She had a dream from Prospero the angel. In the dream Prospero instructed her to resume her regular partaking of the Eucharist. In it he also assured her of Edwin's innocence. When she awoke she felt much relieved. One thing puzzled her. "Why didn't the angel mention whether Edwin was safe?"

She arose, threw on a robe and walked to her father's sleeping quarters. The guards stood at attention. She knocked on the door. Her father must have been awake as he opened the door only a moment later. Surprised to see her, he motioned her to come in.

"Father, I had a most happy dream visit from Prospero. He told me Edwin is innocent and that we must resume taking the Eucharist on a regular basis."

"Dear, I'm sure you would like it to be so simple, but how can you be sure you didn't conjure this dream through wishful thinking?"

"No, Father, this truly was Prospero appearing to me. I have no doubt."

Erith sat in silence contemplating his daughter's response. Thinking to himself, "Obviously she is so distraught she is now hallucinating what she wants to hear."

"Dear, I cannot take a chance on the Kingdom's future based on one dream."

"Why not? You, Percival and Edwin all relied on dreams for direction, with great results."

"Times have changed. Everything is different. What I once believed is all uncertain. I don't know what to believe anymore."

"Father, you can at least resume taking the Eucharist. I believe your beliefs will become clear once more."

"I don't have time to go to the church. I have more important uses of my time."

"Father, clearly you have been impacted by dark forces. You need the Eucharist to overcome them."

"That's enough! I won't have you talking to me like that."

"May I be excused, Your Majesty?"

"Greer, you don't have to revert to that. You can still call me Father."

"May I be excused, Father?"

"Of course. Good night."

"Good night, Father. I love you."

Greer turned to go out the door, but before she could open it, her father took her hand.

"Greer, you know I would love to believe your dream. Edwin has been like a son to me. It has torn my insides to think he could have betrayed us. But we must face the facts. Report after report has come from reliable sources indicating he is guilty of heinous acts. My generals would rebel if I chose to side with him."

"Father, start taking the Eucharist. I am going to start taking it twice daily. Join me."

"No, Greer. I won't take it. Our Divine Helper has let us down. I am not going to invest any more effort in that relationship."

"Good night, Father."

"Good night, my dear."

As Greer walked back to her quarters, she struggled with what had just happened. "I know that dream is true," she concluded as she entered her quarters. "I will not be shaken by my father's unbelief. Somehow we will all get through this."

# Chapter 13

Edwin and the other men all looked intently at Iosua as he considered his reply. Several moments went by as he carefully weighed his words.

"I have a clear sense of our being in grave danger by remaining in Evansing."

A groan went around the campfire as this was not something they wanted to hear.

He continued, "We are greatly outnumbered in hostile territory, which is getting more hostile the closer we get to Evansing Town. I believe it would be prudent to reconsider our present intention of going home at this very time."

"But what other options do we have?" said one of the men.

"Not going to Evansing Town is an option," replied Iosua. "Where we would go, I don't know. This is something we will have to consider. I know it must be a place where we can be safe for some time until we can more effectively confront what is happening here in Evansing. Anyone have suggestions?"

Silence lay heavy on the group as they wrestled with the prospect of being fugitives away from home.

One of the men shouted, "Look at the black cloud coming right towards us. We need to get shelter."

Edwin turned to look at the cloud and realized this was no ordinary cloud. It practically raced towards them. He chose to just wait for it and see what would happen.

As it hovered immediately over them, out came a familiar figure. There before him floating to earth was Joan of Arc.

Without any smile or sign of warmth in her greeting, she spoke, "Edwin, as you know you and your men are in grave danger if you remain in Evansing. Therefore provision has been made for your protective care. All of you that want to come, will accompany me to 15$^{th}$ century France for safekeeping. I should tell you however that during your stay you may be recruited into battle against the English. Whoever does not want to come, simply raise your hand and you will be left behind. You have a moment to consider your choice."

The men were flabbergasted at what she said and weren't sure how to respond to what they had just seen and heard.

Edwin realized he needed to make it very clear for them. "Men, this lady is Joan of Arc from the future. Over two years ago she rescued me from certain death. She has been sent by the Divine Creator to help us. You need to realize that if you stay in Evansing your life is in grave danger. She has come to give us safe refuge. We can trust her. The choice is yours. If any of you would rather remain in Evansing, raise your hand."

Five men raise their hands.

"Okay, you shall remain behind. I wish you well. The rest of you mount your horses and be ready to leave."

Then Joan noticed the three ladies. "Who are these women?"

Edwin answered, "They are women we rescued from Tara soldiers. They are decent women and my men have treated them with dignity."

"Alright, they may come."

The men and women mounted their horses. Immediately the cloud enveloped Joan and all the riders wanting to go. The cloud lifted off the ground, rose several hundred feet and then disappeared.

They reappeared in France almost 20 miles south of Paris.

Joan spoke, "You will be able to speak French as though you were born and raised here in France. This is a supernatural gifting given to you. As well you have all been assigned to a special unit of the Army of France. Your commander, Edwin, will answer to me directly."

As she finished, several men of the French army arrived on horseback. Their leader conferred briefly with Joan.

She introduced the leader, "This is Pierre Lecroix, he will take care of your needs such as getting you uniforms and assigning you to tents. He knows you are not from this time and place."

She rode away accompanied by one of the men who had come with Lecroix.

"Edwin, did Joan tell you that your arrival is most opportune for us?"

"No, she did not. She doesn't tend to share anything more than is necessary."

"Tomorrow we are proceeding to Paris and expect to attack it the day after."

"What is Paris?"

"You never heard of Paris? It is the grandest city in all the world."

"Perhaps that is so, but I have never heard of it. My knowledge of the world outside of Ireland is almost zero. Joan did tell us we may be recruited into battle against the English. I did not expect it to be so soon after our arrival."

Edwin turned to his men. "We are going into battle the day after tomorrow. I know it may seem contrary to the assurances of coming here for our safety. Let us be brave and trust it will go well with all of us."

Edwin's men, already feeling strange in this new land and new time, felt like they had been tricked. As it seemed they were about to mutiny against Edwin, a sudden calm came over them. The thoughts of being angry and betrayed dissipated.

Two miles down the road they came to a convent. Here the three women were left in the care of the nuns until it was time to go home.

The men continued another three miles to an army camp containing thousands of soldiers awaiting orders to move out
the next day. They were taken directly to the northwest corner of the camp where they were issued uniforms and assigned their tents.

Edwin and Iosua were given a tent to share together. This happened because Edwin requested Iosua to stay with him. He realized Iosua had a lot of wise discernment. Now that Percival was gone, Edwin had felt a vacuum in his life.

He thought, "Perhaps Iosua could fill at least a small part of that gap. No one could replace Percival. That was not possible. However if I can develop a deeper camaraderie with Iosua and glean much needed insights then that would at least help."

Joan's arrival to rescue them right after Iosua expressed a clear sense of danger gave a rather dramatic confirmation of the truth he had just shared.

"Iosua, how do you feel about our situation now? Do you wish we had stayed in Evansing? Going into battle against the English isn't exactly staying safe."

"I believe we did the right thing. As improbable as it seems, I consider us safer here in battle than if we were to remain on the run in Evansing. Something very dark has taken over our beloved land. We needed to be better situated. I am confident most of us will survive this battle and live to free Evansing. Our odds are better here than there."

"I agree with you, Iosua, as strange as it seems. I too am expecting most of us to make it back. Joan would never rescue us just to bring us to our death."

The next morning the trumpet sounded earlier than expected. Joan and her fellow commanders were eager to get to Paris. After a quick breakfast of hard biscuits and boiled eggs, they mounted their horses and awaited the command to move.

The Irish soldiers had an array of different looks on their faces. Some were obviously not happy about being involved in somebody else's war. Others considered it a bit of a lark. Most had their serious battle face as they embraced the reality of their situation. Edwin surveyed his men and felt quite pleased at how they were responding. He knew he had picked men of noble character. He had confidence they would play their roles well.

The men in front of them began to move and they followed. Iosua rode alongside Edwin.

"Edwin, any thoughts on how we are going to take back Evansing?"

"Not yet, but I am confident something will unfold when the time is right. The only way we will do it is by having extraordinary help from the supernormal. Perhaps Joan will play a role. We sow help in their war and they help in ours. Evansing can wait. Let's focus now on taking Paris."

After several hours they could see the walls of Paris ahead. The men from Ireland were awed by the size of the city. Nothing they had ever seen in Ireland matched the size and grandeur of Paris. Off to the side they could see a company riding with royal banners flying. Some of the troops near them shouted "Vive le roi!" King Charles had come to witness the attack.

Edwin was intently watching the royal party when he heard a familiar voice. "Edwin, come with me." Startled he looked away to see Joan. She smiled. Then she turned her horse around and he followed her.

"Where are we going?"

"To meet the King."

"What's my role?"

"You are my aide de camp today. I gave my regular one the day off. I wanted you to meet the King. I thought you would like to."

"That's it? You thought I would like to?"

"Yes, is that so surprising?"

"Well, yes, it is. You are normally all business."

"I can also be very human."

"That is good. I appreciate this other side of you."

The King was now only twenty or thirty yards ahead and they placed their gaze on him. The King looked in their direction and gave Joan a look of recognition without indicating joy or displeasure. Joan simply nodded acknowledgment.

Joan greeted the King, "Sire, it is good to see you here. The troops are much encouraged to see you present in this taking of Paris."

Charles responded, "Joan, I am expecting you to give me victory." The tone had an underlying sense of demand almost threatening. Certainly not what you would expect from a monarch who owed his crown to Joan.

Joan gave no indication of being taken aback or feeling intimidated. On the contrary she responded in her usual forthrightness and courage, "Sire, it is not I who can give you victory. Only the King of Heaven can do that."

The King said nothing, but almost glared in response.

"Sire, I now must be on my way to confer with the other officers. Au revoir." She turned her horse with Edwin alongside and away they went.

Edwin asked, "How did you feel about the King's way of relating to you?"

"It's not for me to concern myself with such matters. He is the King. He can choose to treat and speak to me any way he wants to. I am his loyal servant and I will serve him as long as I have breath."

Up ahead they saw the Duke of Alencon, the chief officer with which Joan had been planning the attack on Paris. The Duke's face lit up as he saw Joan coming. He loved Joan. Not romantically, but her combination of peasant girl innocence and courageous military command captivated him.

"Greetings, my dear duke. This is my aide de camp today, Edwin. He will attend me during our meeting today."

"Welcome, Edwin. You must be of high quality to qualify as Joan's aide de camp, even if it is only for a day."

"Thank you, sir. I am very privileged to work with Joan."

The rest of the day, Joan and the other officers finalized details for the assault on Paris.

For the most part Edwin sat as an observer, although surprisingly Joan would on occasion turn to him and ask him what he thought. To ask an aide de camp for his military advice was unheard of. They were meant to only assist with administrative matters. As Edwin shared wise insights the other officers began to look at him with new respect. They recognized this young man had acumen for military strategy.

When the meeting ended, Joan rode with Edwin back to his camp.

"Edwin, you rose to the challenge. The other officers liked what you shared. Perhaps we should keep you here in France in our battle against the English."

He looked at her closely to see if she was serious. She smiled in response. "No, I am not serious. Of course neither of us knows when you will return home. You may still play an important role here."

# Chapter 14

The next day Edwin and his men were up before dawn. The assault would begin shortly. They quietly munched on dried blueberries and smoked beef. Each man reflectively considered the possibility of his death and yet hoped he would be spared.

The walls surrounding Paris stood about 20 to 25 feet high, except of course for the towers which were higher. The battle plan entailed getting ladders against the walls and having troops scale them and overrun the defenders at the top. As well, the French archers would be firing into the top of the walls to thin the ranks of the defenders and distract them from the troops coming up the ladders.

Even though they wouldn't engage until the third wave, Joan wanted all the troops ready to go at the same time. As they sat on their horses they watched the blood-letting and heard the screams of men killing and being killed. Joan audaciously ran up the earthworks and demanded Paris surrender. They witnessed an arrow striking her in the thigh. She didn't stop, but continued to lead the battle. The initial wave of troops made little progress in breeching the walls. This was not to be unexpected as the first attack on a city seldom accomplished much in the way of tangible results. However if the men fought bravely it would intimidate the defenders and bolster those coming after them. They accomplished that objective.

The second wave responded with vigorous action resulting in some noticeable gains. Some of them made it to the top of the walls before being beaten back. It had looked so tantalizingly close and then it was snatched away.

Now it was the turn of Edwin and his men as they joined the third assault. Edwin and Iosua rode side by side. They held up their shields as arrows pelted down around them. They arrived at the wall in time to assist with the raising of a siege ladder. Edwin got on the ladder first and started to climb up. He held tightly onto his shield as rocks and other debris rained down on him. A sizeable boulder almost caused him to lose his grip. He thought to himself, "That hurt. Keep climbing."

Edwin felt the intensity of resistance increase as he passed the halfway point up the ladder. He stumbled and slipped a rung. Iosua the next man behind Edwin yelled encouragement. It helped to know he had a faithful friend right here with him. Now came boiling tar which his shield deflected. He kept going. A few more rungs and he would be in sword length of the top. Two of the defenders were using a pole to push his ladder away from the wall. An arrow caught one of them. The remaining defender succeeded in starting to move the ladder. Edwin surged the last several rungs and stretched out his sword to knock away the pole. For a brief second it almost seemed as though the ladder was about to fall back, but Edwin and Iosua both shifted their weight to move back in the direction of the wall. The ladder slammed back into the wall, both men hung on although the man behind Iosua lost his hold and fell off. Edwin swung his sword at the defender above as he climbed the last remaining rungs. He managed to beat the defender back enough to gain access to the top of the wall. As he landed on the walkway, two more defenders started to rush over. Before they arrived Edwin struck a flurry of parries and thrusts at the first defender which resulted in stabbing him in the throat. Then Edwin turned to face the two new opponents. He slashed down on the helmet of the first one to arrive. This blow stunned the soldier sufficiently for Edwin to follow up with a thrust to the man's left kidney, mortally wounding him. The other defender attempted to strike Edwin's back but this Edwin fended off with his shield. The defender then quickly swung again, this time at Edwin's left leg. Edwin managed to deflect the blow with his sword and jumped back out of reach. Then he rushed at the defender. He struck him in the side breaking several ribs. He followed this up with kneeing the man in the stomach, causing him to double up. Edwin brought his sword down on the man's exposed neck, slicing off his head.

By this time Iosua had also landed on the walkway. Three more troops came running towards them. Iosua confronted the man on their left while Edwin faced the two on their right.

Edwin held up his sword to stop the blow of the one and had to step back quickly to miss the slashing sword of the other. Edwin moved to his right and struck the man who had narrowly missed him. The blow struck a crucial artery, blood spurted out and the man fell down moaning in agony.

As Edwin squared off against the remaining challenger he could hear the sound of retreat. He thought to himself, "Retreat? Why would we retreat?" He didn't realize that he and Iosua were the only ones to make it to the top. Both men finished off their defenders and then ran to the ladder and scrambled down. They escaped back to their lines, narrowly being missed by a hail of arrows.

Contrary to their expectations the mood in the French camp was quite upbeat. What Edwin and Iosua thought to be a disappointing defeat had been considered rather successful for the first day of a siege.

The next day another unexpected turn occurred. The King decided instead of regarding the first day as a success he considered it a defeat. He had lost his stomach for further battle. Joan and the Duke of Alencon had tried to convince him that the first day of almost success gave great promise for taking Paris, even in one more day. But the King was unmoved. His shortage of funds and weak character combined to block him in his perceptions of what was best. Joan and the Duke were greatly distressed, but the King had made his decision. Even in this great disappointment, Joan maintained an honoring attitude toward the King.

Joan came to Edwin's camp. He gave her a hug. She looked at him surprised. Then she quietly said, "Thanks, Edwin. I didn't realize how much I needed that."

"You may be a General in the French Army, but you still bleed when you are cut. How can I help?"

"I think you just did." Then she went on to express her feelings over the next hour. Edwin listened intently, applying the listening skills he learned from Greer. Although difficult to execute well he managed to give some sensitive interjections as he felt was appropriate. All those sometimes painful conversations with Greer had formed wisdom in him as to how to relate to a troubled female.

Joan then turned the conversation to what was to become of Edwin and his men. "I am contemplating new assignments, however the King has not given me permission for anything at this time. There has been no new communication from the God of Heaven concerning your return. Therefore I can find a place for you and your men where you can safely wait and provision is provided."

"Could I continue to be your adjutant?"

"I will see if that is possible. I have no command and no specific role other than to remain with the King at his Court. I think he wants to keep me close so he can keep an eye on me. There wouldn't be any reason for me to have an adjutant. Let me ponder it and get back to you. I need to go now. I am exhausted. Good night. Thanks for being a good friend."

Edwin smiled and nodded in reply.

He went to sleep that night aching to see Greer but also contented in how he was there for Joan when she needed him. "Greer would have been proud of..." He fell asleep into a disturbing dream. Or was it a dream?

# Chapter 15

Edwin was abruptly woken by a heavy hand and then grabbed by two strong men and lifted to his feet. A third man bound his hands behind his back. Then they dragged him outside.

Edwin started to protest but received a sharp blow to his ribs. He decided to stay quiet. They put him on a horse, blindfolded him and tied his hands to the horse's saddle. As they rode, Edwin could hear the men talking about him. They kept saying the word spy. He realized they were considering him to be a spy.

"That's preposterous. How could they think I am a spy?" Edwin's mind questioned.

Almost an hour went by before they stopped. Edwin heard someone mention that the King wanted to see him first thing in the morning.

"The King? Why would the King want to question a suspected spy? Wouldn't he simply have his henchmen do the questioning and have them report back to him?"

The escort took Edwin to a cell. It reminded him of the same surroundings he experienced when kidnapped by King Taryn of Merethath. Indeed the filth and smell in this cell exceeded the one in Merethath.

"Who will get me out of this? Only one person, Joan. She will help." That comforted him.

The next morning Edwin was led by his jailers into a room in the same building that housed his prison cell. There the King awaited him, sitting on a makeshift throne. The King showed no malice nor any emotion. He stared momentarily at Edwin before motioning to one of his advisors.

The advisor, a sly looking individual named Nicholas De Sade, started by asking Edwin his full name.

Edwin ignored the advisor and instead addressed the King, "Sire, I respectfully ask you to send for Jeanne d'Arc. She can vouch for me."

The King remained silent.

The advisor became visibly agitated, "Answer the question."

"My name is Edwin."

"Where are you from?"

As Edwin pondered how to answer, he heard himself say "Calais."

"Oh really? Calais is my place of birth and where I grew up. Let us see if you can answer some questions about Calais?" He then proceeded to ask Edwin a series of questions concerning the geographical features and landmarks in and around Calais.

Surprising himself, Edwin answered the questions as though he had lived in Calais all his life.

The questioner, visibly disturbed and frustrated by the accurate responses finally stopped and reconsidered his approach. "Is it not true that you have been engaged by the English to spy on us?"

"No, it's not true. You have just created that thought with your own imagination."

The questioner slapped Edwin. "How dare you be so insolent as to question my integrity?"

Edwin remained silent.

"Answer me. Have you nothing to say?"

Edwin continued to remain silent.

DeSade again slapped him. "Answer me."

Edwin replied, "You are not interested in the truth for this whole affair has been trumped up for reasons only known to you and your fellow accusers. I have done nothing wrong. Why don't you tell me the real reason for why you are putting me through this sham questioning? You are only trying to justify an outcome you have already determined."

DeSade turned purple with rage and started to kick and slap Edwin until the King motioned to one of the guards to pull him off of Edwin.

The King's demeanor started to soften, yet he was not ready to simply release Edwin. "Return the prisoner back to his cell."

On the way back to his cell Edwin asked his escort what was going on. They of course said nothing, but a prisoner in an adjacent cell overheard the question. After the guards left, the prisoner whispered to Edwin, "They're trying to isolate Jeanne D'Arc by removing her friends and supporters."

"Why are they doing that?"

"The King has no stomach to fight and wants to create a treaty with the Burgundians."

"Surely you jest. After all that Jeanne has done for the King, how can he be so ungrateful?"

"I didn't say it was the King."

"You didn't have to. It wouldn't happen without his approval. Besides he was present just now when they questioned me."

"He was present? Now that is interesting. He is obviously very interested in you. Who are you?"

"I am Edwin of Calais."

"I mean who are you really, so as to command such respect from the King?"

Edwin paused for a moment about whether to reveal more information concerning himself. Then he realized that would be foolish. "I have no idea other than if what you say is true it is because of my friendship with Jeanne."

The fellow prisoner said nothing. After a long pause, he said, "I can help you get out."

"You can? When and how?"

"Tonight. As to the how, trust me you will know when it is time. Be ready."

Edwin spent the rest of the morning pondering his situation, missing Greer and wondering how he would get out. Shortly after noon he dozed off for several minutes until his cell door creaked open. In walked four members of the King's special troop. They told him to get up, which he did. They tied his hands behind his back, so tight he almost winced. He kept it in because he didn't want to show weakness. They then roughly grabbed him and walked him out of the prison. He thought to himself, "Back into the sunlight, it feels good. But where are they taking me?"

The guards blindfolded him and then helped him get on a horse. They rode for over an hour with several stops. Then they stopped to wait for what sounded like a large city gate opening up.

Soon the quiet of the country was replaced with the noisy din of a city, causing Edwin to ask himself "What city is this?"

Their destination turned out to be only a short distance from the gates as they soon stopped and helped him off his horse. The guards led him up a winding staircase for two stories. One of them removed his blindfold. There before him sat a rather distinguished looking individual. The man introduced himself to Edwin as Jean de Wavrin.

Before he could ask Edwin any questions, "Where am I and what do you want with me?"

"Edwin, you are of great interest to us. You and your comrade are known to be the only French soldiers to have breached our walls. More importantly, it has come to my attention that you are a great friend of Jeanne D'Arc. As to where you are, you are in Paris."

"Paris? How is that possible? Did you abduct me? Or has Charles made a deal with you?"

"The how you are here is irrelevant. What is important is how are you going to respond to my proposal?"

"What is your proposal?

"My proposal is that in exchange for your life you will agree to follow our instructions to turn Jeanne D'Arc over to us."

Edwin thought to himself, "If I point blank refuse, they will kill me. If I say yes, I can recant later and warn Jeanne."

"What is it going to be?"

"You don't give me much in the way of choice. How do you propose I turn her over to you?"

"She trusts you and I am sure if you suggest to her she come along with you for a ride into the countryside, she will join you. The precise location and time will be communicated to you later by one of our men. If you try to renege on your promise, I can assure you we have many highly placed friends to take care of you. As long as you are in France, you are under our watch."

Once more the blindfold was placed on Edwin. He was led down the stairs and assisted onto his horse and away they rode.

The ride back was not a restful one for Edwin as he wrestled within himself as to what he was going do. After almost an hour, the blindfold was removed and his hands were untied. He looked around and could recognize some familiar landmarks. He was only a few miles from the camp where he had originally been arrested. Or had he been abducted? His guards turned to ride in the opposite direction without so much as a word.

The initial euphoria of release soon evaporated as the reality of his situation became clearer to his jumbled thoughts. "How can I protect Joan without jeopardizing my own life and the lives of my men? Why would King Charles want to turn over Joan to the Burgundians?" Then he reminded himself that he had no absolute proof of the King's involvement, just a strong suspicion.

When Edwin returned to the camp, his men warmly greeted him and expressed great relief at his safe return. They had been told Edwin had been arrested as a traitor and of course with an accusation like that it didn't look good. Edwin explained it had all been a misunderstanding and all was well. He had already determined he could not tell anyone the truth. He didn't know who to trust even among his own men. For all he knew they too could have been pressured to inform on Edwin.

One thing the men conspiring to kidnap Joan failed to appreciate was the extensive intelligence network she possessed among the soldiers and common people. She had already been informed of Edwin being brought to Paris, for what purpose she didn't know for sure, except she suspected it related to her. After all what other reason would there be for such preposterous charges against Edwin. All this Edwin discovered when Joan came to his camp and they rode away together outside the camp. Edwin had shared the proposal he had been given. Joan's response indicated disappointment but no surprise.

"The King's chief advisor has been proposing a treaty with the Burgundians for some time. The King may not have directed such an action against me, but it's unlikely he didn't know of it. The English have pressured the Burgundians to try and capture me. Our friendship presented them an opportunity to do so. Now we must ensure the safety of you and your men. This is our first priority. As for me, it may be God's will I become a captive. I trust his Wisdom for my life."

"No, Joan, how can that be? How can any good come from you being a captive? We must do everything to avoid that."

"Edwin, I appreciate your concern for me. His ways are not our ways. I will accept whatever needs to be. My first concern is you and your men. I have a wealthy woman friend with a large estate about forty miles from here. When I heard you had been arrested, I sent her a message. I expect to receive her reply tomorrow. I believe she will give you and your men refuge."

"If something happens to you how will we get back to Evansing?"

"I'm sure if necessary our Creator has alternative plans for your return."

# Chapter 16

Early the next morning, shortly after Edwin awoke; a messenger came to his tent.

"Sir, a message from Monsieur de Wavrin. I am to await your reply."

Edwin quickly broke the seal and read the scroll.

"Edwin, I trust you are well. Now is the time for you to deliver on your promise. Beginning tomorrow I will have a squad of men waiting five miles outside of your camp on the road to Paris. They will wait for three days. This should give you adequate opportunity to get Jeanne to accompany you. She has no current duties and no assignment to leave her current location."

Edwin looked the messenger in the eye and said, "I will see what I can do."

After the messenger left, Edwin got on his horse and rode into the nearby village where Jeanne was billeted by a kindly old widow.

"Joan, I have received a message to bring you to a place on the road to Paris. There a squad of men await to capture you. We have three days. Have you heard from your friend?"

"No, I haven't."

"That may make things rather interesting. Do you have any other options?"

"Not that I have determined."

"One other option exists."

"Oh, what is that?"

"Take us back to Evansing."

"But I haven't received orders to do so. I can't just will it on my own."

"You can ask."

"I haven't done that before."

Silence as Joan pondered his request.

"I will do it. God of Heaven, I ask you to enable me to escort Edwin and his men back to Evansing."

After several moments, Joan's eyes lit up. "He will do it. We need to go to your camp immediately."

When they arrived at the camp Iosua informed them that five men had been led away by a platoon of the King's men, not more than fifteen minutes before. Edwin sat on his horse momentarily considering what had happened and what his alternatives were. "Everyone saddle up. We are going after them."

The men cheered. They had been cowed by the official nature of the King's soldiers. As well there were over a thousand soldiers of the French army situated only a hundred yards or so away.

"Joan, since you now have permission to help us can you give us a jumpstart in catching up?"

"I will do better than that. I will put us in front of them."

Ten minutes later they were all on the road waiting for the King's men to arrive. When the platoon commander sighted them, he halted his troop. The commander surveyed what was before him. What he saw was an armed troop double the size of his trotting towards him with Jeanne d'Arc in the lead.

The commander seemed frozen not knowing what to do. He asked himself, "Are they friendly or not? Why is Jeanne with them?" Then he recognized some of the men as being at the very camp they had just left. "How did they get ahead of us?" This confused him further. He awaited the arrival of Jeanne and her troops.

"Good day, commander,"

"Good day, Jeanne. How is it that we meet?"

"There has been a misunderstanding. The five men you arrested were taken by you in error. They are to be released into my custody."

"Do you have written orders? I cannot simply release them to you without written authorization."

"Commander, you know who I am. I am your superior in the French Army. I have authority over you. You are in danger of being charged with insubordination."

"That may be true, Jeanne. However I have my orders from the King himself. I cannot dismiss that charge without his authorization."

"Commander, you are putting yourself and your men in grave danger. Turn over the five men and be on your way."

This reply surprised the commander. To hear such a blunt threatening command from Jeanne was totally unexpected. He recovered his composure. "Jeanne, you are interfering with the King's soldiers while on a mission for the King. That could bring you grave consequences."

"Maybe so, but I still must insist you turn over those five men."

The commander again hesitated to consider his course of action, but then he defiantly stated, "No, I will not give them to you. We will fight to the last man if necessary and you will pay with your life, Jeanne."

No sooner had he finished than he was knocked off his horse.

The commander, winded by the fall, looked up to see the angel Prospero.

"I want you to turn over those five men."

"Who are you? What are you?"

"I am Prospero, an angel sent by the God of Heaven."

Meanwhile no one else can see or hear Prospero. The onlookers are thinking the commander has gone mad.

"Take them!" He turned to command his men to release them to Jeanne.

The five men joyfully rejoined their comrades as they all rode away back in the direction of their camp. In the meantime Prospero wiped away the commander's and his men's memory and their encounter and re-wrote their memory so they all recalled not finding Edwin and his men at the camp.

As the Evansing troop were about to be launched back into their own time, one of the men reminded Edwin of the women they had dropped off at the convent.

"They will be better off there than back in Evansing not knowing if they will live or die."

The soldier replied, "Shouldn't they at least have the choice to decide that for themselves? They are only twelve miles from here"

This reply irritated Edwin, but he knew it was true. "Let's go and pick up the women. I will give them the choice."

The troop was within a few miles of the convent when they encountered a French patrol of almost 100 men.

Its commander, curious to see Jeanne out with a detachment of soldiers, asked Jeanne what was the nature of her being out and about.

"That, commander, is none of your concern."

"Pardon, Jeanne, if that seemed out of order, but I am assigned to be aware of what is going on in this district."

"Commander, you are now aware that I am here. That's all you need to know." With that she turned her horse to go around the patrol followed by Edwin and his men.

When the troop arrived at the convent they were warmly greeted by the women they had left there earlier.

Mary, their unofficial leader, spoke, "We were becoming concerned about whether you were coming back for us, or if even you were still alive."

Edwin replied, "Wouldn't you rather stay here where you are safe?"

"Safe? We are not interested in just being safe. We are Irish, not French. We don't even belong in this century. Yes, I know there are uncertainties going back home, but that is where we belong. We want to go back."

"I can't guarantee your safety."

"We will face what we must."

Edwin thought to himself, "She has an unusual courage."

The three women bade a fond and tearful farewell to their hosts and then mounted the horses provided for them. Led by Joan and Edwin they all rode about a mile away until suddenly they were launched through the time tunnel.

Where they arrived, the weather had that dampness so typical of Ireland. Edwin and none of the men and women minded. It felt so good to be back home and in familiar surroundings. They knew they were in Ireland and most likely in Evansing, but none of them could recognize exactly where they were.

Joan stayed only a moment to bid a hurried good-bye before vanishing back in the time tunnel.

Nearby they noticed a solitary farmhouse.

Edwin rode over to the house and knocked on the door.

The door opened and a man with a very familiar face appeared. He smiled, while Edwin stood speechless.

Edwin wondered if he had gone mad.

"Is that, is that really you?"

"Yes, Edwin, it really is me."

"Our Creator decided you needed some help."

Edwin fell into Percival's arms and wept.

91

# Chapter 17

**P**ercival held onto the sobbing Edwin for several minutes before his young protégé could compose himself. It showed the growth in Edwin as he had absolutely no regrets about sobbing in front of his companions. All that pent up grief and suspense had at last an opportunity to be released.

"Edwin, you will have to fill me in as to what has transpired. Nothing was told to me other than you needed help."

Edwin informed his friend of all their adventures and the apparent bewitching of Evansing. When he finished, he looked at Percival awaiting some great words of wisdom.

Silence.

Edwin continued to wait, but Percival was looking intently off to the side, saying nothing.

"I am seeing Erith in a very dark place. What I mean is he is in a very dark place mentally. I am hearing that he is King in name only. Someone has usurped his power and is allowing him to live restricted to the personal quarters of Evansing Castle."

"What about Greer? How is she?"

"I don't know, I am just seeing Erith. At least he is alive."

"Now I am seeing Greer. She is in her quarters with her two ladies in waiting. She looks like she has gained weight. Oh, she is pregnant!"

"She is pregnant? How she must wish I was with her. Oh, how I wish I was with her. My heart aches for her."

"Trust me, Edwin; I am here for a reason. Somehow we are going to resolve this in a good way."

"Even though something very dark has taken over Evansing, we know The Light is with us. We will overcome."

"Hearing that from you does give me hope. It is a very difficult situation, but you are right in saying there must be cause to believe for a good outcome. After all, you coming back to life is not a small thing."

"That's right. Let's start planning what is going to be our strategy for freeing Erith. One question to be answered is who is now in charge? Who was the disloyal subject that would do such a thing?"

"Can't you simply look again and see?"

"Yes, I can try." After a few minutes Percival's eyes lit up. "Hugo is the one who betrayed."

Edwin replied, "Hugo? How is that possible? He has never given any obvious sign of displeasure with the King. He has always demonstrated such loyalty."

"He may have covered his true feelings rather well. If he had resentments towards Erith then he could have been much more susceptible to the dark influences in Evansing. Are you sure you can't think of any reason why he would want to betray Erith?"

"Hmmm, I do recall a time less than a year ago when Erith spoke rather harshly to Hugo in front of several other officers. Hugo's face turned red and it was several days before anyone saw him again. He definitely felt ashamed and now it is obvious he must have also been very angry."

"Precisely. The perfect opportunity for some Druid mischief."

"Perhaps we can simply sneak into the castle by supernormal means and assassinate Hugo."

"We shall see if that is what we are to do. Remember, Edwin, we don't necessarily do things the way we did them before. The thought that comes to me is to have Hugo come to us."

"Come to us? Now that is novel. How so?"

"Ask Prospero to bring him."

"Would he do that?"

"Let's ask. Prospero, could you please come? We have something to talk to you about."

After a moment Prospero appeared in a shimmering white robe radiating with light.

"Yes, gentlemen, what would you like to talk about?"

Percival replied, "We have a special request to ask of you. As I am sure you know there has been a change in leadership in Evansing. Would you bring the new leader, Hugo, to us here?"

"I could, but do you think that is the best tactic at this time?"

"What do you mean?"

"Hugo is not the root problem. You need to first deal with the Druid influence over Evansing."

"Of course you are absolutely right. I should have known better. Can you tell us how to eliminate the Druid interference?"

"I can give you a clue."

Silence.

After several minutes, Percival inquired, "Are you going to tell us?"

"Yes, I am going to tell you. The key issue making it possible for Evansing to be taken over is jealousy."

"Jealousy?" replied Edwin. "What is it that has created such jealousy?"

"Erith, has been jealous of King Chafen of Randar."

Edwin queried, "Why ever so?"

"Do you recall your trip back to Randar?"

"Yes."

"What was one occurrence on that trip that changed Erith from convivial to morose?"

Edwin thought for a moment, then he recalled the one incident most upsetting to Erith.

"It was when Erith viewed Chafen's top two horses. He realized right away they were superior to anything he had. It most disturbed him because he has always been very proud of his horses. To have someone else better him in an area he considers so important quite disappointed him. I didn't think of it being as distressing as it now appears. Although come to think of it, Greer and I both noticed that the King didn't seem to be quite as content as before the Randar trip."

Percival said, "Yes, I also noticed a change and I did ask him about it, but he would just pass it off and say he was fine."

Percival asked, "Prospero, what kind of help can we ask of you?"

"I am glad you asked that. Our Glorious Leader has given me permission to help you in whatever way you need. Say what you need and I will do it."

"Bring us Erith."

Without a word Prospero disappeared.

Moments later he reappeared with a dazed Erith.

"Wha… what happened? How did I get here? Percival! Edwin! Oh how I am glad to see you both. Edwin, we have heard troubling news about you. Is it true you've turned bandit and are harming helpless women and children?"

At hearing such a question Edwin didn't know whether to laugh or get indignant. He paused for a moment to consider his reply.

"No, Erith, I am not a bandit. You have been duped by Druids cursing Evansing. Have you been taking the Eucharist? Without it you are helpless. Does Greer believe it would be possible for me to turn bandit?"

"No, she refuses to believe you are capable of such heinous behavior."

"And you?"

"I must admit I started to believe those reports. They were so convincing. What you mentioned about the Eucharist is the same as what Greer told me. I slowed down and then stopped altogether. I felt our Divine Helper had abandoned me."

"It may seem like it, but His angel Prospero brought you here. That should be convincing proof he is still able and willing to help you and us."

Erith pondered Edwin's words. "Yes, I suppose you are right in saying that. I lost hope. My mind focused on a downward spiral of negative thoughts and disappointments. I couldn't pull myself out of it."

Percival replied, "Now, Erith, we are going to work with all the resources available to us to recover your faith and your Kingdom."

"You think we can do that?"

"Yes, I think we can do that. Your Divine Helper will help. Indeed help is on the way."

Edwin then asked the question most on his mind, "How is Greer?"

"She is distressed about you and the Kingdom… and she is pregnant."

"Oh what sorrow for me to be here and she to be there. Is she well?"

"As well as any pregnant woman can be when her husband is away. I have done what I can to support her, but I admit I have not been in a great mental state to do so. She needs you."

Edwin stood in silence contemplating his pregnant wife being alone and distressed. He choked back tears and steeled himself to stick to the matters at hand.

Edwin and Percival then shared about how Percival came back from the dead with the express purpose of helping. As well Edwin shared of their being captured, reduced to a tiny size and then being restored and escaping back to Evansing with a side trip to France in the 15th century.

"These tales you share are truly amazing. Perhaps we *can* recover my Kingdom."

Edwin and Percival looked at each other quizzically as to how Erith could still doubt. Then they realized Erith needed to take the Eucharist right now.

After taking the Eucharist, Erith's normal confident disposition started to reappear.

Edwin shared, "We killed Clarendon."

"I can't say I am totally surprised to hear that. He did turn out to be a most frustrating stumbling block. I suppose in his mind he was rather clever in his flopping back and forth. We have been cut off from all news outside of Evansing Town. Who is his successor?"

"One of his cousins, I suspect. Greer will be grieved at his death and even more so at the possible death of Kendy. Perhaps she will be spared."

"We will contend with his successor later. Now let us start formulating a plan to win back my Kingdom. Why don't we ask if St. Patrick could come and bring us strategies and other means to help?"

"Sounds like a great idea. Now you are starting to talk like the King I remember you to be."

"Yes, I am beginning to feel like my old self. I am rather annoyed with allowing myself to dwell on negatives and get into such a state of pessimism."

"Sire, I believe it would be best for you to be the one to ask if it would be possible for St. Patrick to come and help us."

"Our Divine Helper, if it is permitted by you, could you please send St. Patrick to help us recover my Kingdom?"

No immediate response. This was not unusual. If St. Patrick was meant to come then he would come when the timing was right.

Percival broke the silence, "In the meantime, Edwin, the men and women accompanying you must be fed and sheltered. I did not come back without resources. Let us walk a little way into that nearby grove of birch trees."

After a short walk into the grove they encountered a small hill. Percival picked up a clump of dirt and grass on the side of the hill revealing a large iron ring. He pulled on the ring and a large door opened up. The three of them stepped inside and there awaiting them in a vast room on several large tables surrounded by benches, was a feast of wines and all manner of meats, breads, cheeses and vegetables.

Edwin, astounded, asked, "Where did this come from?"

"Angels."

"I will call the others in."

As Edwin walked to tell his companions to come in, he considered what he had just seen. In spite of all the miracles they had experienced, he knew many of them still struggled with doubts about how things would turn out. If he was honest with himself he would have to admit that even he struggled at times to believe it could still turn out well for them.

"Ladies and fellow soldiers, I have some very good news. There is shelter and abundant food awaiting us in that grove of birch trees. The horses will have to be secured and we'll need ten men to stand guard. Iosua, select the men we need for guard duty. Food and drink will be brought out to you and you can take turns staying in the farmhouse for shelter. Two of the men will be posted half way between the grove and the farmhouse, so that in the event of an attack they can alert the rest of us to come and help."

The men and women stood there in silence and unmoving, not fully comprehending what they had just heard. Some of them thought Edwin was jesting, but he didn't have a look that would indicate that. Slowly it dawned on them that he was serious. They started to walk to the grove with a growing anticipation of feeling safe and well-fed.

# Chapter 18

In the room, everyone ate and laughed to their heart's contentment. No one was quite sure how to fully believe that this was possible, and yet here it was. They were eating the impossible. They were warm and protected. Erith still had not said anything to the group and Edwin's companions weren't sure what to make of that either.

Now Erith arose to address the assembly, "My loyal subjects you may well wonder how I arrived here. One of our Creator's angels brought me here so that I could be restored to my senses. I had allowed myself to be hypnotized by Druid lies. My self-pity and failure to be grateful for what I had made me susceptible to focus on what I didn't have. As a result I increasingly distanced myself from the Source of Light and Life. Darkness began to dominate my thinking and perspective. I acknowledge my wrong has endangered the Kingdom and each one of you. Therefore I ask that each one of you would forgive me for this."

The listeners were again unsure how respond to this. As Erith stood in silence, it was apparent he was awaiting a response. The people started talking amongst themselves. Finally a young soldier called Cedric stood up.

"King Erith, I forgive you for this wrong."

Then another soldier stood up and eventually all those present expressed forgiveness, except for the women from Tara, who were not Erith's subjects.

After the last person had expressed forgiveness, Erith replied, "Thank you each and every one of you for your gracious forgiveness. I feel relieved and refreshed having received it."

Percival leaned over to tell Erith, "Prospero is waiting outside to return you to your castle."

Erith and Percival both arose from their seats and went outside. There awaited Prospero who exuded greater majesty than before. The angel who normally looked rather sober and even stern now appeared happy and pleased. He laid a hand on Erith and they disappeared. Percival stood there for a moment and considered what he had witnessed, then he went inside and informed everyone of Erith's return to his castle.

The initial response was one of alarm and concern for the King's welfare. Percival responded by explaining the importance of Erith's return in order to turn the present situation around. This calmed the people and they recognized the King now had a new capacity to work with the forces of Light so as restore Evansing to its normal sublime self.

Later that evening as the people began to prepare themselves for a night's rest, Edwin and Percival started to discuss what would be their next steps to assist in the restoration.

"Edwin, I believe we should allow some time to allow the new spiritual atmosphere to take over. Already I can sense the shift has begun. This is very exciting. We will see things we have never seen before."

"Even though I don't sense any change yet, I do believe you, Percival. What do we do now?"

"We wait with anticipation and readiness knowing we may be called to action on very short notice."

"I will have the men train tomorrow morning. We will work on formations most effective in situations where a small force like ours can surprise the enemy. I hate using that word enemy when referring to other Evansing soldiers. However it is our present reality until they have all been freed from these dark influences."

"Yes, Edwin, since I know how much you care for your men, it must be painful."

"Thank you, Percival, I am glad you shared that. I need to know that someone else can appreciate the pain I am experiencing. It is so lonely at times to be responsible for all these people. Of course even more painful is to know that Greer has to go through this pregnancy alone without me at her side."

"Yes, I know it is difficult for her, but I do have confidence in her ability to stay strong. She is so centered. Besides her obvious beauty she also has remarkable strength. I am sure in your deeper moments of reflection about her you realize that."

"Percival, you are so right. I didn't always appreciate it at first because her strength sometimes got in the way of me wanting to do things my way. She wanted us to develop our way of doing things. I initially interpreted her responses as her simply wanting to do things her way. Then it began to dawn on me what she really wanted. When that happened I found it much easier to cooperate with her and to even begin developing our ways of doing things."

"Edwin, it won't be long before you are in Greer's arms once again. Be of good cheer this will unfold well."

Then both men bid each other good night and went to sleep.

# Chapter 19

Greer could feel the baby kicking and decided since she couldn't sleep anymore she might as well get up. As she sat on the edge of her bed she heard a knock on the door.

"Who's there?"

"It's your father."

Greer put her robe on and then said, "Come in, Father."

She noticed her father looked totally different than the last time she saw him. He emanated a hopeful joy on his face and it almost seemed to radiate with light.

"Father, what has happened to you?"

"I have returned only a few minutes ago from visiting Edwin and Percival."

"What? How is that possible?"

"Prospero took me to them."

"How is my precious Edwin?"

"He is safe and he is not the rogue we have been led to believe."

"I knew that. My Edwin would never do the things they accused him of doing."

"My dear Greer, I have been such a fool to doubt Our Creator. I had allowed dark thoughts and lies to plague my soul. As a result I lost my hope and became vulnerable to Druid treachery. I acknowledged my wrong to Edwin and Percival and all those with them. After doing so I have been filled with new hope and joy. Even Prospero had a new visible joy about him. Something else has come to me. It just popped into my head after I had arrived back. I acknowledged my envy of the King of Randar's horses. That envy robbed me of my contentment and gratitude leading to a downward spiral, which in turn created vulnerability to the Druid magic. And now we have this great mess to overcome."

"What an amazing turnaround, Father! I must admit I felt rather pessimistic about you ever coming to your senses. I believe your dark episode was a necessary step not only in your life's progress but also that of Evansing and perhaps all of Ireland. You and I must have a deep assurance that everything has purpose. Therefore you have no need to feel regrets and consider it all loss."

Erith looked at his daughter with surprise and appreciation. "You are such a treasure, Greer, to encourage me like that. I must admit I did not look at this situation from that perspective."

Greer looked into her father's eyes with love and appreciation. Erith breathed in her look.

After a moment had passed, Erith continued,"The situation requires action soon. I am going to start planning my next steps now. The trickiest part is to know who for sure is still loyal. I know the light released by my repentance will grow over the next several days. This requires me to weigh the need for action with the need for the right people to become free to work with me. Pray that I will have wisdom."

After giving Greer a light peck on her cheek he left.

Back in his personal quarters, Erith sat down to consider the course to be taken. As he pondered his situation he realized how imperative it was for him to start taking the Eucharist on a regular basis. It would clear his thinking and empower him to think from a possibility perspective. Right now the only thoughts he received told him how impossible his situation was. He arose and made a request to the guards to summon the priest so he could take the sacrament. An hour later, the priest, Father O'Hara arrived.

"Your Majesty, it is so good to hear that you wanted to receive the Eucharist. I have been concerned about your welfare in not coming to Mass."

"Thank you for your concern, Father, but I have had some matters interfere with my attendance." Erith would not share anything more as Hugo had threatened his life and that of Greer if he were to raise an alarm about the usurping of the King's power.

After taking the Eucharist, Erith could feel his eyes and mind clearing. He noticed a growing sense of hope. He considered how it had now been almost a week since Hugo had committed a de facto coup. What puzzled him is why Hugo had allowed him and Greer to live. "What advantage is there to him allowing us to live? Or is there something or someone preventing him?" Then the thought came to him, "One of the most influential generals must have insisted on this condition in order to support Hugo. Who would that be? Connor, of course, it must be Connor. But why would he agree to such a thing even with such a condition. It must be a strategic move where he was buying time for things to change. Connor is well versed in the spiritual realm. He knows the effect it can have. I need to ask Connor to come and see me."

The next morning Erith asked one of the guards to summon Connor to come and see him.

A reply came in the afternoon "I am unable to see you now, Sire"

Erith considered the curt reply and pondered why it was so. "He must be considering it dangerous to visit me. What now?"

As he sat there pondering his next move, he noticed a light in the corner of the room. The light got larger and brighter. He felt a strange calmness as he viewed with fascination this most unusual phenomenon.

From the light came a voice, "Erith, you have nothing to fear. There is about to be a sudden reversal in your fortunes. Trust me when it looks difficult." Then the light disappeared.

Moments later four burly guards burst into his room and grabbing him roughly escorted him to a cell in the dungeon reserved for the most dangerous criminals. After they left him, he sat in the damp darkness struggling to maintain his composure. He recalled the light's words and chose to believe them. In doing so he felt a strengthening.

A brief time later in came Sean, Hugo's right hand man. He walked up to Erith's cell and said, "Erith, your time is short. You have been weighed and found wanting." Then he turned and walked away.

The King stared at him as he disappeared into the gloom. Sean's words rang in his soul and he once again found himself struggling to keep his composure.

A voice rang out, "Erith, remember the light."

The voice shook him out of his tailspin into worry and fear.

Erith spoke out his confidence, "I am expecting to be restored to my throne."

Immediately after he spoke it out, something was thrown into his cell. Erith turned around and stooped over to pick it up. It was a tightly bound parchment of paper. He untied it and slowly unrolled it. He started to read it, "Sire, you have been weighed and found worthy. You have many powerful friends. Expect things to change for the better, soon."

Erith stared at the words for several moments. He wanted to believe them to be true. But his head kept nagging at him. "Maybe it's just someone trying to jest with me. Oh, why can't I just ..."

Erith's hands trembled as he stared at the parchment and then he slowly put it down. "What a wondrous thing is going on." He had a deep calm come over him. He would stay in peace and await the outcome.

In the morning Erith awoke feeling rather refreshed and expectant. He felt the best he had felt in months. Nothing had changed externally; he was still in a dark dank dungeon. What had changed was his mind. His body was imprisoned, but his mind was free. It was free to receive new ideas. And the new ideas started to come. He started to think about how St. Patrick had helped with their battle in Dagarath. It was almost St. Patrick's Day, the thought percolated for a moment or so and then he decided. "St. Patrick, if it is right and proper for you to come and help me, please come." Of course there was no instant flash of light and appearance of the revered saint. However, Erith clearly felt he had put something into motion.

Later that morning as he visualized being restored to his throne and seeing Greer and Edwin and their child all enjoying life together, a strange thought came to him. Say out loud right now, St. Patrick are you here? He considered for a moment that two guards were standing right outside his cell. Then he said it, "St. Patrick, are you here?"

The guards looked up at him in derision and then collapsed, one falling on top of the other.

Immediately there appeared a flash of light and smoke and there standing in all his holiness was St. Patrick. The saint had a smile on his face, even a mischievous look. "Hello, Erith, how did you like my entry? I like to add a little extra once in awhile."

"I like you being here. How you enter is of no concern to me. I am very glad you are here."

"Congratulations, Erith, my specialty is getting people out of tight places. You qualify."

"Yes, Patrick, I do. What work of wonder are you about to do?"

"Nothing. At this present moment."

"Sir, nothing? Then why have you come? They are about to kill me, I just know it."

"Yes, it is true, Hugo is planning to kill you soon. He has determined a way to do so that will actually blame your friend, Connor. The key for you is to remain calm. This is an important time for you. Pass the test and you shall be restored to even greater splendor. Fail it and you will surely die along with Greer and her child."

"You mean the test is stay calm while I am awaiting death?"

"Yes, Erith, it is as simple as that. The Master's tests are not complicated."

With that the saint began to fade away and soon Erith was left alone with his thoughts once more.

Moments later the guards started to rouse to consciousness. The one under the other pushed the one on top of him away. "Get off of me! What happened? What are you doing on top of me?"

"I don't know. You think I would deliberately fall on top of you? There is some strong magic at work here."

Then they both looked at Erith. "What happened, Erith?"

He looked back at them blankly and said nothing.

"You want us to come in there and beat it out of you? What happened to us?"

110

Silence.

As the one got his key out and started to put it into the lock, he was knocked backward and lay flattened on the floor. His companion looked at his fellow guard noting that the man was out cold. He then looked up with a new level of fear and respect for the King. He said nothing.

Shortly later two new guards arrived to relieve those two guards. The one soldier was still on the ground unconscious.

Of course the new guards asked what had happened. The other guard simply said he saw him fall backward and lay there unmoving. He did not mention anything about his suspicions concerning Erith. The two new guards carried the unconscious one away to the infirmary.

The guard left behind said to Erith, "You, Sire, are the one true king. I pledge to you my allegiance and promise to do whatever I can to help you."

Erith looked in surprise. "What is your name?"

"Ryan, Your Majesty."

"I will remember your pledge."

Ryan then left after his replacements arrived.

Erith considered what he had just witnessed. He thought to himself, "I am being protected even though it looks bleak and impossible. May I start to truly believe that I am well taken care of." With that thought he started to feel a calm, a deep calm come over him.

He looked up as he heard loud footsteps coming in his direction.

# Chapter 20

In came Connor escorted by six guardsman. Their demeanor was grim. As one of the guardsman unlocked the cell, Connor announced that Erith was to accompany them.

Erith thought to himself, "This is not good."

The party of eight proceeded to the back entrance of the dungeon area of Evansing Castle. As they emerged outside they were met by twelve men on horseback. Connor motioned to Erith to mount.

Erith enquired, "Where are we going? What is the purpose of this?"

Connor mounted his horse and then answered, "Sire, we have been ordered to remove you to a more secure area."

The reply was both reassuring and disturbing to Erith. Reassuring because Connor addressed him as Sire and disturbing because what would cause them to believe they needed to move him to a more secure area. He thought to himself, "What could be a more secure area than Evansing Castle?"

The horsemen rode for almost an hour west of Evansing Town before coming to an abrupt halt beside a large peat bog. Then the real leader of the twelve men emerged. He gave the order to Connor and Erith to get off their horses.

As Connor's feet hit the ground he was greeted by a sword thrust through his back and heart. He gasped, groaned and then fell face first onto the ground.

Erith's fate was meant to be the same except the swordsman's thrust was inexplicably deflected off to the side so that he totally missed his target. Dismayed he quickly slashed at Erith's head and again his sword was deflected away. The leader then rode his horse over to Erith with sword raised, but as he approached, an invisible force struck him from his horse and he fell breaking his neck and dying on the spot.

Having witnessed what had transpired, the other horsemen stood frozen afraid to attack Erith.

Then one of them pulled out his bow and took aim to shoot Erith. In a most mysterious flash of reality twisting light the archer struck himself with his own arrow right in his heart. He fell to the ground with a thud.

That was enough for the remainder of the troop. As one turned they all turned to ride away leaving Erith alone with his horse and the dead.

Erith stood stunned for a moment and then kneeled to mourn Connor, who he knew was a faithful subject victimized by a web of occult deception and rebellion.

Meanwhile Greer was placed under tighter restrictions as Hugo considered how to dispose of her. He had this inexplicable internal resistance to simply killing her. He couldn't understand what was holding him back. Little did he realize the war going on all around him. The forces of light moved to create this resistance while those of darkness relentlessly promoted her death. There was another force on Greer's side. That was Hugo's wife Fiona who had great affection for Greer and had spent many hours in delightful conversation with her. She always appreciated the down to earth authenticity combined with grace displayed by Greer. This added to the indecision and hesitation for Hugo. He tried to tell himself that she would get over it and besides he was the husband and leader, he had the right to do what he wanted without considering his wife's needs. And yet that nobler side of him could not completely dismiss his reluctance to displease his wife for he did so love her.

"Oh! Damn! I must resolve this. I know. I will exile her to the Kingdom of Aldred. They will welcome her and take good care of her. I will be rid of her and my wife while not totally happy will at least not be devastated by her death. I will send a messenger to King Barris immediately."

Shortly after, the troop that escorted Erith returned from their mission. They requested an audience with Hugo.

The second-in-command officer reported the bewildering events. As Hugo listened to the report a great fear came upon him. An awareness came upon him whereby he realized he had been treading on a path leading to the destruction of himself, his supporters and perhaps of all Evansing.

While absorbed in these thoughts he began to see two lights in the corner of the room. They swirled around and around and grew bigger and bigger. Terrified he cried out to his men and asked if they saw them. No one else was seeing them. This response disturbed Hugo even more.

"What do you mean you don't see them? Look they are there in plain sight over in that corner."

The second-in-command officer replied, "Yes, sir, I am sure you do see them. Perhaps you are the only one meant to see them."

"What do you mean perhaps I am the only one meant to see them?"

"Well, sir, if I may be so bold to say, you have rebelled against the King and attempted to have him executed today. Those lights may well be sent for those reasons."

"I could have you executed on the spot for insubordination."

"How is it insubordination to tell you the truth?"

"I determine what is truth. What you are saying is treason."

"How can a traitor accuse me of treason?"

Hugo was taken aback at such a reply. With that he went into a rage and ordered his guards to strike down the second-in-command officer. No one moved. Again Hugo ordered them to strike him down. The officer drew his sword, stepped toward Hugo and thrust him through his heart. The tyrant coughed, wheezed and slumped to the floor all the while spurting blood from his wound. Then the officer looked around to the guards. "Let's go and retrieve our king."

After burying his friend, Connor, Erith had mounted his horse and pointed it in the direction of where he knew Edwin and his companions were situated. Before he could motion the horse to ride, Prospero appeared.

"Erith, the evil in Evansing has ended. Wait here for the men who are coming to restore you to your throne."

"Why don't I start riding back now to Evansing Town?"

"There are still enemies of yours who would harm you if they saw you. Wait here!"

A couple hours later, Erith could see riders approaching him. He thought to himself, "Are these friendly or not?" He tried to assure himself that Prospero wouldn't have instructed him to wait if it would result in harm to himself. As the riders got closer he recognized the second-in-command officer, this caused him to stiffen because his first thoughts were that he came back to try and kill him again. However, as though reading his thoughts the officer in question called out to him saying they wished him no harm and that they came to restore him to his throne.

Upon hearing this, Erith relaxed and smiled. Perhaps all things were going to work out for good after all. When the troop of twenty men arrived, they dismounted and bowed before their king. This greatly moved Erith whereupon he embraced each of the men. He enquired of the leader "What is your name?"

"My name is Bartley, Sire."

"Well, Bartley, you and your companions shall be rewarded handsomely for your loyalty."

"Sire, Hugo is dead. However his right hand man Carrick still has a loyal following."

He had only just finished speaking when an arrow grazed his head and two other arrows struck two of the twenty men killing them instantly. Erith and the others ducked behind some trees that created a protective cover. Several more arrows followed.

Carrick yelled out, "Bartley, you are a traitor to your Lord. You deserve to die and you shall die."

Bartley bleeding from his wound replied, "I have only one Lord, he is the King not some despot."

"You had an oath to Hugo, you cannot simply dismiss it."

"Hugo broke the terms of the oath by deciding to kill the King. I was freed from that oath. You are battling not only against the King but also against Heaven. Surrender now and I am sure the King will grant you and your companions mercy."

"Surrender? Surely you jest. You are outnumbered two to one. You don't have a chance. You will surely die and all your companions with you."

"You don't see that those with us are greater than those with you."

"Get down and close your eyes, everyone," yelled the King.

Seconds later an intense flash of light burst in between the two forces.

The forty two men with Carrick were blinded by the light and thrown to the ground by the force of its power. They started wailing in dismay and distress at their blindness.

Erith and his men opened their eyes to discover their attackers were all helpless and vulnerable in their inability to see.

Several of the men said this is our chance to rid the Kingdom of these vermin. They were about to start killing the blinded men.

"Stop!"

The men turned to Erith who had issued the command.

"There must be a better way to resolve this than simply killing blind men. Bring me Carrick."

Carrick was practically dragged by two men as he resisted and rained curses down on his captors.

"Carrick, you would be advised to make a more conciliatory response to your situation. Tell me why would you agree to side with Hugo against me, your Lord and Master?"

"Hugo offered me an opportunity for wealth and position you would never have offered to me."

"Wealth and position. You would betray your King for wealth and position. You have condemned yourself with your own words."

Erith asked for a sword. He raised it and whacked off Carrick's head.

116

"Gather the other men to stand before me."

All of Carrick's men were set in front of Erith. The King then walked up to the first one and asked him, "Will you renounce your traitorous ways and swear allegiance to me your King?"

"Yes, Sire, I will."

After the man made his renunciation and swore allegiance, Erith continued on to the next man and on through to all the men. Every man proclaimed his renunciation and swore allegiance to their King. Moments after the last man had spoken each one of the blinded men started to see again, although it took twenty to thirty minutes before they received their sight back fully.

Each one of the men looked at their king with new affection and loyalty. They were truly grateful for his mercy in sparing their lives. Some of the men who had wanted to kill them were still not totally convinced that sparing them was the best response. However they kept their thoughts to themselves.

# Chapter 21

E dwin awoke in the morning. It was still early as the sun had not yet come up and he could hear the people around him snoring and breathing deeply. He lay there wondering what the day would bring. It had been several days since they had seen Erith and no word had been sent back to them. This concerned him because it could mean that Erith did not have full control of the Kingdom or else he had no one he could trust to send a message. As he continued to lay there he found himself almost wanting to slip into a dark pool of despair and fear but something held him back. In some ways it seemed like it would be appealing to fall into a deep depression, but he brought himself back away from that abyss by reminding himself there were people depending on him. Edwin knew he could not indulge in the luxury of being depressed. He forced himself to get up, get dressed and go outside. His body shivered in the damp cold of the early morning. As Edwin walked over to the house, he called out to the sentries standing guard to let them know it was he so they wouldn't shoot their arrows at him out of fear he was an unwelcome intruder.

The sentries were surprised to see Edwin up so early, but they were glad for the company and diversion of standing guard.

Edwin chitchatted with them briefly including enquiring how the night went. They informed him that nothing much had happened except him showing up unexpectedly.

"I am glad I could add something to your experience," he chuckled. "I am eager for us to move on to Evansing Town. Today Percival and I shall make a decision to stay or go. If we go it will be early tomorrow."

All four sentries voiced their desire to go as well. It had been way too long since they had seen their loved ones.

"Edwin, how will you know if it is safe for us to leave?"

"Truthfully I don't know for sure whether it will be safe. Another option is for a small band of scouts to survey the situation first. Yes, perhaps that would be a better option than all of us leaving together. We shall see. Percival has great discernment and I am sure his insight will help us make the right decision."

Moments later Percival walked toward the house where Edwin and the sentries were standing guard. "Good morning to you all." Edwin and the sentries responded with like greetings.

"Percival, I am thinking it is time to move on toward Evansing Town and the men here are eager to move on as well. The only thing I am not totally certain of is whether we should all go as it exposes us to significant risk. Or should we now only send a scouting party."

Percival looked a little surprised and even a little irritated at being faced with such a question first thing in the early morning. Then he settled himself into a thoughtful mode, saying nothing.

"The wisest move would be to send out a small party, say a dozen or so scouts and survey the land."

"That does sound like a prudent approach. Now to select who should be in that party. I will lead it and will leave you in charge of those left behind."

Edwin sat down at the table in the house, grabbed some parchment and started to write down names of men who should come with him. After he had written down eleven names he stood up and walked back to the hiding place where the rest of their group was starting to rouse from their sleep. When he arrived he announced the names of the men and asked them to meet him outside.

After the last man showed up Edwin started to share the plan to go to Evansing Town to discover what the state of affairs were. He also asked if anyone did not want to be part of the group going. No one spoke up as they all wanted to go home and be part of this momentous mission.

The first step for the group going entailed reviewing their resources. They needed three days of rations and each one needed to be fully assured they would all come back alive and be able to succeed as long as they were all looking out for each other. After sharing these requirements he asked again whether everyone felt certain they would all return alive. All raised their hands except for one. Edwin thanked the man for his honesty and asked him to leave. Edwin decided he would not replace him but work with who he had.

"Men, we are going to leave in one hour."

Everyone left immediately and reviewed their weaponry, prepared their horses and got their rations and whatever else would be important.

In one hour they were all waiting by the house ready to go.

"Men, we are about to enter territory where we don't know who is for us and who is against us. We all need to be alert to the possibility of trouble and yet not go looking for it when it doesn't exist. Any questions?"

One man replied, "That will be difficult to discern. Hesitation on our part could be deadly."

"Yes, it will, but I have confidence we can do it and believe our loyalty to King Erith will protect us."

With no response after that, Edwin gave the order to ride and away they went. The first five miles were uneventful until they noticed a small army detachment riding toward them. As it rode closer they could see it was about forty soldiers. Edwin stopped his men and considered what their options were. He gave the order for everyone to pull out their bows and load, in case of attack

The approaching party slowed as it came closer. For a moment their commander appeared unsure. Then all of a sudden they charged with their swords drawn.

"Ready. Aim. Fire."

Ten riders went down.

"Ready. Aim. Fire."

Another ten riders went down.

Now the riders were almost upon them. Edwin and his men drew their swords and prepared to ride in to meet their foes. Outnumbered two to one, it didn't look good. Yelling to grow their courage and intimidate their enemy they waded into their opponents their swords swinging.

Edwin could see two enemy riders coming directly toward him; one had a short lance aimed right at Edwin's head. Edwin rode in between the two of them deflecting the lance with his shield and defending against the other with his sword. Then with a sudden turn he rushed the soldier with the lance who was trying to pull out his sword. Too late for him as Edwin struck him hard severing his arm causing much blood to spurt out. The soldier cried out in pain and rode away from the fray. Then Edwin looked up to face the other rider. Edwin held his sword by the handle and near the tip to hold it in place against the overhand slash from his opponent. The blow rang hard against Edwin's sword as the man had great strength. Edwin then tried to strike the enemy's left side, but the man shifted his sword to deflect Edwin's sword. The rider turned to slash at Edwin's leg which Edwin managed to knock aside with his sword. It very nearly caught Edwin by surprise as he hadn't expected such a quick turn. The rider came back again, as he rode past Edwin he cut a blow against Edwin's horse cutting it severely on its upper left rear leg. The horse neighed in pain and stumbled. Edwin almost fell off with the unexpected shift. Edwin jumped off knowing his horse couldn't maneuver. The rider came back swinging his sword which Edwin ducked to avoid and then he returned the previous favor by severely gashing the enemy horse's left rear leg. The horse fell over on top of its rider killing him instantly. Edwin turned around in time to face another rider who had a battle ax which he swung and took Edwin's sword out of his hand. While feeling the stinging from the force of the blow, Edwin stooped to pick up his sword and positioned himself for the return of the man with the axe. This time he avoided contact with the axe and allowed the rider to go by, but he pulled out his dagger and threw it into the back of the man's neck so hard the tip of the knife was visible in the man's throat. The man grabbed his throat and screamed as his horse kept riding away with its rider in death throes. Edwin looked around and could see that the odds had evened up somewhat, in fact it looked as though his men now outnumbered their opponents. Then one of the opposing soldiers shouted retreat and they all started to ride away. Edwin signaled his men not to follow. To his amazement not one of his men was killed or even wounded in any serious way.

They all gathered together, dismounted and started to hug one another. Even though exhausted, they shouted with joy at their victory and protection. The cuts and bruises were tended to. Then they decided it would be best to detour to the west several miles away from the direction the enemy soldiers had retreated. After several moments of riding they noticed ahead a large number of crows circling. Edwin stopped everyone to consider the next move.

# Chapter 22

E rith, his rescuers and his would be assassins rode back to Evansing Town in one contingent. Bartley felt with Carrick and Hugo dead there would be no further resistance for he was not aware of any other leaders capable of maintaining the rebellion against Erith. As they got closer to Evansing Town they did notice a change in the atmosphere which seemed to indicate a return to normalcy. Nevertheless there was some unease as to how they would be greeted. The men riding together who only an hour earlier were wanting to kill each other, had not yet come fully to terms with such a sudden turnaround. The rescuers kept a wary eye on their recent foes.

When they got to within about 500 feet from the city gates they could see a large number of soldiers waiting for them. Erith signaled his troop to stop. He asked Bartley what he thought.

"I am not sure, Sire, perhaps I should go up ahead alone and investigate."

"May you be safe, Bartley."

Bartley continued on alone at a trot. As he got closer to the gates the men waiting there stood silent and unmoving.

Bartley thought to himself, "They all look like they are slightly stunned." Then he realized they were all under a spell. He turned his horse around and returned at a gallop

back to his troop.As he did so a horse cavalry of 50 men came charging out of the gates. Erith and the rest of the men drew their swords and started to charge the cavalry. As feared by some, almost half of the 42 men turned on Erith's men and began to attack them. When Bartley caught up he
immediately slew two of the turncoats. Erith had a guard of loyal guardsmen surrounding him and thus protecting him from harm.

The situation looked dire but Fortune smiled on Erith and his companions. Just prior to the 50 horse cavalry reaching them a wide and deep gorge opened up and the riders and horses all fell headlong into it. The fighting continued with great intensity except that those who betrayed trust were noticeably deflated with such a loss to their cause. Soon their will to fight completely drained away and one by one the loyal soldiers killed them off. None of the turncoats surrendered for they knew they wouldn't get a second chance. Erith's troop suffered seven deaths and three wounded.

When it was over, Erith knelt before the body of one of the faithful fallen and wept.  He moaned, "It is all so senseless. This loss is so senseless." He not only lamented the loss of the loyal but the rebels as well for he knew they had been driven to do something they would not normally have done.

Erith surveyed the scene. He now had thirty-one men capable of fighting. At this point he still didn't know if they had a large opposition or whether they could continue to the castle. The latter choice carried the most risk as there was no certainty as to how they would be greeted. Erith pondered why there was such opposition. Could he have contributed to this insurrection by being insensitive to his followers? Like all people he had his blind spots. However when the King has a blind spot it can have serious ramifications. He started to recall specific attitudes and actions over the past two years where he did not execute justice consistent with what the situations required. Instead he had made some rather poor judgments based on what he felt like doing. In other words he figured since he was the King he could do as he pleased. He started to feel regret for what he had done. He started to speak out loud to his men those wrongs he recalled doing. When he completed his confession he asked them to forgive him. They all responded with an affirmative. At that moment Erith could feel a surge of well-being and a knowing he could now return and have no fear of further resistance. The legal right of the resistance had been removed.

"Yes," he thought, "this feels much better. I realize now again how much I have contributed to my own state of discontent and unhappiness. Unfortunately since I am the King I have also contributed to the unhappiness of my subjects."

This time as they got closer to the gates of Evansing Town they all felt much more relaxed. When they were within 100 yards of the gates a joyous cheer could be heard coming from the guards on the walls. "The King is returning! The King is returning!"

Erith started to weep at the sound. Embarrassed, he tried to will himself to stop. But then he decided to just weep. He didn't want to hold back. All the tensions he had kept inside came out.

The most important person waiting for him by the gates was his beloved daughter Greer. She had tears streaming down her face as she waited for her father. She had experienced her own whirlwind of uncertainty. At times she seemed on the brink of being executed only to have the rebel leaders change their minds. She was now in the final stages of her pregnancy. It took all her strength to stay calm and remain in a place of mental rest for she knew her baby's well-being depended on it.

Father and daughter embraced and hung onto each other for several minutes. Both were weeping with relief and joy. Then the King took Greer's hand and led her inside to the cheering throng of townsfolk, who now were free to celebrate the return and restoration of their king. It had been an oppressive time while the rebels were in control. Now all returned to gladness and hope.

126

After the two royals returned to their private chambers, they considered what their next step would be.

"We need to get Edwin back here but who knows what marauding groups are still out there interfering with his return."

"I so hope he can be back before the birth of our baby."

# Chapter 23

Edwin and his men considered the crows circling ahead. It could only mean one thing. People or animals were dying or dead. They debated whether to investigate and possibly assist or should they divert around it. After a few minutes Edwin decided it would be a distraction. For the sake of the others left behind and for the Kingdom of Evansing it would be best to avoid it. They took a wide berth around it in the direction of Evansing Town.

As they continued riding they noticed how warm it started to become. Unseasonably warm. Most pleasant and yet it caused concern about what was happening. The men started to notice flames around them, but they weren't being burned. This had to be the work of a Druid priest for no other explanation made sense.

The temperature continued to increase until it no longer felt comfortable. Even though they kept riding, the heat and the flames stayed with them. Then before them stood a familiar figure, it was St. Patrick.

"Patrick, you must be here to douse these flames."

"Yes, I am, Edwin, but not in the way you may think. These flames are all literally only in your minds."

Edwin and his men looked at Patrick quizzically and then started laughing. As they did so the flames disappeared and the temperature returned to normal.

"Patrick, you are the ultimate Druid slayer."

"Yes, I still have my touch."

"Thanks for showing up. Much longer and it could have been dangerous."

"This has been one of the Druid priests' favorite stunts," replied Patrick.

"Would you join us, Patrick, on our ride to Evansing Town?"

"Yes, thank you, Edwin, for the invite. I have been impatient for another adventure with my young warriors."

"Good, you can be our protector against Druid magic."

"I am hoping you like me for who I am not just for what I can do for you."

"Of course we are happy to see you again, Patrick. I am eager to get to know you even better."

"Now that is heartwarming."

"I am glad we brought a couple of extra horses from our last skirmish. Their riders no longer needed them."

"That is convenient for me. Of course strictly speaking I don't need horses to get around."

"Yes, but it will make us feel better if you are at least a bit normal in how you do things around us."

"You think so? My value to you isn't my being normal," replied Patrick.

"True enough. Yet until you need to be supernormal it is good for us to see you normal."

The riders all continued until dark at which time they dismounted. Due to concerns of a fire being spotted they didn't build one. They chewed on some raw potatoes and smoked meat. The men were happy to be heading home. Their minds were focused on something greater than their circumstances.

The next morning Edwin and the others arose with the initial rays of light. They forewent having breakfast as they all were keen to get going. In less than forty minutes they sighted a lone rider coming in their direction. They warily kept eye on him and also looked to see if other figures were about to appear as well. Edwin noticed how the man seemed quite unsteady in the saddle as though he were ill or wounded. As he got closer it was obvious he had been wounded for he was bleeding profusely from a head wound. He couldn't have ridden far because with a wound like that it wouldn't take long for him to bleed to death. As the man pulled up to them, one of Edwin's men grabbed the man to keep him on his horse. He swayed and could barely speak.

"Six armed men came and attacked our village and I was the only one to get away."

"What is the direction of your village and how far?"

The man mumbled something incoherent and then gasped his last and died.

A couple of men dragged him off his horse and set him down in the grass.

"Patrick, do you have a sense of where his village is and whether we should get involved?"

"No, I don't know exactly and I don't believe we are to be involved."

"Good because I don't think so either. Let's stay on track. We can be in Evansing Town by this evening if all goes well."

After two or so hours of solid progress they started to hear a high shrieking just a hundred yards to their left in the nearby forest. They all stopped to consider what it was about. Out bounding toward them was a most strange creature looking part human and part animal. Edwin and several of his men pulled out their bows drew back their arrows and let them rip right into the creature's upper body. The creature slowed to a crawl, stumbled and fell over. Edwin and his men released another round of arrows into the creature. Confident now it was dead they came up close to it. Patrick smiled in recognition.

"Edwin, do you remember how my companions and I showed up as elephants in the battle against Dagarath?"

"Yes, of course."

"This is what is called a baboon. It is an animal from a far off land like where elephants live."

"Why do you think it is here?"

"I suspect this is the work of Druids."

"What purpose would they have for an animal like this here in Ireland?"

"I have heard that baboons are regarded as having magical powers."

"Well this one was loud but seems to have been short on power."

"I don't think his attacking us was part of the plan. He probably escaped from the rest of the group."

"You mean there could be others?"

"Yes," replied Patrick. "I think there could be many others."

"What possible advantage could these create?"

"That, Edwin, is probably something we are going to find out."

The party mounted their horses and resumed riding. After an hour and a half they stopped to have some sustenance and rest their horses.

Patrick asked Edwin, "What plan have you got for where you are going? What do you want to accomplish?"

"Basically see whether Erith is back on the throne and we are welcome to return."

"That is the objective. How are you going to accomplish it?"

Edwin didn't answer but considered what he must do to ensure a successful mission.

"I have you here, Patrick. What would you do if you were me?"

"I would consider sending me to go and you and your men remaining here."

"Patrick, if I were to do that, how long would you take?"

"One hour."

"One hour! We are at least a half day away."

"Yes, but I can travel there and back in an hour. After all being dead has its advantages."

"Then you go and we will remain here and wait for you to return in one hour."

With that Patrick quietly disappeared before their eyes.

A short time later Patrick entered Evansing castle and stood before a guard asking him to fetch the King. "Tell his Sire it is Patrick here to see him."

Erith came almost immediately. "Patrick, what a pleasure to see you here. What brings you to my castle?"

"Edwin has sent me."

"Edwin! My daughter and I are most anxious to see Edwin again. Where is he?"

"A half day's ride. I have been sent to see if you were restored and if he is welcome to return."

"Yes and yes."

"There is a matter of their safety. Druid attacks and roving rogue Evansing troops pose a risk to their safe return."

"I will have a troop of one hundred and fifty men sent within the hour to escort them."

"They will be waiting at the south west corner of the Eireann forest. I must return now to rejoin them. The bulk of his force is still another half day ride away from where Edwin is waiting, so don't be concerned if he and your troops don't return for two days."

Patrick then said goodbye and left.

# Chapter 24

Meanwhile Percival and the others continued to wait. In the distance they could see what appeared to be a herd of some sort of animals. But they were not like any they had seen before. These animals were running towards them.

Percival shouted out orders for the men to get their bows ready. Others without bows got their swords ready. As the animals got within range they released their arrows. Even though struck none of them went down. Again they shot their arrows and now some of these creatures had two or more arrows and still they were running toward them. They had fierce faces and were screeching loudly. Now they had time for only one more round of arrows before it would be hand to hand battle. This time some of the animals stopped when struck again, but well over half were still coming. The men steeled themselves for a most unusual sword fight. As the animals got to the men they leaped towards them. Many were stopped by swords. Others severely bit and scratched their victims. After a few minutes the last one was subdued. Seventeen men were injured and of those five so seriously it was unlikely they would survive.

Knowing of Percival's healing power, the men all looked to him to do something. Percival with a pained look on his face said he was not able to do anything at this time. This angered some of the men and distressed others, but they had too much respect for Percival to question him. Within several hours two of the most seriously injured men died. Grief hung over the camp from this loss. What began to restore their spirits was the progressive improvement in the other three severely injured. In fact the progress noted was most remarkable. So much so that men started talking about divine mercy at work. Percival did not say anything except it would be good to give thanks for their improvement.

The men had just finished burying their comrades when a lookout shouted seeing a host of horsemen coming their way. Everyone scrambled to their positions bracing for an attack.

As the horsemen drew closer they made out the familiar figures of Edwin and the men that had left with him. Cheers went up and everyone demonstrated joy at being delivered. This was a day that seemed as though it would never arrive.

"Men, Erith is back in power and we have his troops to give us safe passage back to Evansing Town. Since it is late in the day we will remain here one more night and then leave early in the morning without breakfast."

Percival greeted Edwin with a hug, "Well done, Edwin, you accomplished your mission."

Edwin replied, "We had some timely help from St. Patrick."

"St. Patrick? Well that is interesting. What brought him?"

"He showed up to dispel Druid flames. Otherwise I am not sure we would have returned for we would have all been slow roasted. He also told us we would probably come across more of those baboons you battled today. We had one renegade baboon run at us."

While they continued to chat, unknown to them and their comrades, they were being watched. The eyes watching them were not the usual pair of eyes. These were the eyes of the top Druid in all of Ireland. His name was Alcana and he was angry with the turn of events in Evansing. He had so precisely plotted and planned the takeover. Now it appeared to have completely unraveled. As he considered his options an idea came to his mind. This might be turned to his advantage yet.

The next morning everyone rose early and as the sun barely showed on the horizon they were leaving their camp for Evansing Town. The mood was jovial. They had gone down the road for almost an hour when they came across an old man who looked like he had been beaten and left for dead. The two medics with the soldiers dismounted and examined him. He appeared to be in a lot of pain. They dressed the cuts and bruises. The man said he could ride so they strapped him into a saddle and assigned a soldier to lead the horse. Another one rode alongside so as to keep an eye on him.

After riding four hours the travelers stopped to rest the horses and eat some of their rations. While stopped the wind picked up and started gusting from the north-west. Then a rain started which added to the misery. Everyone huddled together for warmth and protection.

A dozen or so arrows streaked out of a nearby forest striking four of the soldiers and two of Edwin's men.

A rage came upon Edwin. He grabbed his shield and mounted. "Men, get your shields and ride toward that forest."

They thundered toward the forest, yelled curses and waved their swords. Several more arrows hit shields or missed. The force rode into the forest, but whoever had shot the arrows seemed to have vanished. Edwin would not leave it. He would kill those raiders. They continued to search for their trail for a half hour or so until one of the searchers tripped on a handle on the forest floor. He called the others. Edwin came to survey what he had found. "This is a handle to a door and I am sure we will find our quarry on the other side."

As one of them opened the door, others including Edwin were waiting with bows ready. The door led to a tunnel. This created a high risk situation for whoever was first would face a high risk of being ambushed.

Edwin ordered most of the men to spread out around the area in case the raiders popped out another door.

He then decided to address them, "Who are you and why did you attack us?"

Silence.

"Let's smoke them out. Find what we have that is dry enough to light and we will put it down the hole."

After ten minutes enough wood was found to light in the hole. When it was burning quite fiercely they closed the door. In the meantime the others were also scanning to see if smoke was rising from somewhere else. One of them did notice smoke trailing upward leading them to find another door in the forest floor almost thirty yards from the other one. So they lit another fire at the other end and closed it once it was burning. In the meantime they opened the first door and stoked it some more to keep it going. After about fifteen minutes the second door lifted and two men crawled out coughing and pleading for mercy. Shortly after a third man came out as well. The soldiers then closed the door.

"Are there any more?"

One of the frightened men nodded yes. A little while later the fourth man emerged coughing.

Each of the men were bound and placed on their knees to await their fate. They would not have long to wait. First Edwin questioned as to who they were and why they attacked.

After initial hesitation one of them answered they were part of a group of rebels headed by a leader called Lencraft.

"What is the object of this group?"

"To overthrow Erith and place Lencraft on the throne."

"Who is supporting Lencraft?"

"Merethath"

"Why would you fight your fellow Evansing men on behalf of Merethath."

"We were promised riches and positions of power."

"Where is this Lencraft?"

"He is north of here about twenty miles."

"How many men does he have?

"Between 800 to 1,000 or so."

"Can you lead us to where they are camped?"

"Yes."

"You are going to come with us."

Edwin then addressed the soldiers and asked if any of them had not killed his first man.

Two soldiers not much more than boys who had entered the army only a few days ago raised their hands.

"Come here."

He stood them each in front of one of the captured men. Then without warning Edwin thrust his sword through the throat of the third man. "Do likewise."

Both did as commanded.

"Let's go."

When they returned they discovered that two of the struck soldiers and both of Edwin's men had died. The other two soldiers looked like they would recover. They buried their dead and resumed their journey to Evansing Town.

# Chapter 25

They were now seeing Evansing Town in the distance. One of the soldiers had ridden ahead to alert the townsmen and the King. They could see flags and banners unfurled and hear the blowing of trumpets welcoming them home.

Edwin thought to himself, "I at times thought I would never be back home and now here I am."

Edwin and his men who had travelled with him started to weep as they got closer. The traumas they had experienced started to come to the surface. The thought of being safely back home with their loved ones unleashed great emotion.

Edwin started to look for the one person he was most keen to see again. He scanned the walls and the gates. "There, there she is." He kicked his horse to go a little quicker but not too much as his mount was due for a well-deserved rest.

Greer all smiles and very pregnant was waiting by the gate for her hero prince.

Edwin dismounted and ran up to her, hugged her gently so as not to injure the baby. They looked into each other's eyes and then both wept with joy.

Erith came and also gave Edwin a hug. He didn't want to freely cry but his eyes glistened with kept back tears. "Edwin, what a joy to see you safely here and able to be present for the birth of your first child."

"Sire, I am most pleased to be back. It is good to see you restored to your proper place as monarch of this realm."

"Yes, I am pleased as well. My subjects have been most gracious to me."

Greer started experiencing some discomfort. "I feel some strong contractions. I need to get to my room. Call the midwife to come."

Edwin escorted his wife to their bedroom. He was so excited and nervous all at the same time. His main concern was that both child and mother would come through this well. Many mothers died in childbirth and so this was always a concern in 11th century Ireland. He stayed with Greer while the contractions progressively got more and more intense. The midwife indicated he should leave, but Greer held his hand tightly and said no he should stay.

As the pain got more intense she squeezed Edwin's hand tighter and tighter. He almost let out a yell from the pain, but he gritted his teeth and withstood it silently. In the meantime Greer was groaning with each painful contraction. Then the release as the baby came out. Seeing the baby covered in blood along with the placenta almost caused Edwin to lose consciousness, but he steadied himself and stayed standing. The midwife announced the baby was a girl, wiped her off, cut the umbilical cord, wrapped her in a soft blanket and gave her to Greer who placed her on her breast. Edwin watched transfixed at what he had just witnessed. He gingerly reached out and tenderly touched the head of his newborn daughter. The midwife announced that both mother and daughter appeared healthy and should fully recover from the ordeal of giving birth and being birthed. After having been on Greer's breast for ten minutes or so she was handed by her mother to Edwin to hold. He held her so lightly not wanting to crush her and certainly not wanting to drop her. Edwin gazed several minutes into his daughter's eyes simply adoring her.

The King was at the door and was wondering if he could come in. Greer covered herself so as to be more appropriate in receiving her father into the room. Erith came in overjoyed at becoming a grandfather and seeing his daughter had survived the experience. Edwin offered the little girl to his father-in-law who gladly took her. He too looked with great delight at his little granddaughter. He started to coo and make other sounds not normally associated with a king. In this moment he was just another grandfather who was enjoying his new special role.

After a few minutes the baby was handed back to Greer and both men left the room.

"Edwin, she is beautiful like her mother. I think she has your elbows and knees."

Edwin chuckled and then replied, "Then she will have strong elbows and knees. I am good with that."

Then Edwin announced that he and Greer had decided to name their girl after Greer's mother, Orla which in Irish means gold princess.

Erith was pleased with the selection and how it honored his deceased wife.

After a few more minutes of reflecting on what they had just witnessed the conversation turned to what needed to be done with Lencraft and his rebels.

"I need two thousand men to ensure we have sufficient advantage and I would like to leave in a week's time."

"That should be about right in order to give time for gathering the men and giving you more time with Greer and the baby. I will have other officers in charge of the preparations. I don't want to rob you of your time with

Greer and your child. Besides you have had a rugged time. It would be good to give you some rest."

# Chapter 26

The day to go to war against Lencraft had arrived. Edwin had said his goodbyes to his wife and daughter, told Greer not to worry, he would return. Edwin was assisted by two of the other generals. The first was Warren who was about five years older than Edwin. He had been one of the other fighters who experienced St. Patrick and his friends showing up as elephants. Edwin and he were quite close as friends as well as comrades in arms. The second general was Murphy who was almost fifteen years older than Edwin. Sometimes it seemed as though he resented this young upstart Edwin assuming a senior and privileged position in such a short time. He was part of a noble family with a rich tradition and history. Edwin overlooked the occasional slights he received from Murphy as he was a capable officer.

Accompanying the soldiers was the captive taken from the tunnel who said he could show them the way to Lencraft's hideout. This young man whose name was Errol looked rather miserable and even contrite as he rode. Edwin's attitude had softened slightly towards him. He now considered the possibility of another option in what to do with Errol. In some ways the young man reminded Edwin of himself. It could have been he who was in Errol's position. Only the grace of divine intervention made his present good fortune possible. As Edwin pondered this, Murphy came to him with a recommendation.

"Edwin, I am thinking I should take eight hundred or so men on a separate route to avoid unduly concentrating all our forces in one location. It will give us greater options in maneuverability."

Edwin looked at him without saying anything immediately. Then he replied, "Let me consider that and I will get back to you. I may also ask Warren his thoughts."

Murphy looked chagrined but without saying anything rode off to rejoin his men.

As Edwin considered the request he started to have grave doubts about whether it was a sound strategy. The idea of greater maneuverability options may be true, but it came at a cost of dividing up their force. While Murphy saw concentration of their force into one body as a disadvantage, Edwin saw it as an advantage. They would outnumber their opponents by two to one. It did not make sense to him to have the smaller force risk ambush from a force more or less equal in size.

Next Edwin considered how best to share this with Murphy. He knew he needed to be diplomatic so as to soothe Murphy's oversized ego. He briefly considered getting Warren's support for this decision. But he knew that Murphy would dismiss that as both of them banding against him.

"Drat, to have this harassment at the very beginning of this is highly annoying. Maybe I should have taken one of the other generals. Oh well I have to deal with this." Edwin muttered to himself.

He summoned a messenger and asked him to send for Murphy to come to see him. He knew he needed to maintain authority and couldn't simply ride over to Murphy.

When Murphy arrived his face didn't betray any thoughts one way or the other. "What have you decided?"

"I have decided to leave the force as one. You are correct in saying we would have more options for maneuverability. However I do not want to leave a smaller force vulnerable to an attack from a roughly equivalent sized force."

"I want to go on record as being in disagreement with your decision."

"That is your right to do so and it shall be noted."

Murphy rode away without a further word.

Edwin thought to himself, "Something will need to be done about Murphy before he creates real problems. I am beginning to wonder whether his skills of command are sufficient to overcome his bad attitude." The force continued to travel until early afternoon at which time it took a break to rest and eat. Edwin called his two generals to consider their next move.

"Gentlemen, I am thinking we should camp in another two hours or so and send scouts ahead to determine exactly how the enemy is situated. I don't think it would be good for us to go directly into battle after travelling all day."

Warren replied, "Yes, I agree, Edwin, I think it would be more advisable to know what we are facing and be rested for the battle."

Murphy retorted, "Let's continue and take them by surprise. Our horses and men may be a bit tired but certainly we are not exhausted after one day of travel."

"True, but we do not yet have any ideas as to what we are facing and neither do we know exactly where they are. We are relying on Errol to lead the scouts to their camp, but it has been over a week and they may have moved."

"We could send the scouts up ahead now and by the time we get close to where they are the scouts could get back to us with what we need to know."

"Yes, that is possibly true assuming they find the camp and are able to meet with us and give us the information we need to formulate an attack. Thank you for your further input. I will stick with my original plan." At this point Edwin noticed his own tone moving a bit more to the stern side.

This was not unnoticed by Murphy. He turned and walked away without another word. Edwin looked after him with a hard look, struggling with unkind thoughts and intentions. He did his best to get rid of them and not let himself dwell on carrying out an extreme response.

After two hours the troops came to a spot suitable for camping and defending if necessary.

Four hours later the scouts arrived with some disturbing news. They told of a force of at least three thousand. As well they had moved a mile further west into a more fortified location.

Edwin called for Errol. "Why did you tell me there were 800 to 1,000?"

"Because, Sir, that is what was there when I had last seen them over two weeks ago."

Edwin glared at him looking deep in his eyes to see if there was a sign of him lying. He saw no such sign.

Talking to his assistant he ordered him to bring Murphy, Warren and also a couple of the lower ranking commanders.

When the other officers had all arrived Edwin gave them the scouts' report. Their initial response was rather grim. From a two to one advantage they now faced a substantial disadvantage.

"Gentlemen, we have three readily available options: Go back and come back with more men; send for more men and wait here for them; and finally we could devise a clever attack plan and go after them with what we have. What do you think?"

Murphy spoke up, "I think we should attack."

Edwin spoke to the chief scout and asked him to draw a sketch as to how the enemy camp was laid out. The scout then also indicated where he thought the best infiltration point was. He had noted a steep hill on one side of the camp. He also noted steps up the hill and no sentries posted on the top. This could be an entry point taking them into the center of the camp and giving a decided advantage to stage a night ambush.

Edwin asked, "How many of our men do you think should mass at the top of the hill before we attack?"

"I would say around a thousand troops," replied Warren and Murphy in surprised unison.

"We will need to narrow the gap in forces. Everyone in the first group will be ready to shoot half their quiver of arrows into the sleeping camp before we commit ourselves to hand to hand battle."

The officers all liked what they had heard and decided to attack that night.

# Chapter 27

Edwin and his men were ready to go shortly after midnight. Twenty of the more mighty warriors were sent up the hill to check for sentries and if necessary to eliminate them.

The night was quite dark which made for good cover but would also increase possibility of Evansing soldiers mistaking each other for the enemy once the battle began.

After about forty minutes one of the vanguard of troops returned indicating the few sentries in the vicinity of the hill were killed. Edwin led the rest of the troops up the hill. When they got to the top they could see the fires and the enemy force camped in zig zag rows. When the thousand or so troops massed on top of the hill, Edwin passed the command for the archers to be prepared to release their arrows.

The command was made to fire. Hail after hail of arrows were released into the sleeping figures by the fires and the sentries further away. Then the order was given to charge into the camp. The Evansing troops ran into the camp to mop up whatever resistance they encountered. Surprisingly it was quite light. Were most of the enemy killed by the arrows? Suddenly, wave after wave of other enemy troops came out of nowhere. They had been sleeping elsewhere, hidden and without fires leaving only a lesser force in the main camp. As it turned out many of the sleeping figures were dummies made out of straw. The tables had been turned for the ambushers were now being ambushed.

Mayhem ensued as the Evansing troops were set upon by the numerically superior force. The other Evansing troops continued to come up as quickly as possible. The climb was steep and many of them were forced to stand their ground against the enemy so as to protect their comrades still coming up. The battle raged for almost half an hour with many casualties on both sides. Edwin engaged two enemy soldiers. With his shield he fended off the blows from the one on his right and as he did so he surprised the other foe by thrusting his sword deep into his opponent's chest. Then he gave his full attention to the one remaining. His opponent kept backing up overwhelmed by the fury of Edwin's blows until he tripped over a rock and went down with Edwin following up to strike a death blow that shattered his skull.

One important thing in Evansing's favor was that they were technically much more skilled than the rebels. Even though outnumbered, they were able to whittle down the enemy's force to the point where Evansing started to have a significant advantage in numbers of still fighting soldiers. Then, as though a dam had broken, the rebels sensing all was lost stopped fighting and started running. Evansing soldiers pursued and killed without remorse. No mercy or quarter was given to rebels except for one rebel who they didn't kill immediately, Lencraft. He was wounded and brought to Edwin for judgment. Edwin began by questioning him as to why he was leading the rebellion and who his source of support was.

Lencraft remained silent until Edwin ordered him to be tied to the ground and stripped. Boiling water was then slowly poured over the man's bare feet and legs. The man writhed and screamed in agony. Edwin ordered the pouring to stop and then asked again.

Lencraft started speaking, "Alcana the Druid is working with Merethath to come against you. I am a subject of Merethath and was commanded by my King to lead this rebellion."

"Alcana? I have never heard of him. What can you tell me about him?"

"He is the most powerful Druid in all of Ireland, but he works undercover so most people never hear of him."

"Do you know where he is now?" asked Edwin.

"He is in Evansing. Where I don't know, but I know he is here. I have never met him, but I have felt his presence and have received his instructions."

"How do you receive his instructions?"

Lencraft replied, "He gives me his thoughts. They are unmistakable."

"Are there other rebel forces in Evansing besides the one we routed tonight?"

"Not yet, but plans are underway to create more."

"Who are they planning to work with and where in Evansing?"

"I don't know. I swear it, I don't know."

The man was still in great discomfort from his burns. Edwin looked at him wondering whether anything more could be gained by questioning. He motioned to the other two generals and the other two commanders. "Do you have any other questions to ask?"

They shook their heads.

Edwin turned to one of the guards, "Kill him."

The guard stabbed Lencraft in the heart with his sword.

After another twenty minutes the Evansing soldiers who had pursued the rebels began returning. They reported most had been killed. However, some had gotten away. They estimated perhaps four or five hundred of the three thousand had escaped.

Evansing had suffered 186 dead and 142 wounded. The wounded were tended to for several hours.

Edwin then gave the order to get ready to return to Evansing Town. Soldiers loaded the wounded on horses or on wagons as necessary. They continued until late morning at which time they stopped to rest, eat and water the horses at a nearby stream. Permission was given for most of the troops to nap for a half hour or so. Altogether they stopped for about an hour.

During this time Errol was brought to Edwin.

"What are your thoughts about being a rebel now?"

"It was totally wrong, Your Highness. I should never have given into such an impulse."

"Impulse? You became a rebel on impulse?"

"Yes, Your Highness, I did. I know it was foolish, but I did."

"What should I do with you, Errol?"

"I know I deserve to die and I would not fault you for ordering my execution."

"Errol, you have answered well. I have decided to spare your life. I will make you my personal page."

Errol looked shocked and unable to speak. After gathering his thoughts and emotions he spoke, "Truly, Your Highness, did I hear correctly, you are going to make me your page?"

"Yes, Errol, I am."

When the news got out that Errol, a rebel, was made a page not everyone was happy. Some were friends and relatives of the men who had died from the arrows released by Errol and his fellow rebels. One of his arrows may well have struck at least one of those men killed.

Several of those men came to Edwin and pressed their case against Errol.

"Much blood has already been shed. I believe Errol can be an asset in our Kingdom. I ask each of you to seek to forgive him for his transgression."

This did not mollify everyone completely, but something was on those words. They didn't seem like ordinary words. They had a power on them to touch the hearers' hearts.

When the Evansing troops resumed their journey, Errol rode behind Edwin available as needed and indicating his new position.

In the late afternoon they arrived in Evansing, triumphant and somber all at the same time.

Triumphant for having won in convincing fashion and somber at their losses. Another 12 soldiers died from their wounds enroute home.


# Chapter 28


The next day Edwin stayed in late with his wife, making up for lost time in their bedroom. As they lay in each other's arms they both luxuriated in enjoying one another.

"What are you going to do about King Taryn of Merethath?"

The question took Edwin by surprise.

"We are having a lovely time together, why would you bring that up?"

"Because I have been thinking about it. To me the only solution is to kill Taryn."

"Wow, that is pretty dramatic. We go from making love to plotting a death. What brought that on?"

"I saw how distressed you were with all those men having been killed. I realize it has to be put to an end and it needs to be done quickly. The simplest is to kill the head of the snake."

"Greer, your bloodthirsty expressions excite me."

With that he embraced her and they continued where they had left off.

Later in the day Edwin went to visit Percival to discuss the idea of assassinating Taryn.

"Greer gave me the idea."

"Greer? Sweet Greer? She gave you the idea to kill a king?"

"Yes, I was surprised when she brought it up. Especially given when and where she brought it up."

"Well, Edwin, we need to go see Erith and run this idea by him first."

They then went to see the King. Fortunately he was available so they were ushered into his private chambers and discussed the idea with him, of course, only after they had taken precautions to avoid being eavesdropped on.

"You say my dear Greer gave you this idea? She has been through a lot of trying times. I can only surmise this is her reaction of wanting it to stop. I think the idea has merit. Let's meet tomorrow morning and plan our next move. As well, we need to discuss how to contend with this Druid Alcana."

The next morning the three of them met again along with several senior officers.

"Gentlemen, as you know, we have a chronic and serious threat from Taryn. The purpose of this meeting is to discuss specific plans on how to eliminate him once and for all. In other words, how to best kill him?"

Edwin spoke up, "One way would be for me to take a special team of five men and we would infiltrate Merethath. We would ride at night through Nerland and Merethath to his capital. We would rest and hide in the woods during the day. I need maps with enough detail so as to plan the route and timing of our trip."

Percival then asked, "Do we have reliable intelligence sources on the ground in Merethath to give us up to date information on the security around Taryn?"

"It is pretty minimal, but with some extra help we may be able to fill in the blanks," replied Edwin.

Erith then asked, "Who did you have in mind?"

"Prospero. This should be a mission he will help us with. I will ask him for an intelligence report and also ask him to accompany us."

"Good, you may as well. The least he can say is no."

Erith then asked the other officers whether they had any comments or suggestions. They basically agreed with what had been planned.

The King then continued, "Next we need to resolve Alcana, reputed to be the most powerful Druid in Ireland. Percival what information do you have about him?"

"I have put in a request to one of my trusted colleagues who keeps a close eye on the Druid community. It will be a few days yet before I get a reply."

"We will wait for the report before we consider further action regarding Alcana."

"I will try to establish contact with Prospero later today. I will also see what maps are available," Edwin added.

The meeting ended and Percival and Edwin walked over to the Records Office to check out maps. When they entered the Office they could feel a strange presence. Both of them looked at each other with a quizzical and a knowing look. This presence indicated Druid activity. The clerk came to the desk.

"Your Highness, how can I help you?"

While seemingly respectful there was a certain tone to it that didn't ring sincere.

"Where is the clerk who normally works at this desk?"

"He is ill today, Your Highness. We don't know when he will be back."

Edwin looked deep into his eyes and asked, "What is your name?"

"Kenterra."

"Kenterra, what?"

"Your Highness."

"If you want to keep your position you will need to mind your manners."

Silence.

"What do you say when you have been rebuked?"

"Sorry, Your Highness, pardon my manners."

"Wait here, Percival, I shall return in a moment."

A few moments later Edwin returned with two guards. "Arrest this fellow behind the counter."

Kenterra was about raise his voice in protest when one of the guards securely gagged his mouth and the other tied his hands behind his back. They escorted him away.

"Edwin, that was a wise move. We need to find those maps ourselves without raising suspicions about our mission."

"Precisely. When I looked in his eyes I knew he couldn't be trusted. Same eyes as Yaworth had. The subtle surliness gave it away."

Both men searched in the backroom and after an hour of hunting around came across the maps leading to Merethath. They gathered four maps that seemed most relevant and helpful. Then they left to return to the castle for a closer study. On the way back they stopped at the Sheriff's office and asked him to check on the supposedly ill counterman.

Upon returning to the castle they discovered that one of the maps had an entirely different route than any they had previously been aware of.

"This one does not smell right. Can it be that the Druids have already sensed what we are up to and they have set up a dummy map to trick us?"

155

"They did have a dummy counterman."

"This will make the mission more difficult as they are going to be lying in wait for us."

"Let's ask Prospero now if he will come and talk to us."

"Good idea."

"Prospero, we need your help. Please come."

They waited a number of moments before Prospero slowly appeared in full form.

"What can I help you with?"

"Thank you, Prospero, for coming. We have need of your assistance for a very important mission to kill King Taryn of Merethath. It now looks like they know we are coming for him. Our original desire for your help simply entailed you telling us the security arrangements for Taryn and how to overcome them. Now we also need to find the best way to get there without being ambushed or discovered."

For a moment there was silence as though Prospero was quietly considering their situation. In truth though he wasn't. He already knew the answers they needed because he had listened in to their previous conversations. Prospero wanted them to realize he wasn't at their beck and call and would help because he could, not because he had to.

"The map you have second from the end is the one to use. There is one spot however where you will need to do a detour. Bring me the map."

Edwin fetched the map, unrolled it, and presented it to Prospero.

Prospero placed his finger on a specific point on the map and drew an alternate route which went several miles before reconnecting with the route indicated on the map.

"As far as the security arrangements, I will meet you here," as he pointed to a position only a few miles from Merethath Castle.

"Thank you, Prospero, for your help. Your willingness to meet us there and personally work with us is much appreciated."

Shortly after Prospero left, a messenger arrived with news that the regular desk person at the Records Office had been found killed by a vicious slash to his throat.

# Chapter 29

A week after the visit with Prospero, Edwin and his five special team members left after dark for Merethath. The day before, news came confirming Alcana, the powerful Druid, was last known to be in Evansing. That along with what had happened to the Records clerk was certainly unsettling. For now they had to be extra aware of what dark forces they may encounter. Also how much advance warning would be given to Nerland and Merethath forces enroute? Edwin hoped that Prospero factored that all in when he told him which route to take and where he was to meet them.

As the six men rode toward the Nerland border they kept their guard up even in Evansing territory. They stopped just prior to dawn to camp in a thick clump of trees which had a clearing in the middle. The clearing provided barely enough room for their tents and some grazing on grass for their horses.

They slept four and two stayed awake standing on guard at either end of the clearing. Then after four hours they rotated. Other than hearing some farmers yelling at their horses in the distance it was very quiet. Perhaps too quiet. The Nerland boundary was only a bit over a mile away so it was certainly possible for Nerland agents to cross the line into Evansing.

The evening came and after the sun went down they set out to leave. They were at the edge of the clearing on their way out when something struck one of the men as not right. His name was Jeffrey. He was known for special discernment ability when it came to the unseen realm. Edwin knew this and decided this ability would make him a valuable team member for such a trip and such a time.

"Stop! I think something is not right. Let's just stay here for a moment as I consider further what is going on."

They all stood quietly for several moments while Jeffrey tried to discern why he had this feeling. Then he stood a little straighter. He had this quizzical look as though he was receiving instructions but didn't quite understand what he was hearing.

The men were intrigued and impatient to get going all at the same time. However they stood still and remained silent. After several more moments he spoke.

"There was a troop of Nerland soldiers going right by our exit point and the voice spoke to me to wait. In a few more minutes it will be safe to leave. The voice seemed to speak so quickly I had difficulty understanding it. I am not

159

sure if the voice spoke so quickly or whether my ability to hear was making it sound like it was so quick."

After a few moments the men resumed leading their horses out of the woods. Once out of the woods they all mounted and continued on with their journey. Soon they were in Nerland. They needed no signs to tell them they were no longer in Evansing. The atmosphere had definitely changed. In Evansing there was a peacefulness that had been restored when Erith came back to his throne. In Nerland the atmosphere felt chaotic and malevolent. Edwin stopped everyone and pulled out some blessed wine and bread for the Eucharist.

"Gentlemen, we need some reinforcement so we aren't susceptible to the environment we are now in." Each man then participated in the Eucharist. As they did so a new sense of well-being came upon each one as though they were being kept in a bubble of protection.

As they rode on, each man felt a growing sense of anticipation as to what lay ahead. To take out a king would be no mean feat. They definitely would need Prospero's assistance. To what degree he would help was unknown. Hopefully sufficient to keep them all safe and sound so they could return to their families.

After four hours the men and horses started to get weary. A short 20 minute rest stop was ordered. As the men and horses rested they started to hear owls in the distance. Normally that wouldn't raise much concern. But given the circumstances anything that could possibly be considered a signal raised the riders' alertness.

Edwin considered what he heard. It sounded like it could be real owls but he wasn't completely sure. He asked Jeffrey his opinion.

"There is some Druid activity in this area. I can sense it. Whether they are the ones doing the calls I cannot say."

The men were stopped next to a wood. The almost full moon shone more brightly than they would have preferred. They had a clear view of their way ahead for some distance. The road was surrounded by open fields on either side. What could they do to increase their safety?

As Edwin considered his options a very large bird came into view and landed next to them. This was a total surprise. He knew this had to be Percival, but how would he help them? Then he noticed what appeared to be two harnesses and ropes that the bird had wrapped around its neck and upper body. This could be used to attach two horses and their riders and then the bird could take them both. He sprang into action by pointing to two of his men and having them get harnessed up. The large bird then lifted up with the two men and in a matter of moments disappeared into the sky. They were taken to a safe spot about 25 miles down the road. By doing so they avoided the Nerland patrols in the area and also detoured around the location Prospero had indicated. That location was especially treacherous as an ambush was lying in wait.

Almost an hour later the large bird returned to pick up another two and then repeated the cycle to take Edwin and Jeffrey as the last two. When the unusual travel ended Edwin thanked the large bird for his help and then with no further fanfare the bird lifted off into the night sky. The men with Edwin had all heard of this unusual creature and two of them had actually seen it before. Nevertheless they were all in the process of regaining their calm after riding high in the sky.

They continued on for several more miles before they found a wooded area with some terrain which lent itself to being easily defended. The Merethath border was less than five miles further west. Another five miles or so beyond the border was where Prospero said he would meet them. As the sun came up the men rested and stayed alert at the same time. They slept as well as they could, but everyone knew they were in the heartland of their enemy and anything could happen. Knowing an angel would meet them did give a greater assurance. They also knew that didn't necessarily indicate there would be no problems. Prospero was known to help in problems, not always prevent them.

As the sun went down, the men had something to eat and mentally prepared themselves for the next leg of their journey.

161

# Chapter 30

Tonight they were going to meet up with Prospero. They only needed to go about ten miles to the location where he said he would meet them. Of course he didn't say when he would meet them. Edwin figured he would ask him to show up when they arrived at the designated meeting place. Prospero may show up some time later. Edwin decided they would wait as long as they needed to. He had confidence in Prospero and he liked him even though he was a bit crusty and unpredictable.

When they crossed the border into Merethath everyone noticed the atmosphere got even darker. Their evil king radiated evil throughout his kingdom. It made the Evansing team shiver in dismay and discomfort with the change.

As they got closer to their rendezvous point with Prospero their environment turned progressively more and more pleasant. To Edwin's surprise they could see a light up ahead and there was Prospero waiting for them. The light was Prospero's robe glistening in the dark.

"Prospero, what a delight to see you here waiting for us. We do appreciate it."

"I know you didn't expect it. I wanted to surprise you."

With that he got into explaining how King Taryn was away from his normal castle and had moved his court to a fortress castle twenty miles further west.

"Prospero, are you going to come with us?"

The angel looked at Edwin gazing into his eyes and that of each of the men with him. After several moments he replied.

"I will accompany you visibly until you are within five miles of Taryn's castle. At that point I will make myself invisible and continue to be with you. Before I go invisible I will give you final instructions on how to get into Taryn's castle."

Edwin and his men all felt a sense of relief at knowing their special guardian would continue on with them.

With Taryn's move it meant they had over 20 miles to get to his new location. They could do about 14 more miles before dawn. The troop of men and the angel who hovered above the ground found a large cave in the side of a hill just prior to daylight. A grove of trees sheltered the entrance from passing eyes.

Edwin found it curious that Prospero would hang out with them the way he did. Never before had he been around for more than moments at a time. He would deliver his message and leave.

"Prospero, I am curious about something. "Won't other people see your glistening robe?"

"No, because you and your men have all been given the ability to see me. As you should well know, people do not normally see angels. Only those who have been equipped to do so can see angels."

The next night had the special quality of knowing they were about to breach a castle to kill a king.

Everyone was ready for their part to be played in the slaying of Taryn. Soon they had gone the next five miles at which point they stopped to hear what Prospero would tell them.

"Gentlemen, there is a small doorway behind the castle. It has basically been forgotten about. The door has been unlocked for some years and no one has thought to check it. The doorway leads to a set of stairs leading to the main floor. From there you can go up a second flight of stairs where Taryn is sleeping. On the main floor there are five guards at night which you will need to take care of if you are going to go up the stairs. On the second floor are another five guards standing by Taryn's bedchamber. As I told you earlier I will be with you although you won't see me. My role is to cause one of the first set of guards to fall unconscious to the floor. This will cause the others to be distracted as they come to his aid. That will present the opportunity for you to quietly eliminate them."

"On the second floor I will mimic the King's voice in making a call for help. This will result in the guards rushing into the King's bedchamber. While they are in a state of confusion and distraction you can rush in and kill them and the King."

Prospero then left. The men now felt very confident that this would be a successful mission.

Edwin pondered what they had heard. Something didn't seem quite right. It all seemed too easy. Never before had Prospero laid out a plan to be so easy. Just then arrows flew and his companions all went down. Edwin was confronted with a dozen men aiming their bows at him. Discretion can be the better part of valor and so Edwin threw down his sword.

King Taryn himself appeared out of the darkness. Smiling his cunning and cruel grin he commanded Edwin to get off his horse.

"My dear Prince Edwin, what a desperate surprise for you and what a great pleasure for me. Your King Erith won't find me as obliging this time as to terms when it comes to your life."

Edwin said nothing. He determined to maintain his courage and dignity. At the same time his innards were aching at the loss of his companions. He thought of their wives and children and the huge loss their deaths represented.

Taryn commanded two of his men to bind Edwin in leg and arm chains. They then placed him on a cart drawn by a horse. When they arrived at the fortress castle he was taken to the dungeon and left there alone in the dark.

As Edwin sat there in great discomfort his thoughts were twirling in trying to understand how this could have happened. His only conclusion was that Prospero wasn't actually Prospero but rather an imposter. The spiritual realm is a difficult realm to figure out. Sometimes it seems it is all resolved as to how to make it work. And then bang the unexpected happens and you know it isn't as simple as previously thought. He continued to mourn the loss of his men. They were each a prince of a man, mighty warriors with noble spirits. Then he started thinking about Greer and their child. What if he didn't get back to them? When he realized what he was thinking he stopped himself. He knew he couldn't go down that track or he would start to unravel. He needed to focus on staying in hope and remain calm.

Edwin continued to consider the events that had happened. He then thought about how Prospero or his counterfeit had taken time to lay out a very specific plan just before they were attacked. "What was the point of all that? Why not just lead us to the point of being attacked without wasting time in giving a bogus plan?" It was all very perplexing to Edwin.

As Edwin continued to ponder the situation he actually started to lighten up a bit. "Perhaps there was more to what happened than what appeared to be the case."

The cell door swung wide open and in walked four burly guards. Two of them forcibly grabbed Edwin and practically dragged him with them. They walked down the dimly lit hallway and then proceeded to walk up a set of stairs. At the top was a large room with Taryn sitting in the middle.

The guards brought Edwin before Taryn and remained tightly holding on to his arms. Everything was quiet as the King surveyed his captive. Taryn had a bemused look on his face.

"Edwin, I have so many options with you that I haven't yet decided which one is the best. Be sure though I will get great value from you being my captive even if it is only seeing you die."

With that Edwin was led away back to his cell. After the door closed he sat there considering what to do next.

"Prospero, I need your help."

No reply. Only silence.

"Patrick, I need your help."

No reply. Again silence.

Four weeks dragged by and Edwin continued to remain in his cell. His daily food rations were only a few pieces of moldy bread and a potato. Once a week he would also get a piece of dried meat. A small cup of water was also his daily ration. During this time Edwin had moments when he struggled to keep his hope. Sometimes a sense of grief came on him so strong he almost felt overwhelmed. Each time he would stop himself by envisioning his triumphant return to Evansing with Taryn's head in his hand high and lifted up above his own head.

The cell opened up and this time he was brought out for the first time since his audience with Taryn in the large room. The guards led him outside to a post in an open field. They tied him to it. As Edwin looked up he saw six bowmen lined up about thirty feet away. King Taryn appeared and walked toward Edwin.

"Edwin, my negotiations with Erith have not gone the way I needed them to go for me to feel good about releasing you. Mind you, I asked for a lot. I wanted his crown so that I would be the ruler of Evansing."

Edwin said nothing.

"This is the end of the line for you, my boy. I have chosen to give you a merciful death. To tell you the truth I don't know why I have been so easy on you. I could certainly think of more entertaining ways to see you die. Goodbye, Edwin."

Taryn turned around and walked back to where the archers were waiting the signal to fire.

The sergeant-at-arms yelled, "Ready. Aim. Fire!"

Six arrows thudded into Edwin. His body went limp.

The body was taken from the post and dragged to a freshly dug grave where it was thrown in and covered with dirt.

# Chapter 31

Greer woke up in her bedroom from a nightmare. She was shaking as she recalled what she had just dreamt. In her night vision she saw Edwin trying to get to her but he couldn't. He was blocked by a wall of darkness and then he disappeared.

The days continued to pass with still no news of the fate of Edwin and his companions. It had now been almost six weeks since they had left. There had been rumors of their deaths at the hands of Taryn's men but no confirmation. This of course placed the people of Evansing in a state of apprehension and grief. Greer was comforted by her family and friends and they tried to assure her that Edwin would return. She tried to hang onto that hope and part of her did have an unexplainable peace but she also struggled with a sense of dread of the worst possible outcome.

Meanwhile the spiritual realm experienced some serious conversations and debates about whether the lives of Edwin and his men should end the way they did. Prospero and St. Patrick both argued for a major turnaround. The experience was most upsetting for Prospero as he had felt as though he had betrayed his trust to Edwin and his friends. He called them Edwin's friends for he knew that is how Edwin perceived his men. In actuality he hadn't betrayed them, as he had received last second orders to withdraw. Those orders came from The Chief Lord of Ireland. Why they had been issued was the point of debate. The dark side had successfully argued in heaven's courts they had the legal right to kill Edwin and stop him and his men. The arguments were legally valid. But Patrick and Prospero argued a higher legal right existed. It was the Law of Grace.

Patrick asked, "Who presented this petition against Edwin and his men?"

"Alcana, the Druid," replied the heavenly representative.

"What gave him the legal right to make such a petition?"

"Edwin's grandfather on his mother's side had made a pact with the Druids that his grandson would become a Druid by the time he was twenty-one. If he didn't then they would have the right to kill him."

"What can we do to revoke that pact?"

"To revoke now when he is already dead is highly irregular. Normally the only ones to have revoked it before would have been Edwin or his parents, but of course they didn't know about it."

"You indicated normally. What does that mean?"

"It means in some cases we can change what happens normally. Because I like you, Patrick, I will let you in on a loophole. There is now one person who can still revoke the pact. It is Greer. If she does so in the next twenty-four hours there is a chance the Chief Lord will grant your request for a reversal of what has happened."

The representative had barely finished his sentence when Patrick and Prospero had left for Evansing Castle to see Greer.

Greer sat nursing her baby trying her best to stay in a place of hope. She knew being downcast would not be good for her daughter.

She had just finished nursing and covering herself when Patrick and Prospero appeared. Just before they appeared they had released a calming influence over Greer so she wouldn't be unduly shocked. They had also waited until she had covered herself. They knew she was having a difficult time and they didn't want to make it any worse.

"Hello, Greer", greeted Prospero.

Patrick nodded and smiled.

Greer looked at them both with a sigh of relief as she expected they would have something good to share with her.

"Is Edwin alive?" she blurted.

"That is dependent on what you do next," replied Prospero.

Greer looked at him like he had two heads. "What do you mean?"

"It's complicated, Greer. What I need you to do is a simple renunciation of a pact entered into by Edwin's grandfather on his mother's side."

Again she looked at him like he had two heads. "How does that have any bearing on whether he is alive?"

"Trust me, Greer, it has a lot to do with whether he is alive."

"What do I need to do?"

"Simply repeat after me. I, Greer, as wife of Edwin, and having the authority on behalf of Edwin, do revoke and renounce the pact entered into by his maternal grandfather with the Druids. I break its power over Edwin and his daughter and all future children."

Greer repeated these words. When she came to the end she felt a shiver go through her and her daughter laughed.

Both Prospero and Patrick were beaming and then they left.

The breaking of the pact now allowed for a complete reversal of the curse of death over Edwin and his companions. As a result a time warp was created during which Edwin and his men were now approaching the location where Prospero would give them instructions and become invisible. This time however, there was no ambush awaiting them. As a result they proceeded to the back of the fortress as instructed by Prospero.

They walked up the stairs to the main floor and on cue Prospero caused one of the guards to fall unconscious. The other guards rushed over to see what had happened to him. As they did so Edwin and his men came from behind and quietly subdued them with their knives.

Then they began the walk up the next flight of stairs to the second floor where Taryn's bedchamber was. Prospero mimicked Taryn's voice calling for help which led the guards to rush into his bedchamber. Edwin and his men then came in and attacked the guards and Taryn. Two guards with their backs near to the door were taken down immediately by the Evansing troop. Edwin lunged at one of the other guards who managed to parry away the thrust. He then lunged back at Edwin. As he did so one of Edwin's men sliced off the guard's head.

The remaining two guards were also quickly dispatched. This left Taryn by himself with Edwin's five men pointing their swords at him within inches of his body.

171

Edwin relished this moment. Even though the time warp occurred as though Edwin and his men had never died, there nevertheless was a remnant of that experience which made the desire to get revenge against Taryn a lot more personal.

"Well, Taryn, the tables have turned. I am happy to say for us this is where your interference in our affairs is going to end."

"Do it." The five men thrust their swords into Taryn.

Edwin and his men then returned down the stairs to exit back the way they had come in. By doing so they avoided the other guards posted in the fortress. The men returned shortly after dawn to where they had spent the previous day. Prospero met them there.

"Gentlemen, you now have a clear path to get back home. I am now going to leave you on your own." He then disappeared.

Edwin and his friends sat around their campsite relishing their recent conquest.

One of the men asked Edwin what he thought Merethath would now do with their King dead.

"Taryn had no immediate male heir. He has a teenage daughter who will not assume the throne. He did not designate an heir for he probably did not expect to die so soon. That leaves several nephews who will most likely battle for the throne. A civil war may well ensue. This now creates an opportunity to more readily take Nerland back into our sphere of influence. An assassination of Prince Gondar would now be the most efficient way to resolve Nerland's sympathies. King Keltic is still imprisoned and has broad support from his citizenry."

The trip back to Evansing went without a hitch, a pleasant change from their journey out. Mind you, the worst part of their journey was miraculously reversed as though it had never happened.

As they got close to Evansing Town they could see a large black cloud resting on top of Evansing Castle.

# Chapter 32

E dwin and his men looked with alarm. This was no ordinary storm cloud.

The name Alcana sprung to Edwin's mind. "Men, this is the work of Druid sorcery."

"What can we do?" one of the men asked.

"Trust the Chief Lord to protect us."

As they got closer to the gates they could feel a whirlwind of evil swirling around them. It threatened to fill them with fear but Edwin shouted, "Courage, men, we shall overcome."

He led them into the city where they were greeted by soldiers and townsfolk. They looked confused and full of fear.

"Who can tell me what is going on?"

One of the soldiers spoke up, "Sir, only a matter of a half hour or so ago the black cloud came out of nowhere and released its dark energy. We all feel helpless."

"What is happening in the Castle?"

"When the dark cloud showed up an invisible wall went up around the castle blocking anyone from entering or leaving."

Edwin and his men rode up to the point where the force of resistance was so strong their horses stopped. They dismounted and tried to penetrate it but to no avail. They could see through it but could not physically go through it.

Next step was to cry out for help. Something stopped Edwin from doing so. An inner knowing revealed things had changed again and he needed to come up with a new solution.

He asked himself, "What is that new solution?"

A simple solution came to him. "Dig under it," sounded a voice in his head.

Edwin cried out to the soldiers and townsfolk near him, "Bring your shovels. We are going to dig under it."

Within ten minutes a team of shovelers had assembled by the force field and started digging underneath. They had selected a spot where the dirt was relatively soft, but it was

175

slow going. They needed to make a deep and wide enough trench so a significant number of men could crawl under the invisible wall. Finally they had dug a trench deep and wide enough for two abreast to start crawling under the mysterious wall. Edwin and one of his special team members led the way. He had told them to wait for his return before sending more men. When they had gotten through underneath the wall they entered into an atmosphere of utmost malevolence. They were bombarded by all kinds of evil, murderous thoughts. Once they returned back to the other soldiers, they warned them of what they would encounter and that they would need to resist those thoughts.

"If any of you feel you cannot handle it or you are feeling unduly afraid then don't come under the wall."

A number of the soldiers backed away and chose not to go under. About a third of the original number indicated they felt they could handle it.

Before they started crawling under, Edwin stopped to consider what they would encounter.

"We will most likely encounter enemy spiritual beings. How will we deal with them?" he mulled. He raised his hand indicating everyone to simply wait until he sorted out what they would do. What came to him was that they needed to exercise authority to rid the castle of these evil beings. All they needed to do was tell them to go and know they had the power to do it.

"Men, we aren't going to encounter many flesh and blood soldiers. We are mainly going to face invisible beings of pure evil. I am now giving you authority to be able to say to them: Go now and never return. I remind you to not give in to the thoughts and feelings they will throw at you. Just keep telling them to go and never return and don't doubt the authority given you to do so. We will go throughout the castle and as we do so keep saying what I told you. I am however expecting that we will encounter some of the castle guards and castle servants who have been bewitched by the evil and who will attack us."

Edwin and one of his men then led the way of crawling under the spiritual wall. When the men all had gone under and through to the other side, they didn't see anyone around. It actually was eerily quiet. Edwin had decided it would be best for them to stick together to avoid smaller groups getting ambushed and overwhelmed. First thing they encountered were the closed castle gates. Edwin and his men wrestled with what they should do.

Finally Edwin recognized his authority and he stepped up to the gates and commanded, "Open the gates now!"

After several minutes the gates started to open. The men were surprised as many thought Edwin had lost it. This response to the exercise of authority encouraged and strengthened their confidence in their own authority. As the hundred and fifty or so men walked through the gates they met twenty-two guards who attacked them even though greatly outnumbered. Unfortunately they were so impacted by the evil influence they could not be coaxed to lay down their arms. They all fought to the death with the rescuers suffering twenty-four casualties.

Edwin led the men to where the royal residences were located. When they arrived, there was nobody there. Greer, the baby and the King were nowhere to be found. In the meantime as the men were telling the spirits to leave, the evil presence got lighter and lighter. As they continued to walk through the castle they came across bodies of servants who had died at the hands of the affected guards. Others were walking around in a daze wondering what had happened. Eventually other members of the extended royal family came out and along with them, Percival. They had all barricaded themselves in one of the large rooms with heavy doors. Percival had acted quickly to do his best to help but by the time he got to where Greer and Erith were, they were already gone.

Edwin of course was glad to see Percival and the others, but he was also distressed at not finding Greer, Orla and the King. Yet something inside him said to not worry, things would work out. He decided he would focus on that feeling and not let fearful thoughts overtake him.

"Percival, what are your ideas on what we do now?"

"I suspect your family has been transported via a spiritual highway to a Druid stronghold."

As they were discussing their whereabouts, the evil cloud and its presence lifted off completely.

Now they had a new clarity in their thinking not previously available to them.

Percival said, "Let's go for a ride. Meet me outside in ten minutes."

Ten minutes later Edwin crawled onto the metamorphosed Percival and together they lifted off into the skies. They flew for an hour northwest and then landed. After Percival reconfigured into his normal state they started to confer further as to the next step.

Percival spoke first, "I felt it was important to get away from Evansing to enhance our clarity of direction. As well I had a very strong leading that going northwest would lead to finding your family. I recall years ago of hearing of a Druid fortress about thirty miles further north. There is a monastery only a few miles from here. A friend of mine there should be able to help us. He has had a lot of successful dealings with Druids. Let's walk the few miles. It will do us good."

As they walked they talked about how the past several years had been most remarkable.

Edwin shared, "To think I would have the life I have, given where I started is most amazing. Sometimes I still wake up and look at Greer and ask myself how did I ever stumble across a life like this?"

"Your noble heart attracted good fortune."

"There were nobler hearts than mine and many noble hearts never attract good fortune. Why me?"

"Remember you had other qualities that added to the attractive power."

"You mean my being a warrior?"

"Yes, you had a value needed by Evansing. Nobility with valuable qualities created an irresistible force."

At that point they came to the gate to the monastery. Repeated knocking on the gate resulted in a man's head appearing at the gate's grated opening.

"What do you want?"

"We want to meet with Darcy."

"Who should I say wants to meet with him?'

"Percival, his old friend."

"Percival? You are Percival? Come on in."

The gate opened and Percival and Edwin entered the monastery.

The man who had greeted them excitedly shared how they had heard many stories of Percival in their Divine Services. They came to the main building on the monastery grounds and entered. As their eyes grew accustomed to the dim light a man with a large engaging smile came up to Percival and gave him a huge hug. They then spent ten minutes or so catching up.

Edwin patiently stood listening with a bemused look on his face. These two men clearly had great affection for each other. Many years earlier they had shared tough experiences which had knitted their hearts in ways only enduring hardship together can do.

Percival stopped to introduce Edwin to his friend, "Darcy, here is my good friend Prince Edwin of Evansing. We are here to seek your help in rescuing his family who I believe are being held at the Druid fortress just down the road from here. His family are his wife, Greer, their infant daughter and his father-in-law, Erith, King of Evansing."

Darcy looked at Edwin for a moment without saying anything.

"Edwin, be of good cheer we will work something out although it may not be exactly what you hoped for."

# Chapter 33

Edwin wasn't quite sure how to receive that statement.

"What do you mean it may not be exactly what I hoped for? Do you have some special insight about my family?"

"I don't know specifics I am simply sharing what is coming to mind. Stay in hope and peace."

"I am not sure if your statement exactly encourages me to stay in peace. It is creating an element of angst about something happening that I don't like."

"Yes, I know. It is important you be able to handle truth even when it isn't completely what you hoped for."

"What do we do now?"

"I have a special passageway available to access the Druid fortress. We can leave tonight."

Later that night the three men left for the fortress. Since the distance was too great to walk or ride in one night, Percival provided the transportation in his own unique way.

They landed a mile from the fortress. There they reviewed the plans they had developed earlier. Everyone knew their roles and expected to fulfill them to the letter including the timing.

They walked to the passageway entrance. This entrance was no normal entrance. To the untrained eye it looked like part of the wall. As well, it had been anointed with holy oil so that no Druid or their accompanying spirits could detect it. Darcy led the walk through what appeared to be the solid wall. When he noticed he wasn't being followed he stuck his head out through the wall and asked if they were coming. Even though Percival and Edwin had had all kinds of weird and wonderful supernatural experiences, this particular one seemed to create a partial paralysis in their ability to just walk through the wall. With the prompting Percival took a step and to his half surprise he didn't hurt himself. Edwin then followed, feeling a little more confident that he could do this. The dungeon cells were in the basement and close to the passageway. Each of the men had been thoroughly blessed with holy water and oil, took the Eucharist and had the monks bless them with protection. They had a feeling of invincibility and were ready to take on whatever they faced.

Edwin would take the lead followed by Darcy behind him to the left and Percival right behind to the right. As they crept along in the shadows they could hear two guards speaking.

"What are we going to do with this King and his daughter?"

"Alcana wants to keep them for ransom so they are going to be with us for a while."

"Ransom? What sort of ransom would incline Alcana to give up these two prizes. I would think he as soon kill them outright instead."

"That may happen soon enough. The ransom demand is that Evansing pay 50,000 pieces of gold and Erith and his daughter give up their positions and be transported to the other side of Ireland."

Edwin thought to himself, "Why is there no mention of baby Orla?"

The other guard responded, "There is no way Evansing will be able to pay that much gold. It will bankrupt them."

"If not, then Erith and Greer will die."

The guards continued towards the three men who were hiding around a corner. As they were walking straight across and not into the corridor Edwin lunged out with his sword to skewer the one closest to him. Darcy simultaneously leapt out to plunge his sword into the chest of the other guard. Both guards died immediately. The three men then turned right up the way the guards had come from. As they proceeded they noticed a darker and darker haze in the passageway. They smelled it. It was smoke. There must be a fire up ahead where the cells were.

They quickened their pace. When they entered the cell area there was a fire in the one corner with several of the guards working to put it out. On the other end of the cell area was where Greer and Erith were located in adjacent cells. Edwin, gratified to see them was also alarmed to not see the baby. Since all the guards were engaging the fire none of them were by Erith and Greer. Now how to open the cell doors?

Darcy pulled out a special key made to be a passkey in the event they needed to free a prisoner. First Erith and then Greer were released. Edwin hugged them both and then taking Greer's hand he started walking quickly back down the way they had come with the others following.

"Where is Orla?"

"I don't know they took her away a few hours ago."

"Darcy, what are we going to do about the baby?"

"We will have to find her later. We must take what we have now."

Just before they were to turn down the corridor leading to the exit they encountered six guards coming from the opposite direction. Edwin pushed Greer into the corridor and attacked the nearest two guards with Darcy and Percival joining in to attack the others. Edwin slashed the throat of one of them and quickly stabbed the other one in the heart. He then faced a guard who though rather large was surprisingly quick. Edwin had to defend himself against some rather deft moves aimed at his own heart and head. Their swords pressed against one another and both were pushing for superiority. The strength of the guard was great and Edwin was starting to feel the strain of it. He pulled out his knife and shoved it into the guard's stomach. Blood spurted out but the guard continued to push with his sword. Edwin continued to dig around with his knife in the man's stomach until the guard convulsed and collapsed.

The other guards were dispatched by Percival and Darcy, although Darcy did sustain a moderate wound in his side. Percival placed his hand on the wound and the bleeding stopped. They all escaped through the exit and fled into the nearby woods. There they found a shelter invisible to all outsiders. Percival could only transport two at a time so he made two trips.

When they all had arrived at the monastery they were exhausted and yet not ready to go to bed.

"Darcy, do you know what they are planning to do with Orla?"

Darcy did not answer immediately. He carefully considered his response.

"There is no other way to say this except to tell you that Druids only do two things with captured babies. They secret them away to be raised up and trained as Druid priests or priestesses or….."

"Or what?"

"They burn them as a human sacrifice."

# Chapter 34

“Oh God not that. We must get her back.” Greer started to sob at the prospect of losing her little girl.

Edwin and Erith both put their arms around Greer to comfort her.

Percival started speaking with Darcy, “What can be done about recovering Orla?”

No reply. Then he spoke, “This is something that I will have to sleep on and see if I get a dream of revelation about it. You can do that too. Together we will hopefully get something definite to work with.”

In another hour or so with the sun coming up, the weary and sad group of people went to sleep.

Edwin lay in his bed next to Greer but he wasn’t sleeping. He had woken up after only a couple of hours. Greer’s gentle breathing irritated him. “What is she doing sleeping? She should be awake like me wondering what is going on? Where is Orla? What is the point of this happening?”

Then he sat up in bed and started ruminating about all the experiences since they had decided to resume the Quest. Nothing but obstacles. Everything was a struggle. Hardly anything just came together without some sort of resistance. “Why! Why! Why! Maybe the Quest is not what we are meant to accomplish after all. The easiest thing for us to do is simply be comfortable and build ourselves a nice secure prosperous kingdom. Perhaps I should let go of all thoughts on something greater, it is too hard. What is the point?"

Finally exhaustion overtook the grief and anger and he fell back to sleep.

When Edwin woke up in the morning Greer was not in her bed. Momentarily Edwin panicked thinking she had been kidnapped again. Then he told himself to relax and that unlike himself she slept and woke up earlier and got up.

Edwin walked into the common dining room and there was Greer with Percival and Darcy.

"Hello," he greeted trying his best to be cheerful.

The others gave a response back although it was subdued as they all keenly felt the loss of Orla.

"Any ideas on what we do now about Orla!"

Percival replied, "Nothing has clearly come as of yet. There seems to be a block. We could pull out all the stops and ask the usual allies to help us, but I don't believe we are meant to do that."

"Why not? I can't think of a better time to draw upon every resource we have to rescue Orla."

"Yes, I appreciate your view and normally I would agree but things have changed."

"What has changed?"

"The old ways of doing things are no longer available to us in the way they used to be."

"What do you mean the old ways are no longer available to us?"

"The spiritual realm has changed the rules. It is a different season."

"So what are the new rules?" Edwin questioned, his voice rising and tinged with anger.

Darcy interjected, "That is precisely what we are trying to get insight on."

Greer took her husband's hand and started to gently rub it. She looked into his eyes and said, "Edwin, try and stay calm. Something will work out. We shall see what shall happen."

Edwin looked at her and thought to himself, "How can she be so calm about this? Doesn't she realize our daughter is in grave danger?"

Edwin did not reply to Greer as he did not know what to say.

Percival spoke up, "Now is the time for us to explore new options. One thing that comes to mind is that we should seek to have St. Brendan come to visit us. He is a new personage we have not worked with before and I am sure he could bring us the fresh revelation we need, not only for saving Orla but also as to how to navigate these new times. I will ask right now for him to come. Brendan, would you please grace us with your presence?"

As is frequently the case there was no instant response, but the request had been made and so now they needed to wait and see what would happen. In the meantime they had to decide whether to simply wait for a response from Brendan or should they consider another avenue of pursuit.

Edwin spoke up, "I think we need to consider other options as well. Who is another respected saint from long ago? Or who would be another angel to consider asking to come see us? I know, I will ask the Archangel Michael. He is fierce, but he did send Joan of Arc to help us."

Percival said, "Yes, go ahead. He directed Joan to help us, but his direct involvement with us was minimal."

"Archangel Michael, we need your help to rescue our little girl Orla. Would you please come or send someone who can help us?"

Again they waited and no response.

Edwin expressed his frustration, "Why can't these spiritual beings show up now when we need them, not later when it could be too late?"

Darcy replied, "These are majestic beings, not our personal pets to be at our beck and call. Try to trust that whatever needs to be worked out will be."

"Are you saying then we will get Orla back unharmed?"

"No, I am not saying that. I don't know what the outcome will be. Just believe that what needs to happen will happen and there is a deep reason for it."

187

"I am not concerned about some higher spiritual good. I want our daughter back."

Greer spoke up, "Edwin, something besides our daughter missing is affecting you."

"Let me have a look at you." She then rolled up Edwin's sleeves and asked him to take off his shirt. He protested weakly, but he knew better than to resist Greer when she was so determined. As she looked at his back she noticed a large red mark that looked like the result of a bite, probably of a spider.

"Didn't you notice any pain when you got this bite?"

"No I didn't notice anything."

"We have got to undo the effects of this bite. Sometimes spider bites can cause reactions resulting in the person bitten to act rather excitedly and you certainly are doing that."

Darcy indicated he would go to the monastery infirmary and see what he could find.

A short time later he returned with a jar of ointment. He handed it to Greer and she rubbed it onto the bite mark and surrounding area. It felt soothing to Edwin.

Fifteen minutes later Edwin began noticing a substantial increase in his well-being.

"Thanks, Greer, I do feel better. You are so wise."

Greer smiled, "You are very welcome, my dear."

"I am still interested in knowing what other steps we can ..."

Michael the Archangel showed up just as he was speaking.

"Edwin, I have heard your request. I am assigning El Cid from Spain. He is a contemporary of yours." Then he vanished.

Everyone was struck with awe in experiencing Michael, who radiated a strong presence unlike anyone else they had encountered.

After several moments of silence Darcy spoke up, "I am expecting El Cid to make us successful in our goal to rescue Orla. I have heard of him from travelers who have been to Spain. He is a renowned warrior ruler."

"I appreciate your confidence, Darcy, I trust it is well placed."

King Erith spoke up, "I need to get back to Evansing. Percival can you bring me back?"

"Yes, Sire, I can. We can leave in about ten minutes. Edwin and Greer, I will return as soon as I drop off the King." He then left to get ready for the departure.

Erith then spoke directly to Greer and Edwin, "Dears, I regret to leave you in this situation. My prayers are with you for the rescue of Orla." He gave them each a hug, with an added tender kiss on Greer's right cheek. They exchanged a few awkward words of nothing of consequence and then he took his leave.

Greer looked at Edwin.

# Chapter 35

Edwin looked back at Greer.

He spoke, "This could be the worst case scenario for us right now except we still have hope."

She replied, "Hope, yes, we have hope. Let us believe there is an agreeable purpose to this El Cid coming to help us."

A voice from behind them answered, "Yes, let us hope my purpose for being here is agreeable to you and His Divine Purpose."

Greer and Edwin, startled, turned around and met face to face someone they had never seen before. His armor and apparel were strange so he wasn't a native of Ireland and he certainly wasn't a monk.

"I am El Cid. I have been assigned to you with the express objective of rescuing your infant daughter. I have cause to believe we will be successful."

"Hello, El Cid, I am Edwin, this is Greer my wife and this fine gentlemen is Darcy, a resident monk. I am sure you already knew that, but I wanted to keep up with formalities of polite society. Do you have an initial plan we can start on?"

"Not exactly a plan, more like some ideas."

"Well then, what are your ideas?" Edwin replied sounding slightly disappointed.

"I have been informed about the situation and have received a deposit of understanding useful for formulating an approach. Together we can create a plan to follow. One piece of information I have been given is that your daughter is being kept in a village twenty-one miles west of here called Ballymun. One idea is for us to go disguised as travelling wine merchants. The monks here are renowned for the wine they have imported from Europe. We can get a wagon from them and transport wine to Ballymun. When we get there we will set up a stall in the market and also one or two of us will call on the people in the village."

"Well, El Cid, by my standards that is a plan and sounds like it could be a good one at that. Darcy, could you arrange for the wagon and horses, the wine and some suitable clothing for us?"

"Yes, I can and I will get on it right away." He then left.

"As soon as Percival gets back we can leave. You do know who Percival is?"

"Yes, I was told he is your wise counselor with some rather unusual gifts."

"That he is. When he gets back the four of us can leave hopefully within the hour."

"You mean the five of us."

The two men turned to face Greer.

"You are not leaving without me. Besides it will seem more natural and less threatening if you have a wife with you. In any event I want to be there."

Edwin looked at El Cid and they nodded in agreement.

"El Cid, what additional resources as to protection from Druids and their minions do we have available?"

"I have been assured by the Archangel Michael himself that we have a cloak of hiddenness over us so that the Druids and their evil spiritual cohorts will not be able to detect who we truly are. As well he indicated we have a company of angels travelling with us. However we will not see them or detect their presence. It is a test of our faith that they are going to be with us and will help as necessary."

"That sounds good enough for me."

"Greer sweetheart, what do you think?"

"Well, dear, thanks for asking. Yes, it sounds very promising. I have one addition I would like us to make. I would like to have Joan accompany us."

"Joan? I thought we were now meant to work with new people."

"Yes, I know we have worked with her before, but this would be a new way for her to work with us. As you have told me Joan is a simple peasant girl at heart. She could pretend to be El Cid's wife and that will add to the ruse."

"I tell you what Greer, you ask Joan if she will come and if she does, very well. If she doesn't then it's not her assignment."

"I can do that."

"Joan, this is Greer. I have a special request for your help. Could you please come?"

Almost immediately Joan appeared in a simple woman's garb. This quite surprised Edwin as he had never seen her aside from looking very much the warrior.

"Joan, as soon as she asked you came."

"Yes, a simple polite request from Greer carries great weight with your Divine Overseer. This particular mission has been give high priority. Together we shall see what can be accomplished."

Over the next several hours preparations were made for their departure. Percival had returned a bit later than expected. Erith and the Evansing Council required decisions on some urgent matters and his valuable counsel was needed.

The preparations for departure were now in place and the hopeful, expectant crew of people got into what were now two wagons in order to comfortably accommodate the females.

Greer asked Darcy, "What kind of village is Ballymun?"

"First it is large for a village, both in area and in population. It has over a thousand inhabitants and is almost a square mile as it is somewhat spread out. But most of the people live in the central part within a half mile of each other. The size will create some challenges for us, but given our resources I am sure we are more than equal to those challenges. Another characteristic of Ballymun is the curious mixture of light and dark. Certain sections in it are quite inculcated with beliefs in faeries, elves and Druidry. Consequently the darkness is almost palpable in those areas. Others are filled with light as though they are the doorway to heaven itself. This gives us some grid as to how to proceed. We could connect with the light sections first and see if anyone knows of a new baby arrival. If no news there then we still expect most likely Orla is being kept in one of the dark sections. Knowing this will narrow our search efforts."

El Cid spoke up, "Those are valuable insights, Darcy. What a great question, Greer."

Edwin seized the opportunity, "Yes, she is brilliant, isn't she?"

Greer thanked them both and gave Edwin an affectionate rub on his back.

Darcy signaled the horses to begin pulling and off they went. Edwin had kept his good cheer even though the time of leaving was delayed beyond what he had anticipated. Now they were leaving and everyone was filled with expectation of a successful recovery.

The next day the group arrived in Ballymun. They drove to the market place and set up their wares. Not too many people were around that day. They did make a few sales and engaged some of the locals in conversation about the latest news in the area such as whether new babies had been born for they had knitted booties to give as gifts. These were knit enroute by Joan. She came up with the idea that it would make a much more plausible reason for enquiring about new babies.

Darcy and Percival started to call upon the houses in the 'light area' of the village. On their sixth call they encountered a talkative young woman. She mentioned how she had noticed a woman in the 'Druid believing' section who had been carrying a young baby. The remarkable thing about it was that the woman had been barren for ten years of marriage. This young lady had seen her only months earlier with no sign of being pregnant.

"Perhaps she would like a new pair of booties for the baby. Please give us directions to her house," said Percival.

After receiving directions, the two men left for the market to first get Greer and the booties. Darcy stayed at the market with Joan, while Percival accompanied Edwin, Greer and El Cid. As they walked toward the house in question they could feel the darkness envelop them. The house did not have any sign of life inside. They knocked on the door. No response. They walked around the house and yard looking around for evidence of something noteworthy. Everything was strangely quiet around them. No sign of movement in the nearby homes. Could it be everyone was gone working in the fields? Edwin forced the door open and stepped inside. There on the floor lay the body of a young woman. Her throat had been slashed.

# Chapter 36

The blood was still quite fresh so she hadn't been dead long. No sign of a baby. He stepped back outside and shared the news. This disappointed Greer and her hopeful demeanor changed to one bordering on despair. Edwin gave her a hug.

"Stay the course, honey. Stay in hope."

El Cid peered more closely into the surrounding homes and yards. He noticed some interesting movement in a home several properties over. Someone was looking out the window at them, but when they realized El Cid noticed them they quickly closed the curtains.

"Let us pay a visit to that house over there. It may be nothing, but it also could be the people who were just here or at least saw who was just here."

As they walked over, the intensity of dark forces grew stronger. It felt like tiny needles on their faces. The men and Greer walked a wide circle around the home to see if there were any other exits. None were noted. Then the three men approached the door with Edwin knocking on it. No answer. Knocked again. No answer.

Edwin walked up to the door, lifted up his right leg and kicked it in.

This time they were met by three men with swords who came charging at them. Behind them were two women hanging back into a corner of the home. Was one of them holding a baby?

There was no time to look closer. Edwin, El Cid and Percival each took on an opponent. Edwin backed up out the door to make more room for swordplay as the quarters were tight in the house for such action with six men. One of the men approached Edwin with an eerie gleam in his eye. He thrusted rather quickly and had a certain flair about his movements. Edwin noted a deceptiveness about him. The man feigned to Edwin's left only to come back to Edwin's right and grazed Edwin's side due to having his thrust partially deflected. This upset Edwin which sparked a flurry of thrusts and slashes as he rushed his opponent. The man continued to maintain his calm demeanor and gleam as he successfully fended off Edwin's attack. Then he returned the favor by mounting his own offensive play. His sword tip caught Edwin's shirt near his neck, no blood drawn. Edwin determined to keep his cool. Instead of mounting another attack Edwin stepped back. This drew his opponent in for another play for the kill. However this time Edwin stepped aside and caught the man off guard by thrusting deep into the man's lungs. The gleam disappeared and was now replaced with terror. He was gasping for air and coughing blood. Edwin kicked the man down onto his back and left him to gasp and choke in his blood. In the meantime El Cid and Percival were in the process of defeating their own opponents. When they finished all eyes were on the two women in the corner.

Indeed one of them was holding a baby, a young baby. The women looked defiant and afraid at the same time.

Edwin ordered both of them to come out of the corner and toward the door. They hesitated then walked slowly toward the men. Edwin took the baby and his eyes lit up as he knew it was Orla.

"Greer, come here, our treasure has been found."

Greer squealed with delight and took her daughter in her arms.

After ten minutes or so of Greer and Edwin delighting in holding Orla, it dawned on them to get moving and get out of the village. First what to do with the women? They decided to tie them up and leave them in the house.

As they returned to the market they noticed several men following them some distance away. Darcy and Joan had already hitched up and loaded up the wagons in anticipation of a quick getaway. They started the teams of horses and turned them in the direction of the monastery. The men who had been following had stopped. Little did our band of heroes and heroines know but those men had been stopped by a large angel who appeared to them and paralyzed them with fear.

Greer studied Orla to see if anything visible had been done to her. Nothing visible, but she did notice Orla seemed frightened, understandable given her separation from her mother and father. Greer prayed there would be no lasting effect.

The trip back was uneventful which they suspected could only be attributed to the angelic force guarding them.

Once back at the monastery El Cid and Joan returned to their homes. This left the question of how to transport Greer and her baby. It didn't appear feasible to have either Edwin or Greer hang onto the bird and the baby while flying on the back of the big bird. It was decided to have Percival return home and bring a troop and a wagon for Greer and the baby. The next day Edwin and Greer were playing with their daughter when Darcy showed up with a concerned look on his face.

Edwin asked, "What is the matter, Darcy?"

"We have a band of unknown soldiers knocking on our gate and wanting entrance."

Edwin considered what he had just heard. Nothing immediately came to him as to how to respond.

"What are you and your colleagues wanting to do?"

"We would like to skewer each and every one of them for they don't look very savory."

Edwin sighed. For a moment he thought to himself how nice it would be to have everything work well with nothing gumming the works or creating another challenge to be faced and resolved.

"Let me go to the gate and enquire further," replied Edwin.

As he went to the gate he considered what he would say.

Speaking through the opening in the gate, "What is the nature of your business?"

The leader of the band of soldiers answered, "We have no need to tell you why we want entrance except to say this. If you don't let us in then we will kill all inhabitants as penalty for not letting us in."

"That is very severe. I should tell you though that we have five cases of the plague and you will put yourself and all your men at risk by entering through our gates."

# Chapter 37

The leader did not respond but went to his men and conferred with them as to what to do next.

He returned and said, "How do we know what you say is true?"

"Would you like to examine one of them up close and expose yourself to the plague?"

Again no reply. Their leader seemed stumped as to how handle this situation. The men with him were adamantly indicating they had no stomach to risk catching the plague. The leader realizing he was risking a rebellion to his leadership and not so sure he himself wanted to risk contact with the plague, finally relented and the troop of soldiers marched away in the direction of the Druid fortress.

"Well done, Edwin, what inspired you to say that?"

"It just came to me, Darcy. Initially I thought as you did, let's skewer them and then I started considering how perhaps we could avoid battling them and risking all the potential loss that action could entail."

"The Divine Creator's Grace was on you to get such a revelation. And His Favor had them respond like they did."

Edwin looked at him. "You think so?"

"Yes, I do think so."

"Why would you say that?"

"Well it was totally uncharacteristic of how you would normally respond. You said yourself you originally thought to skewer them. And having them leave so readily without greater resistance is certainly not the usual response by such a gang of ruffians."

"You know it *is* interesting, I had been thinking how it would be nice if things would work out without another challenge to face. Perhaps His Mercy was demonstrated in this matter."

"Good for you, Edwin, in your acknowledgement that it wasn't purely your brilliance. Mind you it was brilliant and I do acknowledge you handled it very well."

"Thanks, Darcy, I do appreciate your approbation."

"Approbation? Now that is a fine sounding word to use. You have come a long way from being an illiterate warrior from Elfereth."

"Yes, I surprised myself when that word came out of my mouth. Percival has been a most excellent tutor for me. I am amazed at how he progressed so greatly from very humble roots as a peasant warrior himself. How long have you known him?"

"Percival and I grew up together in the same village. In fact we were both serving as warriors at the same time. He left only weeks before I decided I better leave as well. The chieftain and others knew I was close to Percival and they had their suspicions of my loyalty. I never married so it was easy for me to pick up and leave one night.

I rejoined Percival and it started a time of many adventures together. The culmination of which was when we both became monks. Given our experiences and beliefs that is stunningly miraculous. Has Percival not shared with you about his life?"

"Very little. He shared about being briefly married and how he decided to leave his village after a dispute with the chieftain on how they did war."

"Yes, that would be Percival. He doesn't like to share much about his life unless there is a purpose to do so. I should let him share what he wants to share with you."

"Speaking of Percival, hopefully we will see him and the troop escort soon. They should be here tomorrow sometime."

Edwin returned to Greer and Orla with a smile on his face and without saying anything to Greer, sat down next to her. Then he sat there in silence.

"Well are you going to tell me what happened?"

Edwin looked at her and continued to grin without saying anything.

Greer, getting a little exasperated swatted him on his arm and said, "What is the matter with you? Why are you not telling me?"

"I just wanted to have a little fun with you. And besides I was savoring what has just happened."

"Yes, that is very nice, now tell me what it is you are savoring."

"I did something today, totally different than my normal approach. It makes me marvel at how it all turned out." He then shared what had happened with the soldiers at the gate and what Darcy had said.

Greer considered what he had said and paused a moment before answering. "You know that is even more than what Darcy said it is. Edwin my dear, you demonstrated a new level of wisdom and sensitivity to doing life differently. Having those in place enabled you to hear and respond to the thoughts the Creator was giving you."

"My sweet Greer, thank you for such a thoughtful response. My greatest wisdom was in marrying you."

"I feel the same about marrying you." They hugged and kissed and went back to playing with their daughter.

The next day in the late afternoon, the Evansing troop arrived with Percival. Their arrival was a welcome sight as both Edwin and Greer were eager to get back home.

"Percival, it is so good to see you again."

"Likewise, Edwin, and you as well, Greer. We had a wonderfully uneventful trip."

Darcy then came up, "My dear friend, I am also glad to see you. Let me talk to you for a moment, just the two of us."

They then walked a short distance away where they could talk privately. "Percival, I think it is time for you to consider sharing with Edwin more of your history. I believe it would be beneficial for your relationship with him and his personal development. Even though you may not see the relevance of most of it, nevertheless it will nurture new levels of wisdom and insight for Edwin."

Percival looked surprised, then a little dismayed, and finally thoughtful.

"I will consider what you say, Darcy. I am not sure if I agree with you but I will consider it."

"Well that is a start. By your initial reaction it didn't look promising."

"It didn't initially feel promising, but I recognize my feelings aren't always a good gauge for what is right. As I reflected on it some more it started to feel more and more like it could be a good thing. Not only felt but sensed. Of course I also highly respect your opinion and input. You are such a good friend and I have missed you so much. We need to find some reasons to spend more time together. Could you come to Evansing for a spell? We could certainly use your wisdom input."

"Thank you, Percival, for your invite and encouraging comments. I must admit I have been feeling a little restless lately and wondering if this is how I am to end my days. I have been asking for guidance. Perhaps this is the answer I have been looking for. Let me ponder this until tomorrow morning. In the meantime I will talk to our abbot to get his input and make him aware of what I am contemplating."

"That sounds sensible and sensitive. Good combination when making a decision."

As Darcy walked to the Abbot's office he felt very betwixt and between as to what he should do. On one hand the idea of striking out to Evansing appealed to his desire for adventure and new challenges. On the other hand, he had responsibilities at the monastery which he didn't feel anyone else was ready to take on. He experienced some regret with that for he knew he hadn't invested time in training someone to take over from him. He knew he should, but a combination of not seeming to find the time and also deep down not wanting someone to know what he knew impeded him from doing so. Another question to consider would be if he went, for how long should he go?

He arrived at the Abbott's office and knocked quietly on the open door. The Abbot looked up and broke out into a smile. He liked Darcy and was happy to see him. He stood up to shake Darcy's hand. Both men exchanged pleasantries for a moment and then the Abbott, called John, asked Darcy to sit down.

"John, I have come to get your advice about something I am considering. I have been invited to go to Evansing for a while. I am not sure how long. It could be a month or it could be a year."

"Or it could be where you end your days," interjected John.

This statement startled Darcy because he had not seriously considered that possibility.

The Abbott continued, "Darcy, I have felt for some time that your time here is drawing to a close. Your passion for the monastic life has been waning over the past two years. The opportunity to bash some Druids and their adherents seems to always perk up your spirits but those activities only take a small percentage of your time. The life of a traditional monk is not what you are meant to live."

Darcy silently pondered what John had stated. On one hand he recognized the statement as true and on the other hand the idea of committing himself wholeheartedly to Evansing felt a little bit intimidating. There was a nice secure predictability about living at the monastery. "Oh, what to do?" he thought to himself.

"I must admit you are right, but it isn't totally easy to pick up and take on a brand-new life, even if it does look inviting."

"I wouldn't know what that is like except when I decided to become a monk and that is many years ago. I do know this, I have sometimes wondered if I should have considered other options. I have asked myself if I simply settled for being a monk or was this truly my call in life. You, of course are the one who must answer for yourself."

"These are hard questions and yet I am sure what you are saying is true. I am going to go for a walk and mull these over further."

# Chapter 38

The day was a typical overcast Irish day with a light off-and-on drizzle. Darcy found the drizzle to be refreshing; there was a sense of newness about it. When he realized how he felt about it, he understood a little more deeply how much his underlying being was looking for newness. Not simply newness for the sake of it but something closely aligned with what he had been created for. At the monastery the options for newness had been exhausted at least as far as he could see and what seemed to be implied by the Abbott as well. As he considered further the benefits of going to Evansing, he realized he had two major supports in his favor for going there. Percival, his dear friend, and the Royal Family of Evansing were truly grateful for his role in rescuing Erith, Greer and ultimately the baby princess. His life should be as secure as any life can be. "I will do it, I will go to Evansing," he said out loud.

Darcy walked over to where the Evansing contingent was congregated and waited for Percival to be free to talk. When Percival noticed Darcy standing nearby he turned to talk to Darcy.

"Percival, if you really want me to go to Evansing I am ready to leave when you are."

"Darcy, that is wonderful. How long can you stay?"

"As long as you want me to. I am prepared to make a permanent move."

Percival's initial response was a large grin. "Darcy, that is way beyond what I expected. Of course you will be welcome to stay as long as you wish. Your insights about battling Druids and the special powers you have developed will be much appreciated as we resume the Quest."

They walked over to Edwin and Greer and shared the news. Both of them had already been informed about Percival's invitation. They too were delighted to know Darcy was coming. They had great respect for Darcy's skill and they appreciated the likable wisdom he had which they knew would come in handy and ensure he fit in with the main personalities at Evansing.

The next day the Evansing contingent gathered in front of the monastery's gates. Darcy tearfully said good-bye to each of his fellow monks. John, the Abbott, was last in the procession and he gave Darcy a prolonged hug, then looking in Darcy's face said, "Darcy, my dear friend, you have made the right decision."

"John, I believe you are right."

Darcy with his eyes full of tears got on his horse, turned to wave one final good-bye before the Evansing party departed for home.

Percival and Darcy rode together continuing to catch up on the years they had been apart as well as reminiscing about some of their adventures when they were young. They laughed and greatly delighted in just being together like soul mates do.

"Percival, you know how in some seasons things work out even without trying and how in some seasons nothing works out no matter how hard you work?"

"Yes, Darcy, I do. This past season has certainly been a lot of the latter with the very important exception of rescuing the Royal Family. Mind you as I say that, ultimately everything has worked out well. But it took a lot of blood, pain and toil to get there."

"Percival, I believe we are in a new season to see a lot of progress with the Quest. I am anticipating more successes than has ever been seen before."

"Really my friend, what makes you say that?"

"I have this strong feeling it is a new season. I believe the relative ease of our rescuing the Royal Family and then avoiding confrontation with those Druid disciples are two very clear examples of a change."

The words were no sooner out of his mouth than an arrow struck Darcy in the chest. Fortunately it lodged into his money pouch kept inside his jacket. The point just barely protruded through the other side and slightly scratched his skin drawing a trickle of blood. The arrow startled everyone around Darcy. Edwin let out a shout to the troops accompanying and they all stopped to look where the attack was coming from.

All was silent. No further shots were fired. Most peculiar. Was this simply the working of a madman or was it the deliberate attempt to murder Darcy?

"Do you think it is possible the Druids already formulated plans for your demise so quickly?"

"I have learned, Percival, that the Druids are able to communicate almost instantaneously sometimes and then other times appear to be very slow. I can only surmise there are divine interventions sometimes and seemingly sometimes not. It is likely they know of my leaving and instigated this attack. Why it stopped after one arrow is most likely due to one of those divine interventions."

"Why do you think sometimes there is an intervention and sometimes it doesn't appear to happen?"

"A higher good is always being orchestrated even when it doesn't seem like it. If we doubt it, then we doubt our Creator's capacity to do all things including bringing good out of evil."

"Interesting to see enough intervention to prevent a deadly attack, but not so much as to totally block the evidence of it being there."

"Yes, enough evidence to show we had help to prevent my inopportune death."

"I am glad for it. You are my dear friend and it would be a sore loss to lose you now."

"Yes, Percival, I am looking forward to the adventures that lie ahead."

"I remember the adventures we had in France when we were in Marseille."

"Ah, Marseille, what an exciting city for two young men! We were so unsophisticated to the locals."

"We were unsophisticated! Two country boys from rural Ireland. We were agog at seeing such a city like Marseille. If we hadn't gone we would never have met Monsieur Toutant."

"I often recall Monsieur Toutant and his mentoring us. Without him we would never have gained the wisdom to know how to live life."

"He certainly gave us a boost in wisdom, but I like to think we had it in us to grow through the experiences and learning we have had since. Mind you, Darcy, his training raised our openness to gaining wisdom. He acted as an accelerator and for that I am extremely grateful."

"Yes, Percival, it was most fortunate meeting him."

"Yes, one of those seeming chance encounters which later you understand was anything but chance. He struck up a conversation with me while in the market place. At first I felt suspicious because he seemed too friendly. The locals were rather friendly but not that friendly. However, as we talked I could tell he was genuinely listening and caring about what I had to share. Also there was his kind face. He had a distinct kindness about him I knew couldn't be faked."

Percival responded, "When you came to our room from the market accompanied by this older man I was at first quite leery, wondering what is this all about?"

"Yes, I know. At first I thought you were going to say something to put him off or perhaps even your initial look would cause him to turn around and walk away. By the time I got back to our room with him I had sufficient conversation to know this was someone we needed to get to know better."

"Darcy, you were right in your assessment and it wasn't long before I also knew here was someone of quality who had an attitude outside of simply caring for his own concerns. He obviously loved people and gained great pleasure in helping others. I sometimes think he gained as much as we did for he was looking for someone to pour his wisdom into. Once he started, it was as though he had been ready to burst and he needed to start sharing soon."

"How do you think he ended his days?"

"He had a thriving business creating leather saddles and bridles with several fine employees. I am sure it provided sufficient income without him needing to be personally involved all the time. And he exuded such a joy of life. Unless something untoward happened he most likely ended his days prosperous and happy. At least I hope he did. He surely deserved to."

"True enough, Percival. Being wise and joyful doesn't guarantee a great end to ones' days but it does improve the odds."

"His kindness alone should have increased his odds to end well. He had such a generosity about him to help others. He saw how we were two lost young men trying to discover what life was all about."

"If we hadn't met him I am thinking we would have continued on the path we were on, leading most likely to an early grave."

"Darcy, you are right about that. We had no sense of what to think about beyond today and maybe tomorrow. Each day was all about survival and for what? To live another day pretty much the same as the other. Monsieur Toutant taught us to start planning and thinking about how our todays determine our tomorrows."

As they continued to ride along a little ways from the rest of the party, a sudden opening in the ground happened and they were both swallowed up as the ground closed up after them.

# Chapter 39

The sudden disappearance of Percival and Darcy created a great uproar in the Evansing party. The troops all went into high alert being prepared for any sort of enemy attack. All remained quiet and no movement was detected around them. Edwin stood near the spot where the ground opened even though Greer had cautioned him about standing too close in case it opened again. He pondered what to do. They had no shovels for digging and surely by now all they would uncover were the corpses. Sadly he came to the conclusion that they were gone and for the safety of everyone else they would need to move on.

In the meantime our two wizened heroes had found themselves in a new realm. Unhurt they arrived in a subterranean world. It comprised of a large tunnel with torches blazing on the walls lighting the way forward. The air was surprisingly fresh. This enlivened their hope for this meant an opening to the surface had to be nearby.

"Darcy, are you alright?"

"Yes, I am. Even though it seemed like we fell a great distance we landed gently. What kind of magic is this?"

"I have no idea. Whether we like it or not we have signed up for a new adventure."

"You know, Percival, I feel surprisingly calm. It's like my brain has switched off and I am going with my heart. It seems to tell me everything is alright."

"Yes, I am experiencing the same response. What else can we do? We need to remain calm. Here we must again trust that Fortune is guiding us and protecting us."

As they proceeded they began to catch a whiff of something cooking that smelled like bacon.

They stopped to consider what to do.

"Shall we just carry on and assume the people ahead are friendly or shall we sneak up on them?"

"That, Darcy, is a question with no clear answer. Given where we are and how we got here I would say they already know we are here."

So they continued and when they turned ahead, there in front of them was a party of a hundred or so people.

A very distinguished looking older gentlemen walked up to them.

"Welcome to both of you. We are glad you can join us for a meal."

Percival replied, "That is very kind of you. Were you expecting us?"

"First let me tell you, my name is Sean. You must be Percival and you must be Darcy, correct?"

"Yes, that is true. Tell me, why did you arrange for us to come here?"

"We have need to recover our lost lands. We have lived down here for the past twenty years, but now it is time to seek justice and the return of our lands."

Percival surveyed where they were. It was a rather large room lit by torches all around.

"Sean, how could you survive underground for twenty years?"

"Angelic support."

"Really? Why would they do that?"

"Our Divine Overseer took pity on the injustice of our situation. He intervened as we were on the verge of starving to death when all means of survival were taken by one of the nobles. A rogue of a man who decided he wanted our lands."

"Who was the noble?"

"Terrence of Bantry."

"I know of him and what I have heard is not good. Darcy, do you know this Terrence of Bantry?"

"No, I am not familiar with the man."

"Sean, how can we help?"

"We would like you to beseech King Erith on our behalf?"

"Why couldn't you have done this yourself? King Erith is a just man and you could have presented your case to him at the time your lands were seized or certainly some time before now. Even now you could present your case to him."

"We tried at the time the lands were seized and we tried several times since, the latest being four years ago. He refuses to hear our case."

"I could understand that response twenty years ago, but King Erith has become ever more amenable to these causes in recent years."

"Maybe so, but he hasn't considered our case worthy of his review."

"Is there something you haven't told us yet? Something that triggered the seizing of your lands?"

"The only thing possible is that in a local competition of hurling our team defeated his team. I remember him being extremely upset. Later I heard he had wagered a large amount of money on his team. Perhaps he wanted to recoup his losses. When he seized our lands he said he had the right to because his family had owned it generations earlier and they had lent it to our ancestors. In other words he was simply taking back what was rightfully his. There is no such record of this ever being the case."

Percival asked, "It's interesting that I have no knowledge about Erith's relationship with Terrence. The King has never mentioned him and I have never seen him at Evansing Castle. What do you know of his relationship with the King?"

"We have checked around and discovered when Erith came to the throne over twenty years ago there were some who opposed him. However, Terrence supported him even to risking his life in a skirmish against the King's opponents. Undoubtedly this has created a strong sense of loyalty by Erith toward Terrence."

"Yes, it may well have. However loyalty should not supersede justice. Why don't you let us go and I will share your case with Erith and hopefully he will realize he needs to intervene."

"Yes, Percival, and we will all live happily ever after. I doubt if it will be as simple and easy as that. Reason being there is other talk about why the King won't confront Terrence."

At this point Sean lowers his voice, "I hesitate to share what may only be hearsay and which besmirches our King's reputation. According to servants in Terrence's household the King stayed at Terrence's castle while Terrence had gone for an extended trip on business in the west of Ireland. During this time Terrence's wife and the King spent a lot of time together. Often demonstrated unseemly affection for one another and spent time together behind closed doors in the Lady's bedchamber."

"Those are very serious allegations even to share as possible hearsay. You could be arrested for treason."

"Yes, I know. It is not without a certain trepidation I share this with you. However it would also help to explain why the King is so unwilling to help us."

"Given the seriousness of your situation, Darcy and I will not reveal this matter to anyone. I may need to indirectly raise it with the King to spark movement on your behalf. Are Darcy and I free to leave?"

"Yes, you are free to leave. I will show you the way."

Sean and several of his men walked with Percival and Darcy along a lighted passageway that turned into an upward climbing ramp until they came to a massive door which Sean's men then opened. It was great relief for Percival and Darcy to see the outdoors again.

"How will we get in touch with you?"

Sean answered, "I will come to Evansing Town in a fortnight to see how you are progressing."

"Very well. Until then I will do my best to help your cause."

The two men rode through the opening and into the dull grey light for it was another cloudy overcast Irish day.

They rode on in silence mulling over what they had experienced and pondered how they would proceed with

Erith. As they came to a thick clump of woods an air of unease came upon them both. The temperature suddenly cooled and even made them shiver. They stopped their horses and considered their options.

# Chapter 40

"What do you think is happening, Darcy?"
"I don't think this is a natural cooling. I am not aware of Druids in this area, but I sense someone with at least some Druidic abilities is nearby."

"Yes, I agree. Any thoughts as how to handle this?"

"Let us take a wide berth around this wood."

"Sounds right. Let's go."

Both men put their horses into a gallop away from the wood. As they did so a Druid priest in his priestly garb came flying towards them with a sword swinging. Both men leaped off their horses and narrowly missed being hit. They drew swords and stood ready to defend themselves. At this point a second Druid also came flying at them.

Then Darcy did something totally unexpected. "I command you both to come down." With that both Druids fell a crumpled heap on the ground not more than twenty feet in front of the two men. Neither one of them moved.

They had been at least thirty to forty feet in the air moving at great velocity when they plummeted. Both men appeared to be dead from the impact. Darcy gingerly poked them both for signs of life. Neither one stirred.

"Darcy, that was great presence of mind to command them out of the sky. I have never heard of anyone doing that since Patrick did it."

"That is what popped into my mind. The story of Patrick knocking the chief Druid out of the sky to his death resulting in him having favor with the local king."

"Interesting they would attack us in this manner for I have never experienced it before nor have I heard of them doing it."

"I have heard rumors of it but never experienced it personally either."

The men looked around to see if anything else could be threatening. Nothing stirred other than a deer bolting out of a nearby bush. This raised alarm as to why the deer came from hiding. Soon they saw the reason. A wolf was chasing the deer, but it soon stopped when the deer steadily gained ground as it bounded away. A sigh of relief came from both men.

"Notice how the temperature has increased?"

Darcy replied, "Yes, you are right. It has increased."

The two men continued on their journey without further incident.

Their arrival at Evansing Castle released a great wave of joy. Everyone thought they had died. Edwin and Erith were especially pleased at seeing their valued friend returning to them.

"Percival, I had such torment wondering what else I could have done. At the time it seemed obvious both of you were lost and I had grave concerns about getting the rest of the party back to Evansing Town."

"Don't fret, Edwin, you did what any prudent leader would have done."

Then Erith came and hugged tightly his closest friend. Uncharacteristically he even hung on for a moment and when he released his grip he had tears in his eyes.

"I am not ashamed to say I was very emotional at the prospect of not seeing you again and not being able to share life with you. You are my dearest friend and it would be bleak indeed to go forward without you."

Percival joked, "I should get swallowed more often just to receive all this affirmation of how much people love me."

Both Erith and Edwin articulated that in future they would make a point of expressing their love more often.

Erith and Edwin also wanted to know what happened when they got swallowed and how did they escape from underground. Both Darcy and Percival said they would share that later as it wasn't best for them to share that just yet.

This surprised the King and Prince but they respected their wishes and did not press for details.

The rest of the day was spent in celebrating the safe arrival of Percival and Darcy. It was also a belated celebration of the return of Greer, Orla and Edwin.

The next day Percival and Darcy met with Erith and Edwin to consider their next move with the Quest.

Edwin began, "With Taryn out of the way we should now be able to concentrate our resources on Nerland. Our original thoughts on this were to assassinate Prince Gondar. I think that is still the best course of action."

Erith responded, "Yes, surprisingly he has not killed his father. Keltic's prospective return to power would be a huge catalyst to simply return Nerland back to being run properly and rejoin the Quest. However there is something interfering with our successfully restoring Nerland to us as an ally."

Percival sensing an opportunity asked, "Oh and what might that be?"

"I don't know. It's a feeling I have had growing over the last few days that something we are not aware of is blocking us not only with Nerland but with the Quest."

"Before we make any strategic decisions about military action we need to identify what the reason is for this block. Erith, may I speak to you in private?"

Erith looked at Percival quizzically but after a moment's reflection said "Yes" and then dismissed the meeting.

"I could tell, Percival, you had something rather deep and maybe even disturbing to discuss with me. It reminded me of the time you and Edwin brought to my attention what happened in that village in the south."

"What I have to share is not that grave, but it could certainly stop the Quest. As you know the  spiritual realm uses legal rights to say no to our desires and plans. Darcy and I were swallowed up by the ground because a man named Sean and several families with him had their land taken by Terrence of Bantry with no compensation. In other words he stole their lands. They have approached you on more than one occasion and you have not intervened on their behalf."

Erith's face at first displayed shock at being confronted with such news. Then after several moments of silence he spoke.

"Terrence has been a loyal supporter of my claim to the Evansing throne right from the beginning. Without him and several others like him I may not have become King. I owe him a tremendous debt of gratitude for his loyalty."

"Yes, Erith, I am sure you do. However that does not give him the right to be unjust with those he is called to protect. He is their ruling local Lord and he has broken trust with them. You are their King and you have broken trust with them."

"Percival, remember who you are and who I am. We are friends, but I am still King."

Unflinching, Percival replied, "Yes, Sire, you are King and I am your servant."

Erith troubled at how he had addressed Percival. "You are more than my servant, you are my best friend."

Silence.

"What do you suggest, Percival?"

"I suggest you call Terrence to Evansing Castle and ask for a full explanation."

"That could be messy."

"Yes, I can appreciate it will be messy confronting someone so loyal to Your Majesty."

Silence.

"Percival, I have something to confess to you. This is not easy for me to share. Around twenty years ago Terrence's wife and I shared a great affection for one another. It seemed at the time she possessed some of the qualities my wife was lacking and she undoubtedly yearned for greater tenderness than what Terrence was capable of giving her. I spent an extended time with her at their castle when Terrence was gone away on a business trip to the west of Ireland. During that time we crossed the line from emotional adultery to physical adultery. When Terrence discovered this he was furious, but of course I was the King so he said nothing to me. I found this out by a note from his wife. I have not seen either one since. It was a short time later I heard of Terrence seizing lands without compensation. I believe he did it out of revenge and knowing he had leverage because of my adultery with his wife. My shame combined with a sense of owing him for his loyalty has caused me to be unmoved by the pleas of the dispossessed landowners."

Silence.

"Erith, that is a long time ago and you are not the same man. Just like you owned up to the massacre of those villagers in the south, you can own up to this as well."

"Yes, you are right I can, but I am afraid of how Greer will respond to knowing I was unfaithful to her mother."

"It may well be difficult for her, but justice must be restored in this situation. The dispossessed people have lived underground in a most marvelous way for all these years. They have had angelic support to survive and even in some ways thrive. Nevertheless they still want their land back. Until you do it, this wound will block the Quest."

"I will send for him immediately."

Erith called for his scribe and instructed him to write up a message to Terrence to instruct him to come immediately for an audience with the King.

After the scribe had left Percival asked Erith how he felt.

"I feel elated and horrified. I am truly glad to expose this shame to the light and right the wrong that has come of it. Also I am truly sad at the pain this exposure will cause my family and those loyal subjects who look to me as a role model of virtuous behavior."

"Erith, remember twenty years ago you weren't quite so virtuous. People have been pleasantly surprised at how you have turned out. There will be some initial distress at this disclosure but it will slingshot you ahead into the Quest once again. You will sense a new flow like we had when we first started."

"Why didn't this stop us at the very beginning?"

"That is a mystery. Most likely the timing didn't yet require you to make amends. You weren't consciously aware of the need to acknowledge it as wrong and make restitution because of it. Now you do. Now you are responsible to do something with your new awareness."

A messenger came to the door with an urgent message for the King.

As Erith looked at the scroll he realized it had the seal of the King of Nerland. He hesitated to open it not knowing whether to be excited or anxious.

# Chapter 41

With anticipation and in trepidation Erith broke the seal and unrolled the scroll. As he began to read the scroll he was informed in blunt terms that Keltic has died and Gondar is now the new King of Nerland. Nothing more was given.

Erith's heart felt very heavy at the death of his close ally. He and Keltic were different in temperament, but he was a faithful ally and even in some ways a good friend.

"Keltic is dead and Gondar is the new king."

"That is indeed unfortunate. I am sorry for your loss and ours. Keltic could be cruel, but he still had a nobility about him."

"Yes, it is a big blow. Somehow we are going to turn this to our advantage. There are several Nerland nobles who have the wherewithal to succeed Gondar as king and who are potentially still friendly towards the Quest. Getting rid of Gondar is still important, but first we need to have someone to install in his place. We need to call a Council meeting so that all our decision makers are aware of what has happened. Collectively we will come up with a strategy as to who we should first approach and how to do so."

Several hours later the Council meeting commenced with Erith sharing the news about Keltic. Uncharacteristically he decided to throw it open to those present to hear their thoughts concerning the news.

One of his senior commanders, named Lothar, spoke up, "This is an opportunity to invade Nerland and annex it as part of Evansing. By doing so we will never have to worry about Nerland turning their back on us again."

The others in the room were taken aback by such a bold statement. Annexation had never before been considered. It may have some advantages but at what cost in lives and the future credibility of Evansing's intentions for the Quest.

Initially there was dismay at such a proposal and then Erith spoke up, "Gentlemen, at this point let us explore all the options available to us. Feel free to share without judgments from the rest of us. I will delve deeper into the merits and potential downside of these proposals and select the ones most likely to succeed. I will then appoint people to investigate each selected alternative."

That settled those present and resulted in a flow of all kinds of suggestions as people felt comfortable in allowing their ideas to be shared without fear of criticism.

When the meeting was over the scribe handed over the ideas to Erith who started to sift through them. The four that struck him as having the most merit were the following:

1.  Assassinate Gondar followed by an invasion and let the Nerland people pick their King subject to Evansing approval.

2. Find a replacement first like they had done in Randar and Dagarath. Then assassinate Gondar and invade.
3. Invade and annex Nerland and execute Gondar.
4. Work to create a rebellion resulting in the Nerlanders overthrowing Gondar without a costly invasion.

Erith then allocated each of the four ideas to Edwin, Percival, Darcy and Lothar to investigate further as to which alternative would make the most sense. He instructed them to each get back to him in seven days with at least some initial indication.

Edwin and Percival walked out together. "You know, Percival, I have a good feeling about our regaining Nerland as our ally. I believe there are possibilities of stirring up those discontented with Gondar's rule and their current state of broken relationship with Evansing. In many ways we have always had close relationship with them. This breakup has been like two close brothers deciding not to talk to one another and not even see each other after a lifetime of closeness."

"I agree with you, Edwin, there must be a strong current of discontent that could be tapped into. It is interesting that this alternative was not even considered until Darcy raised it. This shows you how having someone outside of the normal sphere can have a different perspective. Erith was wise in allocating to each person further investigation into a particular option another person had suggested."

"Yes, he knew if he gave to a person an option that person proposed the investigation could be tainted with only looking for whatever supported that choice. And quite likely only minimal consideration given to uncovering the reasons not to pursue it."

"I am glad I was given the fomenting a rebellion option as it is so different from how I would think. I am eager to create new pathways in my thinking. Sometimes I get frustrated with the same old solutions coming up. This will force me to look at this situation in a fresh manner."

Lowering his voice Edwin then switched to a different topic but with a common theme. "Percival, I have also noticed that my relationship with Greer is experiencing a certain sameness. I seem to have run out of ideas to keep the joy alive of being married to one another. Any thoughts on what to do?"

"Edwin, relationships have a tendency to hit plateaus. These are potentially times when they consolidate for future growth or when they dip out of frustration with one another. You are committed to Greer and she is to you. That is a great protection for both of you."

"Oh, so you say this is normal?"

"Yes, it is. We all would like to have marriages that are continually stimulating and exciting. The truth is, life gets in the way and its demands can drain much of the emotional, mental and physical energy necessary to give the same level of devotion as in the early stages of a marriage. Having said that, it doesn't mean people can't have happy fulfilling marriages. That should be one's desire and all the necessary steps to achieve that objective should be taken. It does require making the effort to do so."

"One type of effort I seem to struggle and stumble with too often is when Greer is really excited about something and wants to share her heart about it. The problem is she keeps adding more and more details to the point where I start getting restless with getting back to what I was working on. Then I will more or less cut her off or change the topic. This hurts her feelings and I feel like you know what, after she leaves the room."

"Ah yes that is a familiar scenario. We as men want to be good husbands, but in the present moments we succumb to the inner pressure that comes from life's demands. We then later realize our wife's well-being is a pressure we need to give top priority. We will never be perfect at meeting our spouse's needs. However we can keep reminding ourselves she is not an interruption. We need to quit making excuses for ourselves about being too busy, stressed or engaged in something to be able to shift over to what she needs from us in that moment."

"You know, Percival, if I succeed in that one area I believe it will enhance the relationship from both sides. It will allow the warmth to come back that seems to have cooled off a little. She feels hurt and I feel guilty. These are not the kind of feelings to create a great connection."

"Good for you, Edwin, in realizing something so profound and essential. I am sure you and Greer will get back on track."

"Thanks for the help, Percival. Now I need to get on with finding the information that supports fomenting a Nerland revolution without the need for us to assassinate or invade."

"See you later."

# Chapter 42

Edwin decided he would rely on his extensive spy network in Nerland to give him some detailed information about the feelings of the general populace towards a rebellion against Gondar. The spy network was extensive due to the numerous family connections existing between the two kingdoms. Gondar knew of these connections and had made a point of imprisoning or executing a number of suspected Evansing sympathizers. Some simply because they had family relations in Evansing. This actually had the opposite effect of what was intended. Instead of curbing the negative sentiment the injustice increased opposition to Gondar.

There had already been numerous reports logged indicating growing opposition to the new Nerland King. One thing was still missing. A key figure needed to be inspired to lead the revolution and become the new king. The only prospects now were ones who were unknown to Gondar as he had executed everyone of King potential. Edwin started to seriously think he should make a journey to test out one particular prospect who seemed to tower above the rest. The one major problem with this prospect was that no one knew on which side he stood.

He would need to convince the King and Greer that this was a mission worth the risk. He would take Darcy with him. He also needed to come up with a disguise as he was fairly well known in Nerland.

"No, Edwin, I do not want you to go on such a dangerous mission."

"I am going with Darcy and I will be wearing a disguise. No one will realize it is me."

Again Greer reiterated her strong resistance to Edwin taking on this dangerous mission.

"What could I do to get you to believe me it will not be a dangerous mission?"

"Not be a dangerous mission? Edwin, I am not stupid. You going to Nerland at such at time as this is very dangerous. You have a responsibility to me and Evansing to stay alive and put your talents to work in the best and most prudent way possible. Yes, I know there will be future battles. That is different. This trip strikes me as a near suicide mission. You will need to figure out another way to make contact."

Edwin restrained himself and did not respond the way he wanted to. He simply said, "Very well." and left the room.

He sat down to consider other options. The one man he could send on this mission with Darcy was a former soldier called Dalaigh. He now ran a business as a blacksmith. It was prospering and he had two employees. He believed Dalaigh's remarkable ability to relate to people and his knowledge of the Nerland landscape would give him a great advantage in this mission. He was also brave which made Edwin believe he would do it. He went to one of the messengers and told him to fetch Dalaigh as soon as possible.

Several hours later Dalaigh appeared with the messenger. "How can I help you, Sir?"

"I have a mission. I believe you are the best man to accompany Darcy, a former soldier who is still very much a warrior. It entails going to Nerland and finding a certain man whose whereabouts are not totally certain. His name is Finbar and he was last known to live in the southern edges of the Nerland's capital. If he has kept a sufficiently low profile he could still be there. If not he may have had to flee for his life. Your mission is to find him and find out if he is willing to be the next king. If so he will have to know that we want to stir up a rebellion against Gondar so we can properly place him on the throne."

Dalaigh looked rather pleased at what he heard. "Yes, sir, I can fulfill that assignment. When do you want me to leave?"

"Tonight would be ideal or else tomorrow morning early."

"I can leave tonight after I make arrangements concerning my shop."

"Very well, Dalaigh. I am impressed by your decisiveness. No need to clear it with your spouse?"

"My wife does not play a role in a decision like this. I decide and I have said yes I am going. I am keen to confront my fears in such a mission. Any special weapons or instructions other than what you shared?"

At that moment Darcy entered the room.

"Darcy, I want you to meet Dalaigh the travelling companion I told you about."

"Dalaigh, this is Darcy. You asked about special weapons. Darcy has some rather unique talents which I am sure will come in handy to ensure a successful mission."

"He will fill you in on any other instructions and of course Evansing will cover your expenses."

"It is an honor to serve my King and his Prince."

"Thank you, Dalaigh. May God be with you."

"He will be much needed on this mission."

Dalaigh left to talk to two of his employees. He advised them of the need for him to leave for a few days. Then he went home, told his wife about a trip he needed to take without telling her where or why.

He and Darcy left by horseback towards the Nerland frontier. It was getting rather dark, but they kept going without stopping until they came to a secure camping site. They ate cold salted boiled back bacon with cabbage and potato in silence and went to bed.

Early next morning they ate again the same cold food, then got on their horses to resume their journey.

When they came to approximately where the border was, they changed direction and rode several miles south instead of continuing west. They had both noted a definite cooling in the temperature and decided to be on the safe side with avoiding what could be a Druidic ambush up ahead. As they rode south the temperature warmed giving them confidence they were circumventing any unfriendly forces.

They resumed travelling west and had continued to do so through a rather thick wood when they started to hear what sounded like an otherworldly grunting. They stopped, listened and noted the sound seemed to be coming towards them. Neither man was immediately sure what to do. One obvious choice was simply to turn around and ride in the opposite direction. Something told them without words that wouldn't be the best option. So they pulled their swords and waited. The sound got louder and louder and they could hear trees being knocked over.

# Chapter 43

Darcy looked at Dalaigh and said, "Be of good cheer, my friend, for we are about to face a dragon."

At that point a white dove flew in and around their heads and then flew away.

"All's well," exclaimed Darcy. "That was a good omen."

Next came the dragon only a hundred feet or so away. Both men drew their swords to face what looked like a certain battle to their deaths.

Unlike the legends of old, this was not a fire breathing dragon but he stood forty feet tall with a tail almost as long with spikes on the end. He swished his tail back and forth and it looked like he used it as a vital part of his attack. Upon sighting the men, the creature gained momentum as it approached. The two men and their horses stood their ground standing side by side. The tail started flicking around and then came hurtling towards them. Instead of hitting them it hit an invisible shield and bounced back. The dragon growled in anger and pain for it had struck hard.

Not seeming to realize what had happened it flicked its tail hard again at the two riders. This time it not only struck an invisible shield but also an invisible knife as the last six feet of its tail sliced right off. Now the dragon howled in pain and rage. It started to almost leap towards the two men. Once it was in range it lunged at them. Then something strange happened, everything slowed right down and as the dragon's head came towards them the two men parted to allow it to fall between them. As its head struck the ground they sliced furiously at its neck just behind the head. After several blows each the head was nearly severed and the dragon was dead.

Both men backed their horses away from the huge corpse fifty feet or so. As they sat there on their horses in silence they knew they had just witnessed a divine intervention.

Dalaigh finally whispered, "What do we do now?"

"We give thanks." So they spent several minutes expressing gratitude for their miraculous deliverance.

They continued on their journey until they came to an inn located in the southern end of Nerland's capital. There Darcy enquired from the innkeeper if he knew of Finbar.

The innkeeper eyed both of them warily, "Where are you from?"

"We are from Tara," replied Darcy.

Again the innkeeper looked with suspicion, but then he softened as he considered that Darcy's accent did sound like someone from Tara.

"How would you know Finbar and what is your business with him?"

"Those are rather interesting questions. Would you consider it right for me to ask you those kinds of questions?"

"Finbar is my brother and yes, I do believe I have the right to look out for his welfare."

"We have no desire to harm your brother. We have important business to discuss with him."

"How would you even know about Finbar?"

"It is through a friend of a friend."

The innkeeper looked around and then motioned them to follow him into a separate room. They followed and the door was closed behind them. The innkeeper stood and stared into the eyes of Darcy for several moments. As he did so his visage softened and he finally smiled. "I believe I can trust you. Your eyes tell me I can. Wait here and I will send a message to Finbar to come here."

While they waited the two men dined and each enjoyed a cup of mead. After an hour or so the innkeeper entered the room and indicated to them to follow him. He led them up the stairs to the second floor and opened a door to a room. In the room sat a man of slight build physically. However they noted the intense gaze of his eyes bright with light. They thought to themselves this man has something special.

The man stood up and introduced himself as Finbar. He then looked at his brother and thanked him and stated he would like to be left alone with the two men. Darcy introduced himself and Dalaigh without stating why they were there.

Darcy started off by saying, "Thank you, Finbar, for meeting with us. I think you know why we are here."

"Yes, I do. I had a most interesting dream last night. It started with seeing this throne and crown and then it transitioned into seeing both of you exactly as you appear now. I woke with a start and progressively it dawned on me what was going on. A friend of mine only a few weeks ago whispered to me once that if anybody should be or could be King of Nerland it was me. I looked at him at first with surprise at such an audacious statement. Not only audacious but also treasonous. He whispered even though we were alone in his house. So when I received that dream I had been prepared by my mulling over his statement. I must tell you it is a combination of knowing this is a call I must say yes to and yet knowing the deadly risks it poses to myself and all my family members. What is the next step?"

Darcy replied, "We represent the King of Evansing and we want to encourage a rebellion against Gondar."

Finbar considered what he had just heard. He took a deep breath. Then he spoke up.

"There is already a core of individuals who have informally banded together to overthrow Gondar. I attended one of their meetings but decided the risks were too high for me to continue."

Darcy replied, "Now is the time to start engaging this group to stir up a mass rebellion to overthrow Gondar. Evansing will provide whatever resources are necessary as to weaponry and finances." With that he pulled out a pouch filled with gold coins.

"This should give you a good start. As well we can provide weapons by arranging their transport to places near Evansing's border with Nerland. We will give you the intelligence as to Nerland military patrols."

Finbar taking the pouch looked at Darcy and Dalaigh and stated, "This will be used as a sacred trust on behalf of the people of Nerland. I will approach my friend who thought I should be king. He is also part of that group I mentioned to you. How will we communicate with you and you with us?"

"We need to have a secure drop area where we can leave messages for one another. We have trusted servants on both sides of the border who can carry messages."

"A little over five miles south of here I have a small farm. There is a rock sign with my name on it. Another 50 yards past that sign on the right side of the path there is an alder tree about forty feet high with a hollow in its trunk. It is easy to see if you know it is there as it is only about ten feet from the path. My property has the advantage of having no immediate neighbors, thus reducing the likelihood of anyone noticing the messengers."

The men continued to talk for hours into the night concerning strategies to be considered.

"Dawn is rising and it is time for Dalaigh and I to return to Evansing. Expect a messenger to arrive in about two weeks with instructions. As well, leave for our messenger an update on your progress to date and any needs you have."

Darcy and Dalaigh then left for Evansing. As they started out the sun was beginning to rise over the horizon. It was a most brilliant red. While beautiful they knew that could indicate stormy weather on the way back. They each sighed at the prospect.

"Hopefully," Darcy thought to himself, "that will be the only kind of storm on the way back."

As they expected the wind picked up, the temperature started dropping and raindrops started falling. It created a most unpleasant trip. Darcy started thinking, "Perhaps this is a good thing. Nerland patrols will most likely stay sheltered and therefore less likely to run into us. If there were plans to ambush us they may well be hindered by the storm." Suddenly his sense of discomfort and even slight anger at the weather disappeared. He realized this storm would act as a protection on their return journey. Now he could embrace it with gratitude as a positive turn in the weather.

The two men continued on for almost two hours before they came upon an abandoned woodcutter's cabin. Since their clothes now had soaked right through to their skin they decided the sensible thing would be to take shelter and see what they could do to dry out. To their surprise there was enough firewood inside with which they could light a fire to warm up and dry their clothes. Even their extra clothes in their packs had gotten quite damp from the relentless rain pouring down.

After an hour inside they were starting to feel human again. The cold had gone to their bones and now they were feeling warm and restored. Their clothes were almost comfortably dry.

Dalaigh looked outside and noticed some movement. He called to Darcy. They both looked but could not see anything. The woods were thick and the rain obscured their vision.

"Could it have been your imagination?"

"I doubt it. Something appeared and quickly disappeared. You know it looked like a woman."

"A woman? Now what would a woman be doing out here by herself? Perhaps she is not by herself. Maybe she is bait to draw us out of the cabin."

"Let's stay in here and let them make the first move. In the meantime let's block the door and secure the window the best we can."

After ten minutes a woman came from behind a tree and started toward the door. The two men looked at her almost in disbelief. Darcy went to the door while Dalaigh remained at the window.

Darcy opened the door as the woman was about knock on it. She had a look of both relief and terror. Relief at the prospect of shelter and terror at not knowing what these men would do with her. Darcy welcomed her in and assured her they would not harm her. He quickly ushered her over by the fire and also went to give her part of their remaining rations.

She shivered almost violently from the cold and rain. After ten minutes or so she began to stop shivering and started to feel the beginning of warmth.

The woman appeared to be in her mid-forties, attractive face and form and beautiful long red hair. Darcy noticed these qualities and it pleased him.

He gently asked, "My dear lady, could you please tell us why you are out here in a remote place in such a storm?"

The lady did not answer as she fought back her tears. After keeping them in abeyance, she finally spoke. "I am a widow. My husband died two months ago of the pox along with our two boys, leaving me all alone and penniless. The landlord forced me out of his house when I could no longer pay the rent."

"What are you planning to do?"

"I don't know. I have no family nearby and everyone is so poor they have no room or way of assisting me."

Silence.

"After the storm subsides you are welcome to return with us to Evansing."

"To Evansing?"

Silence.

"What would you do with me in Evansing?"

"Ensure you have a roof over your head and food to eat. I am sure we will find you something to do to support yourself."

After a further brief silence, the woman replied, "That sounds like the best of the options available to me. My name is Aoife."

The introduction of her name prodded the two men to introduce themselves.

"You certainly have the right name. You have the toughness to be a warrior."

"My mother wanted me to be tough because she knew life was hard. It has been a hard life. Yet I have been able to stay in a place of hope most of the time. It must be Grace."

"Yes, Grace does keep us going through the tough times," responded Darcy.

He continued, "It does look like the rain is slowing down. Hopefully that means it will stop soon."

An hour later it had stopped completely. The party of three left with Aoife riding with Darcy.

Any onlooker would have noticed that Darcy had a broad smile on his face.

As they rode, Darcy reflected how if the storm hadn't happened he would have never met Aoife. Then he noted how often in life he had good things come to him through difficulties. They frequently created opportunities for growth and new relationships.

# Chapter 44

The bond between Aoife and Darcy grew as the miles passed by. They shared with each other their life stories and even secret intimacies of their lives they hadn't shared with anyone else. It made no difference they had just met. The influence of Darcy being her deliverer and Aoife being the delivered created its own attraction difficult to resist.

What made it so easy to share was trust. They both knew they could trust one another. It created an environment of feeling safe and secure with each other. This feeling was special and previously not something either one of them was all that familiar with. Both of them had lived lives where feeling safe and secure only happened in fleeting moments. Even while living in the monastery Darcy felt a certain unease about his role and future there. He couldn't pinpoint it at the time, but now he realized he simply did not belong there. With this woman he felt he could actually start to live a truly fulfilling life. Not that she had everything he needed, but she would facilitate a much greater appreciation of other aspects of his life. She would add that much needed spice to make everything else taste better.

The towers of Evansing Castle were now visible. All three of the travelers looked forward to arriving inside its walls. There had been a continual sense of suspense about whether they would meet an ambush somewhere along the road. Both Dalaigh and Darcy could sense that danger often was nearby but somehow they avoided it. They both figured something beyond the visible intervened on their trip. Perhaps Providence looked kindly on them for rescuing Aoife and rewarded them with a safe return.

While the two men were returning to their familiar surroundings, Aoife now would be starting a whole new life. Equally exciting and daunting. Exciting as to the possibilities with Darcy and a brand-new beginning. Daunting in not knowing how everything would turn out in her new home.

As she pondered her new situation, a beautiful young lady accompanied by a handsome young man approached on horseback. They appeared to have been out riding just south of Evansing Town and were returning from their outing. At a discrete distance behind them rode fifteen or twenty soldiers. She thought to herself, "These must be very important people."

"Good day, Your Highnesses"

The young man replied, "Good day to you, Darcy and Dalaigh. I see you have gained in number. May we have the pleasure of an introduction?"

"Yes, of course. Prince Edwin and Princess Greer let me introduce you to Aoife whom we met on our return trip. She is a recent widow and in need of assistance so we decided to bring her with us and give her shelter and a life in Evansing."

Greer piped up, "That is so kind of you, Darcy. Do you know where she can stay?"

"No, Your Highness."

"There is a vacant cottage on the castle grounds where she can stay as long as necessary.

Aoife, I am dreadfully sorry to hear of your loss. You must join Darcy at the King's Table tonight for supper."

"Thank you, Your Highness. This is most kind and generous of you."

"You are very welcome, Aoife. It is our pleasure to help."

Greer continued to ride alongside with Aoife right into the Castle grounds. As they chatted Aoife thought to herself how unlikely to have a Princess relate to her like she had value. The thought almost overwhelmed her, but she kept her composure.

Later, after Edwin and Greer left them alone, she confided to Darcy how she felt.

"Princess Greer is not your average princess. She has a grace and kindness that surpasses them all. Her inviting you to stay in the cottage on the castle grounds and come eat at the King's Table is a great honor. I have been given a room in the castle so we shall be quite close to each other. I am pleased at this turn of events. I feel so blessed to have met you. My desire is that we shall become very close. I know this is very sudden to say, but I want you to have no doubt about my heart's desire. I want to court you with the objective of marriage. Hopefully sooner rather than later."

Aoife looked at him speechless and then she started to smile. "I would like that very much. If I had been closer to my husband I probably would not have been quite so keen to say yes to you so quickly. However, my husband was a cold man and for years I have wished for something better in a marriage. I can see you are a man of warmth and passion. These are important qualities to me in a man. What about your vows as a monk? Will you not be prohibited from marrying? Will a priest in Evansing be willing to perform the ceremony?"

"Those are valid questions. I left the monastery on good terms with the abbey and he recognized I did not belong there. I am sure he will give me a full release from my vows. In any event I can talk to the local church people with the influence of the Royal Family to ensure a special dispensation. I have no concern about that. But to ensure you and I are both at ease about it I will approach my good friend Percival to see what protocol he recommends."

"Let me now take you to the cottage. I will arrange to get you water to fill your tub so you can be ready for supper."

"I feel dreadful going to the King's Table in rags like these. What will the King think seeing me like this?"

"I will see what I can round up for you."

While they inspected the cottage, which was far better and bigger than anything Aoife had ever lived in, several servants arrived at the door. The lead servant said it was on orders of Princess Greer. They came in with water already heated up and poured it into the bathtub. Also they brought in almost a dozen changes of clothing, all very fashionable and made of expensive materials. As well they brought in fresh towels, bedding and pillows.

Darcy and Aoife both looked quite stunned at what they had just witnessed.

"This is even beyond what I would have expected from Princess Greer. She must really like you."

"I think it's because she and her husband quite like you. You helping them regain their baby is not a small matter."

"Yes, that is probably part of it, but she must also like you. I will leave you alone now to bathe. I will be back in less than an hour to bring you to supper."

Aoife undressed and slipped into the welcoming waters of the bath. She couldn't recall ever having a bath like this. The only infrequent bathing happened in a stream nearby to their cottage and it was always cold. This was warm and felt like the very epitome of luxury. As the water started to cool off she realized she needed to start getting dressed and ready for Darcy.

"Darcy," she thought to herself, "is a dream come true." She caught herself sighing at the thought of him. "I am in love with the man and I have barely met him. Yet I already know his heart better than my husband."

As she pondered this Darcy came to the door. Together they walked toward the castle door where they would walk up the winding staircase to the dining hall.

With each step Aoife felt a little more anxious about how she would be received by the King and his family and friends. She grabbed Darcy's hand for support. He gave her hand a squeeze.

On the second floor they walked another twenty paces or so and they entered the dining hall. They were one of the last to arrive and the meal was about to be served in another few minutes. They walked past the tables to the head of the room where the King's Table was situated. To their surprise Princess Greer stood up to introduce Aoife to her father and the others sitting at the table. The Princess accorded Aoife great honor by standing to introduce her. She motioned to Aoife and Darcy to sit in the seats next to her.

The Princess and Aoife sat chatting quite amiably with one another. It seemed a little surprising given the age gap. Percival observed this as possibly Greer desiring someone who approximated about the same age as her mother. She appreciated the maturity and life wisdom even if Aoife was a commoner and used to a much simpler lifestyle. Definitely Aoife demonstrated qualities out of the ordinary for a peasant woman. There seemed to be an inherent nobility and grace about her. These qualities undoubtedly made her quite attractive to Greer.

Percival and Darcy sat together and chatted about the trip. Tomorrow Darcy and Dalaigh would meet with the King, Edwin and Percival to more fully debrief and plan the next moves.

After giving an initial overview, Darcy asked if he could change the subject to something quite pressing for him and Aoife. Percival of course agreed.

"Percival, as you know I have decided to leave the monastery for good. Now since I have met Aoife I want to also get married. Can I count on your assistance in working out the revocation of those vows and facilitate us getting married by the Church?"

Percival remained silent for a moment as he considered his response. "Yes, I can help you. There is the King's personal priest who is quite accommodating with matters requiring shall we say adjustment. He may require some sort of penance to compensate for the revocation. Hopefully it shouldn't be too onerous. I will talk to him after supper."

"Thanks, my dear friend. I knew I could count on you to help. Aoife and I have had such an amazing connection just in the time we rode together. It truly is Divine Providence to have a storm bring us together. She is delivered from a most desperate place and I am brought to a place of being married and finding true love for the first time in my life. I know it is very quick, but in my heart I know it is right."

"Darcy, from what I have seen and heard of Aoife, I have no doubt she and you will be very happy together."

The meal progressed with the King enquiring of Aoife as to her health and welcoming her to Evansing.

As the meal drew to a close Darcy and Aoife remained seated talking with one another even as the other diners had left. After a while they noticed they were the only ones remaining. Time had flown as it does for new lovers.

# Chapter 45

Darcy walked Aoife back to the cottage. He stood at the open doorway fumbling for final words. As he did so Aoife grabbed him and kissed him. Initially it so startled him he didn't respond, but then he hugged her back and engaged in kissing her back. After a moment they realized they needed to stop so it wouldn't progress to something not right at this time.

"Aoife, that was wonderful. I haven't kissed a woman since I was a young man."

"Darcy, you are an amazing kisser. You must be holding out on me about your background as a monk."

"No, I am not," he said with a laugh. "It must be your influence."

They then both said good night and she closed the door and he returned to his room in the castle.

The next morning after breakfast the King and the others met to discuss the trip to Nerland and what plans to make.

Darcy and Dalaigh were both present to report and they answered questions asked of them.

"Finbar is in our opinion someone we can trust. He already has a base of support and as we move now to support him and his followers we will have a great probability of success. I believe we will see the current Nerland regime overthrown within three months."

Dalaigh voiced agreement with Darcy.

The rest of the meeting then was spent determining a timetable of providing provisions to Finbar. They acknowledged they would be flexible as they received requests from Finbar and as they became aware of new intelligence.

After the meeting Darcy walked out with Percival eager to discuss the outcome of his meeting with the priest. He had been puzzled as to why Percival seemed to avoid talking to him prior to breakfast.

Percival had a furrowed brow.

"Darcy, there is a complication in your request to get married. The priest has told me unequivocally that he cannot marry you and Aoife. Not only that, he will not authorize any priest in Evansing to perform the wedding. He will not offer any alternative solution or penance in place of you revoking your vow. He says your vow as a monk is irrevocable."

A wave of panic and despair came over Darcy as he heard these words.

Both men remained silent as the full import of the words sunk in.

"But, but there must be another way. I will get the abbot at the monastery to approve it."

"I asked the priest if he would accept such an approval from your former abbot and he said no."

"Then we must consider other options. There must be a way. There must a solution that will work. We must talk to the King and see what pressure he can bring to bear."

"I have talked to Erith and he will not interfere."

"Then we must talk to Edwin and Greer."

"Yes, we can talk to them. What they can do I don't know. You certainly have favor with them. I am sure they will do whatever they can."

They walked back to the meeting room where Edwin was still discussing strategies and logistics with some of the other officers. When he noticed Percival and Darcy waiting politely by the doorway he stopped his discussion and told his officers he would resume it later.

"Hello, you look like you are wanting to talk to me."

"We do indeed. Darcy wants to marry Aoife but the King's priest refuses to do the ceremony. This is based on his view of Darcy's monk vow being irrevocable. He will not recognize any possible option nor will he authorize another priest in Evansing to perform the wedding."

Edwin considered what he heard without comment.

"Let us go see what my genius advisor tells us."

"I thought Percival was your genius advisor."

"Yes, most certainly he is. But I also have another genius advisor. Her name is Greer. For such a matter of the heart like this I am sure something will percolate to the surface."

They walked over to Greer's sitting room and shared the problem.

Greer wrinkled her nose slightly and gave an impatient sigh.

"That priest is just plain out of line. Darcy, we will find a way to get around this. My father didn't respond because he didn't appreciate the full nature of this request and the unjust stand by his priest. I will go to him myself this very moment and ensure he fully understands."

"My dear, before you leave let us first consider how and when you are going to approach him. If you bluster in on your father he may well get angry and resist, no matter how much he loves you and likes to please you."

Greer was surprised at Edwin's words and at first she wanted to resist and go anyway, but then she started to consider the wisdom of what he had shared.

"Alright, honey, what do you suggest?"

"Besides your belief that Erith doesn't know the full facts, what other reasons could there be for why he didn't want to intervene? What do we know about his intervening in Church matters? Offhand I can't recall any time where he has tried to get a priest to change his mind. Certainly not while I have been here. Do you recall a time, Greer? Then turning to Percival, "Do you recall a time, Percival?'

Neither one could recall the King intervening on behalf of someone or even on behalf of himself.

Greer spoke up about how two of her family members on two separate matters asked the King to change his priest's ruling on a matter and both times he refused.

Percival recalled how once before he was asked to approach Erith with the objective of getting him to intervene with a priest's unfavorable interpretation. He refused that too.

Edwin asked, "Did Erith ever give a reason for his refusals?"

Both acknowledged that the King never gave a reason. Because he is the King he was never pressed to give a reason for his response.

"What do we know about Erith's relationship with his priest?"

Silence.

No one could think of anything out of the ordinary or even close about the relationship.

"I have always noted my father's relationship with his priest as being very businesslike, no special connection or warmth. I have sometimes thought that was rather odd given they have had this relationship for over twenty years. One time I did see the priest express anger with my father. This shocked me, but what shocked me even more was how my father accepted it without any response."

Percival spoke up, "That is odd. I have never seen anyone express anger with the King outside of his family." He said this while giving a sideway glance at Greer. She looked back at him with an amused look.

"Yes," responded Edwin, "I am sure certain family members have expressed anger with the King." He tried not to look toward Greer.

"All right, gentlemen, this is not about my relationship with my father. Let us stay focused on the task before us and get Darcy and Aoife married. I am going to do some research on the King's relationship with the priest. I can tactfully make some enquiries from my uncles and aunts. I will get back to you within the week."

Edwin and Percival looked at Greer a little startled. They knew she could initiate actions of this type. What caught them was the degree of passion and determination when she stated it.

"Now, my dear, that sounds like wisdom. Good for you."

She smiled back at Edwin without comment.

"I must take my leave of you now." With that she left.

"Well, gentlemen, I think we can safely leave this quest in the capable hands of my wife. She will do whatever is necessary and available to her."

Darcy appeared to be at least slightly relieved and hopeful knowing Greer would be working on their behalf. He couldn't quite shake that tormenting feeling of having the matter unresolved. Percival and Edwin both tried to encourage him to be hopeful and anticipate a good outcome.

"I know gentlemen you are trying to help and I do appreciate it. However I have this deep fear that something representing a deep unfulfilled longing is being blocked by a spiteful clergyman who is unconcerned about our happiness. It makes me very angry."

With that he left.

# Chapter 46

The next morning there was an uproar as news spread that the King's priest had been murdered.

Edwin and Percival were notified and both ran down to the priest's house to observe first-hand what had happened. The body had been discovered by the housekeeper early that morning when she reported for work. When they arrived the Sheriff was still examining the body and his deputy was searching the home for clues.

"Sheriff, what does your examination tell you?"

"His skull was crushed. Most likely with this walking stick the priest would always take with him. If you look closely you can see what appears to be a mark from being struck against his skull. It was left lying beside the body."

"Any ideas as to who did this?"

"Not yet, but my initial thoughts are it is somebody who struck with great force. I would say he must be a rather strong individual. The body has already gotten quite stiff so I would say it was late last night perhaps around midnight."

Percival and Edwin walked outside, off away from the crowd that had gathered.

"You don't think possibly that..." Edwin stopped in mid-sentence.

"I don't want to say it either, but there is a strong link between an angry man and death of the man who he perceived to be standing in the way of his happiness."

"I am going to give our friend the benefit of the doubt, however small that doubt may be. I just can't believe he would do such a thing even if he was angry."

"Do you know why he was in the monastery?"

"He killed a man while angry in France in a quarrel over a woman. To ease his conscience he became a monk and dedicated his remaining life to God."

"He has revoked that dedication, but has God revoked that dedication?"

"That, Edwin, is a question perhaps only Darcy can truly answer. In his heart I am sure he believes he has God's blessing to get married and leave behind his dedication."

"The King will surely suspect Darcy. What do you think he will do?"

"Hard to say. Given the coolness of the relationship between King and Priest it may be a relief for Erith to see him gone."

They then left to tell Greer the news.

Greer was shocked to hear the news and like them she began to consider the possibility it was Darcy. Then she stopped herself and decided that she too would refuse to believe it was him.

"I will go to the King and see what he is considering. At the very least he will want to question Darcy about where he was last night."

Percival spoke, "I will go see Darcy and inform him of what happened."

"Shall I come as well?"

"No, Edwin, I think it would be best for me see him alone. If that is alright with you, Your Highness."

"Yes, of course."

Percival arrived at Darcy's door just as Darcy was on his way out to pick up Aoife for breakfast.

"Percival, what a pleasant surprise! What brings you to my door?"

"The King's priest has been murdered."

Darcy looked shocked and speechless for a moment. Then he realized how his anger last night would undoubtedly create a concern in Percival.

"No, I did not murder him. As much as I love Aoife I would not murder to get her."

"The King will likely want to question you as to your whereabouts last night. Do you have anyone who can vouch for where you were?"

"I was alone in my room."

"That will certainly make it more difficult to prove your innocence but as long as there is no evidence proving you to be out and about near the priest's home then you should be fine."

Silence.

Percival sensed there was something more needing to be shared by Darcy but said nothing.

"I need to tell you I did not remain in my room the whole evening. Approaching nine o'clock I walked toward the priest's home with the thought of talking to him. Instead when I got close I realized it was highly unlikely he would change his mind and given my state of mind it would not have gone very well. I turned around only a few houses from his home so I may have been seen by someone."

"That will complicate things. Hopefully no one noticed or recognized you. We may have to count on you having favor with the King because of your essential role in rescuing his granddaughter and your friendship with Edwin, Greer and I. Surely that will count for something. As you know when he questions you, tell him the truth and trust he will believe you."

They heard a knock on the door and there stood two soldiers sent by the King to escort Darcy to the King's quarters. They were going to walk on either side holding Darcy's arms but Percival intervened and said it was not necessary. The two soldiers walked behind Darcy and Percival as they proceeded to see the King.

When they entered the King's quarters there sat Erith looking rather perplexed. Undoubtedly he had been wrestling with all the implications of what happened and how would he justly deal with it now.

Erith motioned both men to sit down.

"Percival, as you know I would not normally have someone else sitting in here not part of this hearing. However given your relationship with Darcy and the uniqueness of this situation I will permit you to remain."

"Thank you, Sire. I do appreciate it."

Erith then turned his attention to Darcy.

"As I am sure you know by now my priest has been killed by someone sometime during this past night. Given your desire to marry and that request having been refused it does make you the obvious prime suspect to have committed such a crime. Another fact is that whoever killed the priest did not have robbery as a motive. The Sheriff noted there was a full money bag and other valuables readily in plain sight left untouched. What can you tell me as to where you were last night? Any witnesses who could confirm it?"

Darcy then shared everything from his conversation with Edwin and Percival to when he finally ended up back in his own room.

Erith looked at him intently considering all he had heard and the nature of his relationship with Percival and his family members.

Just then a knock was heard at the door. One of the guards opened it and in came a local merchant escorted by the Sheriff.

"Sire, this man claims to have seen Darcy walking near his home in close proximity to the priest's home last night."

Erith motioned for the man to speak.

"Your Majesty, my name is Gudwald and I am a cloth merchant here in Evansing. Last night I was sitting on my front porch and I noticed this man," motioning toward Darcy, "walking in the direction of the priest's home."

"You are sure it was him."

257

"Yes, I am sure."

"Did you see him go into the priest's home?"

"No, the priest's home is around the corner from mine and my view was blocked. Shortly after I saw him I was called into the house by my wife so that was the last I saw of him."

"What time was it?"

"Between nine and ten."

The King thanked the man and said he could leave.

Erith then intently looked into Darcy's eyes for several moments.

"Darcy, this is a peculiar problem. I have the Church wanting whoever committed this crime to pay. They know you have a motive and they know Gudwald witnessed you heading in the direction of the priest's house. Yet, I don't believe you did it. The other challenge for me is that the Church also knows you have a close relationship with Percival and the Royal Family. This creates suspicion of favoritism. I will need to put you in the dungeon for a few days to indicate a willingness to press this further. However I am expecting to release you when further investigation indicates a lack of evidence. The Sheriff will be the one to come up with that conclusion and I will simply agree with him. Even though as king I could simply do what I want it is important to maintain right relationship with the Church and the people at large."

Darcy wasn't sure whether he should be glad or sad. In the end he decided he could handle spending a few days in a dungeon. In any event he had no choice.

The two guards led him away to the cells below the castle.

Percival asked, "Sire, there must be someone else who killed the priest. If we can discover who, then we can clear Darcy without any suspicion of your interference."

"Yes, that is true, Percival, but how will you discover who that might be?"

"I am going to start checking around asking those closest to the priest as to who is aware of someone who

258

harbored a grudge against him, and most likely knew about Darcy's request being turned down."

"I wish you well, Percival. I know this is distressing for you as well as for your friend."

"Thank you, Erith, for that acknowledgment. It is comforting to know you care. If it is acceptable to you I will now take my leave."

"Certainly."

# Chapter 47

Percival immediately went on a mission to find the killer. His first stop was the one priest known to be a good friend of the murdered priest.

Eldon was a man in his mid-fifties, but he looked ten years older. He had a nervous twitch on the left side of his face. Percival couldn't recall if he'd had this for some time or if it had started recently. He did look like he had been grieving and had suffered a recent loss.

"Good morning, Eldon, may I come in and ask you a few questions?"

"I would rather not. I am not in a very good frame of mind for anything at this moment."

"Yes, I am sure you are mourning the loss of your good friend, the priest who was murdered."

"Indeed I am. It is a very grievous blow to lose such a friend."

"I must importune you to dig deeper to answer those questions. It is a matter of the Kingdom to resolve who murdered your friend."

Eldon considered the status of his visitor and what he had said. Then he reluctantly moved to the side to allow

Percival to enter. The room was dark, dank and reeked of alcohol.

"Pardon the mess. I have been out of sorts for some time and have not taken the time to tidy things up."

"Oh you have been feeling poorly even before the murder?"

"Yes, I have felt rather depressed lately. I can't identify exactly why."

"I am truly sorry to hear that. Depression is a painful place to be."

"Yes, it certainly is. What are your questions?"

"When is the last time you saw your friend?"

"Earlier that evening we had supper together at the Last Chance pub just down the street from his home. We had a wonderful time. He shared how he was concerned about his safety because he knew that Darcy was disappointed about being turned down in his request to marry."

"Oh really? Why would he be concerned about his safety?"

"He knew Darcy was not an ordinary monk. After all Darcy does have a reputation as a warrior. He figured if Darcy was willing to renounce his vows as a monk then he could be capable of violence."

"Interesting. In what emotional state was he in when he shared this?"

"He definitely felt afraid. I tried my best to cheer him up but nothing helped."

"What sort of person was your friend? Was he generally up and jovial or mainly more morose?"

"More of the latter. He had been creating some enemies of late and had lost some of his closest friends."

"Oh why was that?"

"I noted that during the past two years his mood definitely had taken a turn for the worse. He seemed to see everything as quite black or white, right or wrong. This new inflexibility started to grate on people and created tensions for him with his friends and others. Some of it was justified by him taking the high moral ground, but some of it was him thinking his personal preferences should be absolutes for others."

"How close would you characterize your relationship with him?"

"I was his only remaining friend so he didn't push his views on me. I would say our relationship was solid and for most part enjoyable."

"What parts didn't you like?"

"When he would attack my family for being louts and layabouts."

"That would be serious. Did he do this repeatedly?"

"Yes. Even though I told him to stop, he wouldn't."

"Why did you remain friends given the seriousness of this?"

"He was the only friend I had. We needed each other."

Percival paused and reflected for a moment on the conversation to that point.

"Do you think it was Darcy who murdered your friend?"

"I certainly think it is possible given the motivation he had."

"Who else had motivation to kill him?"

"There could be two others I can think of."

"Who are they?"

"There is a merchant called Sloane who used to be one of his friends until the priest would not grant him permission to marry a divorced woman from the northern part of the Kingdom. Sloane had to be held back by two others so he wouldn't physically attack my friend. He muttered threats at the priest as they led him away. That was only about six months ago. The other one was a man called Kildare who works as a blacksmith for another blacksmith. He had wanted to start up his own business, but the priest refused permission for him to do so. This much enraged Kildare and he too voiced threats. Kildare almost considered taking the matter to the Sherriff but decided not to."

"Why did he decide not to?"

"He found out the priest had an arrangement with Kildare's employer and was protecting him from losing a valued employee and also from a future competitor."

"Why would Kildare accept the interference from a priest who had no authority to interfere?"

"He was visited by some toughs sent by a party unknown. They warned he would be killed if he resisted the priest's order."

"Hmmm. Who would have the thought the priest had some kind of racketeering activities on the side?"

"You know, Percival, the priest probably would have said yes to Darcy if he had been given a bribe."

Percival looked at Eldon and said nothing.

Finally he muttered his thanks and a quick good-bye to Eldon and left to return to the castle.

At the castle he went immediately to see the King.

Erith was available so he granted Percival an audience.

"Sire, I have been talking to Eldon the closest friend and perhaps only friend of the priest." He then went on to share what he had learned from his conversation with Eldon.

"That certainly puts a different perspective on who could have murdered the priest. I will order Darcy's release first thing tomorrow morning."

Percival thought to himself, "Why not now?" But he knew better than to question Erith.

The next morning Percival went to accompany the guards who were releasing Darcy from the dungeon.

Darcy's face lit up with joy at seeing his dear friend. "Good morning, Percival, it is good to see your handsome face."

"Good morning, my dear friend, you are being released."

"Oh, what a pleasant surprise. I expected at least another day or two."

"Yes, it is a little earlier. I have discovered you aren't the only person to have a motive to murder the priest. Come let us have breakfast in the dining hall. First let's go to your quarters so you can change your clothes and wash up."

"I hope I didn't catch any lice in this place. It's filthy as you would expect a dungeon to be."

"I have a special tonic you can put on your hair and kill any lice in short order."

The two men proceeded to Darcy's quarters.

"So the King didn't bother waiting for the Sheriff to give his report?"

"He decided he had enough reason on his own to release you earlier. After all he is King."

Neither one was about to ask the next obvious question about why Erith was no longer concerned what the Church and others would think.

At the dining hall Darcy was warmly greeted by Aoife and the others.

After the initial euphoria about Darcy's early release there still remained the unresolved matter of him and Aoife getting married. With the priest no longer a hindrance it did create the possibility of his successor being more amenable to give permission.

"Percival, what is our next step?"

"Erith has yet to appoint a successor, but I believe he is considering your case and will appoint someone who has a more flexible view of your situation."

Edwin walked up to the two men with a smile on his face.

"I have good news for Darcy and Aoife. Erith has just informed Greer and myself that the new priest he has appointed is willing to marry them upon some performance of penance."

Both Darcy and Percival's faces lit up with delight.

"I need to tell Aoife this good news."

As Darcy walked over to Aoife he could see Greer was already informing her of the good news. He walked up to them and Aoife looked into his eyes. The eyes of both of them glistened with tears of joy.

A messenger arrived from Nerland and went straight to the King. Erith took the scroll and began reading.

Everyone's attention was drawn to the King's countenance. Initially he looked a little concerned and even confused. Then he looked up and motioned to Edwin and Percival to come up. They both reviewed the message. They all looked at each other and each one started to smile.

Edwin was asked by Erith to make an announcement of the message contents.

"Ladies and gentlemen, I have important news to share. Gondar has been assassinated and replaced with a new king whose name is Finbar. He is friendly to Evansing and we have been supporting him in overthrowing Gondar."

Initially there was almost a stunned silence. Then as people appreciated what had happened they started to cheer at the prospect of being reunited with loved ones and once again enjoying a friendly relationship with Nerland.

"How is it the situation changed so quickly in Nerland?" asked Edwin.

Percival replied, "The only thing that makes sense is that the critical mass of discontentment with Gondar had reached a point where it could no longer be tolerated. Even those thought totally loyal to Gondar participated in the plot. It became so widespread it was no longer hidden. The opposition became so great nothing could resist it. The setting up of Finbar as an alternative, even though few people knew of him, released the energy for change necessary in the atmosphere over Nerland."

Edwin considered for a moment what Percival had said.

"I don't totally understand your explanation, Percival, but it certainly sounds like it could be right. Sudden shifts of seeming intractable positions have always been a mystery to me."

Erith entered the conversation, "Gentlemen, we now need to formulate how we are going to support the new Nerland regime and unobtrusively regain their support for the quest to unite Ireland. I do recognize the need to be subtle and allow some time for the new government to take full control and acceptance. As well, due to all the stress that Gondar put on the people, they need some calm to be restored. We may need to wait at least six months before endeavoring to forge ahead with the Quest."

"In the meantime I think it is important for us to reestablish our links with our allies to ensure they are all on board for the next thrust. I would like to propose that Percival and I go to Aldred and visit King Barris within the next four weeks. Sire, if you could send a courier this week to propose a meeting that would expedite it," Edwin replied.

"I agree with your thoughts, Edwin, except I would like to propose you also bring Greer and Orla along to visit with the Crown Prince and Athandra."

"Yes, Sire, that is an excellent recommendation. Greer will love the idea of visiting her dear friend. I had briefly considered it, but didn't think you would want to expose Greer and Orla to the risks such a trip would entail."

"Risks? What risks are you referring to?"

"New anti-Quest activity has been noted in the region of Aldred bordering onto Evansing. It is the most direct route to Aldred's capital."

"My understanding is that the activity is very minimal. Has this changed to something greater?"

"Yes, new intelligence indicating a surge arrived only yesterday and I hadn't discussed it with you yet. Pardon me for the delay, but I hadn't thought it critical enough to bring it to your immediate attention. Now that this change with Nerland has happened it has become of greater importance."

"You are right in considering this a risk for Greer and Orla. But what about the risk to you and Percival? Evansing would be sorely harmed at your loss and our enemies would dearly love to inflict that loss."

"I have confidence that we can deal with anything that should arise. Besides I was considering an alternative route which would lead us around the area considered most troublesome."

"I appreciate your courage and confidence, Edwin, but in this case I think you are being unnecessarily reckless. There is no need for you to expose yourself and Percival to such personal danger. I will send a courier with an armed escort on the alternative route to Barris and propose we cooperate in wiping out all this opposition."

"Yes, Sire."

"Edwin, I know you are keen for battle, but in this case I am going to send one of our senior officers to lead any incursion.

Percival, do you have any insights about this you want to share?"

"None at this time except I think it is important for you to gain a feel for where Barris is at. My sense is that the hold on the Quest has cooled his ardor to resume the fight for a united Ireland."

"Oh, what makes you say that?"

"Nothing I can nail down as to specifics. It is simply a sensing I get when I consider Barris' personality. I am sure you recall how Barris and almost his entire kingdom were vulnerable to take over by dark forces. This time they may well be working more subtly. Therefore the danger levels of going to Aldred could be greater than they appear. This is coming to me now as I speak and I have confidence that it is accurate. Sire, your perception about danger to Edwin and myself I believe is accurate. It would be good to send a larger escort than normal but not too large as to attract questions."

"Sound advice, Percival."

Erith summoned one of his senior officers and told him to get a troop of 200 men to go to Aldred. He then began to dictate a message to King Barris.

"Dear King Barris,

I wish you and your family good health and all manner of good things. Your daughter, Chandra is in excellent health and she and her husband are expecting their first child.

The purpose of my letter is to ask your input as to how to proceed with the growing anti-Quest activity occurring in the area bordering onto Evansing. We have just been informed of the overthrow of Gondar and his replacement with a king favorable to us. This raises the very real possibility of resuming the Quest within the year.

Hopefully within six months. This makes it imperative for all opposing forces in Aldred to be eliminated as soon as possible. I would like to contribute forces of 2,000 men to enter Aldred and combine with your forces to carry out the necessary operations. Upon completion it would be good if you could visit us here in Evansing so we can begin to discuss preparations for the next phase of the pursuit of the Quest. Please provide a reply to the officer bearing this message.

Yours truly,

Erith"

The next day the troop was ready to be dispatched. The King, Percival and Edwin saw them off and wished them a safe and successful journey.

As they left there seemed a growing heaviness over Edwin as he watched the troop disappear into the distance.

# Chapter 48

The senior officer commanding the horsemen riding to Aldred was a 36 year old seasoned veteran called Terence. He had a wife and three young children. As he and those under his command left on their mission they noticed the sun receded behind a thick cloud. So thick it actually almost seemed to be dark. A curious sensation of being devoid of light.

Terence shivered involuntarily at the shift in the atmosphere around him. He halted his horse and his men. Speaking to his second in command he asked him what he was sensing. His officer turned to him, smiled, and plunged his twelve inch knife deep into Terence's chest. The mortally wounded Terence gasped for breath while clutching his chest, then collapsed dead off his horse. The killer officer then turned to his men and said there had been a change of plans. None of the men protested or made any move to challenge what had happened. Everyone seemed to accept what had happened as reasonable and normal. The only one who struggled with it was a young 19 year old soldier called Colm. He had been tempted to ride up and attack the assassin, but his better judgment told him this was not the time. He had this internal conflict. A classic evil versus good struggle as to his thought patterns. The good was focused on supporting his King and Evansing's Quest. The evil was focused on the destruction of the Quest.

The rebel officer's name was Alby. He had been an officer for two years and was highly regarded. What he presented to his fellow officers and his men and those in his public life was opposite of what he was conjuring up in his private life. He lived alone and had been practicing Druidry for the past year. In the course of doing that he increasingly experienced greater and greater measure of darkness and dissatisfaction with the idea of pursuing a united Ireland. He began receiving telepathic messages from a powerful Druid, called Tarabel who lived in the Kingdom of Tara. The assassination of Terence was in direct response to those messages. Unbeknownst to Alby his will had been progressively taken over by Tarabel. What had started as a curiosity about the dark spiritual realm had now become a chain around his neck leading him as Tarabel directed.

It was Tarabel who created an environment of submission in the 200 soldiers. The influence came from the dark cloud over their heads. The reason Colm had a capacity to consider attacking Alby was because he had the most noble heart of all the soldiers. Whereas the others were not evil they had not taken steps to establish a truly noble heart. Colm had been purposely focused on being a noble man. This inspiration came from his father who would spend time with him to teach him what it meant to truly be someone who would live well in every sphere.

The troop continued to ride on the road to Aldred. Unbeknownst to the soldiers following Alby their mission now had taken a very dark turn. No longer would they simply be delivering a strategic message to promote Irish unity. Rather they were now to be used to destroy the alliance with Aldred.

In the meantime the heaviness that Edwin experienced had gotten heavier and heavier until he could not simply ignore it. He realized something had to be very wrong. He went to Percival and expressed to him what he had been experiencing. Percival initially looked concerned and then started to look very concerned.

"Edwin, that troop sent to Aldred is in grave danger. Meet me at our usual place for the big bird in 30 minutes or so."

"Will do."

Edwin was excited about the prospect of a ride in the sky. He was also pleased his senses were accurate and he hadn't just dismissed them.

By the time Edwin arrived at the usual spot there was the bird ready for takeoff. He hopped on, wrapped his arms around its neck and away they went. In ten minutes they sighted what looked like a body on the road. They landed nearby to take a closer look. Edwin walked over to the body and was shocked to discover it was Terence.

"It's Terence. There is no sign of a skirmish. He looks like he was simply stabbed by one of his men. How is it possible that no one responded?"

Then he considered how the heaviness he had sensed must have interfered with the troops' ability to act. They must all be under the influence of what was most likely a Druidic spell.

Edwin hopped onto the big bird and away they went in search of the troop. In a matter of moments they encountered the swirling dark clouds and the strong negative influence. Due to the high nobility of their hearts

270

Percival in his bird form and Edwin were able to resist coming under its influence. On the ground below they saw the troops continuing on their journey with Alby in the lead. Edwin could see a dark aura surrounding Alby. None of the other men had this aura. He did notice an aura of light around one of the men. As he looked closer he recognized it being Colm. "That's curious," he thought to himself.

Percival kept flying further ahead to land in a spot about an hour's ride from where the troop was presently. After changing back into his human self, Percival and Edwin started to consider their options.

"If I take out Alby with an arrow it could very well break the darkness over the rest of the men."

"Yes, it may, but it may also result in chaos."

"How so?"

"Right now they are being kept in line with the mission given to Alby so they follow him in an orderly manner. If Alby is dead then that orderliness will be gone. The darkness may release in the men a surge of violent desires resulting in them rampaging through the countryside and wreaking havoc amongst ordinary folk."

"So what do we do? Oh, I did notice one of the men named Colm had an aura of light around him."

"That is interesting. We may well be able to exploit that."

"How do we do that?"

"I will send him messages and hope he has enough light to receive them and understand."

"What thoughts will you send him?"

"To quietly bless all the men with light and to release more light. He can say it to himself until he notices the atomosphere has shifted. He will know when that has happened. Then he will ride to the front and slay Alby."

"What will happen then?"

"One of two things, the men will then slay Colm or they will follow him."

"It's our best option."

"Sounds good, communicate with Colm."

Percival closed his eyes and quietly within himself started to speak from his mind to Colm's mind. After several minutes he stopped and reopened his eyes.

Colm was quietly riding along wondering what he was going to do when he started getting strong thoughts identified as being from Percival. He listened to the message. The dark influence all around him wanted him to resist to responding to the message. However he still had enough light to counteract it. He decided he would respond and do as it instructed. As he blessed the men with light and released more light, there was a progressive shift in the atmosphere. Everyone's mood got increasingly more upbeat from the previous sullen and morose moods that had dominated. The dark cloud overhead got lighter, smaller and higher up thus diminishing its power to affect.

Alby started to look around in dismay wondering what was going on. He barked a command to ride faster. After several miles the horses were getting tired from the extra exertion. Soldiers near Alby told him they needed to rest the horses. At first he resisted their advice, but then his own horse started to breathe rather raspily. He commanded the troop to stop and rest.

Colm took a deep breath, pulled out his own twelve inch knife and concealed it under his gear. He rode to the front. He greeted Alby, who looked irritated with this unexpected encounter with one of the men he liked the least.

"What do you want?"

In one motion Colm pulled out the dagger and thrust it into Alby's heart as he stated, "To avenge Terence."

Alby stared in disbelief at what had happened. The dark powers at work in him prevented him from dying instantly, but they could only delay the inevitable. He tried to mumble something and then fell down dead.

At the sight of what had happened one of the soldiers pulled his sword and took a run at Colm. Before he could reach Colm another soldier knocked him off his horse with the butt end of his sword. The rest of the troop stood there motionless, not knowing what to do. A soldier named Alva spoke up.

"Men, we have just witnessed the rightful punishment of Alby for his slaying our commanding officer, Terence. I don't understand why we allowed it in the first place. Colm has set things right. We still have a mission to complete. I say we appoint Colm to be our new commander."

After several moments the men came into agreement that appointing Colm the commander was the sensible thing to do even though he wasn't the highest ranking soldier present.

Colm addressed the men, "I appreciate your confidence and recognition. I will do my best to be worthy of this role as your commander on this mission."

After another twenty minutes of rest the troop resumed their journey to Aldred.

Edwin and Percival hid in the trees by the side of the road waiting for the Evansing contingent to ride by. With great relief they witnessed Colm in the lead and Alby nowhere to be seen. They remained silent as the troop rode by.

After the cavalry had disappeared into the Irish glade, Edwin congratulated Percival on his genius insight and execution. "Percival, well done! Truly you are a master. Where would Evansing and I be without your wisdom?"

"Thank you, Edwin. I owe it all to Divine Providence. I couldn't do it otherwise."

With their mission accomplished they started their journey back to Evansing. After a short while they could see smoke in the distance rising from Evansing Castle.

# Chapter 49

As they came closer to Evansing they could hear shouts and see people scurrying around. The large bird landed nearby in a grove of trees just outside the castle walls. After allowing time for Percival to be restored to his human form, they both entered a secret door to gain access to the castle grounds. The fire was in the north part of the castle. A line of men had been formed to pass buckets along from the nearest well to throw on the flames.

Edwin and Percival each stood and assessed the situation to see what was the best way to deal with it. While what was being done was good and admirable there was one major flaw in this approach. No one was making an attempt to remove the flammable items such as wooden furniture and the cloth curtains. Edwin ordered twenty of the men in the line to come with him. He led them to the edge of where the fire was raging and they started to remove anything that would burn. Since the castle walls were made of stone they of course were not flammable.

The men continued to approach as close to the fire as possible in order to remove materials. Edwin took care to ensure they did so without endangering their lives. A few of them did suffer some minor burns as they valiantly tried to be as thorough as possible. Within the hour the flames started to die down as the fire had lost its fuel for burning. An hour after that the flames were quenched except for some embers that continued to glow until they were doused with water.

King Erith congratulated Edwin on his quick thinking. "Edwin, if you hadn't initiated robbing the fire of its supply the damage could have been much greater."

"Thank you, Sire. I am glad I stopped to consider whether there was a better way. I have to acknowledge it is Percival's influence for me to be more thoughtful and less impulsive. Sometimes immediate action is not the best response."

Percival spoke up, "Thank you, Edwin, for your kind comments. Now we need to identify why this fire happened in the first place. It would be good for the Sheriff and his men to examine for clues as to the cause."

"Oh, do you think there could be treachery, Percival?"

"Yes, Sire, I do. There is something in my gut that tells me not all is right with this. It would be good to enquire of the guards all the people who were seen prior to the fire in this part of the castle. Since it is primarily used as a storage area there should not have been many people authorized to be in this section. A review of the guards would also be prudent."

"Very well, Percival, I will issue orders for this to be carried out."

"We need to also assess what specific objectives could be achieved by such a fire as to what supplies were destroyed and what advantage could have been created through distraction by the fire."

"I will order the Sheriff and his men to determine what inventory of supplies have been lost. As well I request you and Edwin to investigate the effects of the distraction on the security of the castle and Evansing Town."

"Yes, Sire, we will investigate."

Percival and Edwin started to walk toward the main gates.

"I believe the first place of potential advantage for a distraction is at the front gate of the castle."

"Don't you think the guards there would be all the more on full alert when the fire came to their attention?"

"Possibly, but I think it would be wise for us to at least see what we can discover."

When they arrived at the gates the changing of the guards was in process.

Edwin spoke up, "All the guards who were just on duty come over here. We need to ask you some questions."

All twelve men along with their commander lined up in front of Edwin and Percival.

"Commander Liam, could you recount to me exactly what happened at the gate while the castle fire burned?"

"Sir, we closed the gates at the first fire alarm and all the guards stayed at their post. We know from the protocol established that we don't leave our posts unless a superior officer tells us to do so."

"Did anyone notice unusual activity outside the gates?"

Silence.

One of the troops stationed in the lookout tower spoke up. "Sir, I do recall seeing four foreigners standing near the gate entrance. They had been stopped when the gates were closed. They looked rather agitated."

"How did you know they were foreigners?"

"By their dress and tone of their voices I could tell they weren't local. I had never seen them before."

"What did they say?"

"I couldn't understand specific words, just some of the voice tones."

"Did you see where they went?"

"After several minutes they turned around and walked toward the center of town."

"What would be your best guess as to where they could be from?"

The trooper considered the request for a moment. "I would say they came from Tara."

Percival spoke up, "Yes, Tara is the place that came to me as well. I believe there is mischief being stirred up by someone in Tara."

"Given the fire started inside the walls and if someone deliberately started it then they must still be inside the castle grounds."

Edwin then turned to the on duty commander and issued orders that no one was to leave the castle grounds without his personal authorization except of course for the Sheriff and his men. Next he ordered the trooper who had sighted the four men to take a squadron of eight guards and go look for those four strangers.

Edwin and Percival started to walk the grounds and the castle hallways to see if anyone or any thing seemed to be out of place.

"Percival, I am relying to a large extent on your discernment while we walk."

They had spent almost an hour poking around the castle and its grounds when they came across a door previously unknown to either one of them. Percival stopped and seemed to be sensing something.

"What is it, Percival?"

"I am feeling darkness behind this door."

"I will get some guards for support."

Several minutes later Edwin returned with four guards. However Percival was nowhere to be found.

"That is strange. Would he have left on his own or did something happen to him?"

Edwin turned the door handle but it did not budge. He motioned to two of the men to attempt to break the door down. No success. The door stood unmoved by the pressure and jolts. The other two men were then sent to get a large pole to ram against the door. When they returned it took several attempts before the door swung open. It revealed a surprisingly large room. It had evidence of recent habitation. But who? Most troubling for Edwin: still no sign of Percival.

Edwin left the four guards to stay behind and watch over the room. He then went to find the Sheriff who was still conducting his investigation of the fire.

"Sheriff, I have discovered a room previously unknown to me that apparently was inhabited by someone, but who, I don't know. Percival had indicated he felt a darkness behind the door. I went to get some guards for support and when I returned Percival was no longer there. It could be a link with the fire. Come with me and see if your expert eye picks out anything left behind that could provide a clue as to who and for what purpose this room was inhabited. Of course most importantly I am hoping you can find a clue about what happened to Percival."

"Certainly, Sir."

Both men returned to the room and started to look around. The Sheriff noticed an item stuck in one of the corners. He picked it up and examined it closely.

"I am not sure if this is what I think it is, but it certainly looks like a Druid ceremony ring. It's strange to have been left behind. Makes me think it may have been left on purpose to steer us in the wrong direction."

Edwin took the ring and examined it as well. As he did so he sensed a peculiar force come over him. He threw it down.

"What's wrong?"

"Something or someone started to come on me."

Edwin continued to feel unsettled and felt a little panicky. "This may have been set up as a trap for me. What did you feel when you held it?"

"Nothing that I noticed."

"I will leave you to continue your examination. I need to find Darcy."

# *Chapter 50*

**E**dwin hurried to where he believed he would find Darcy. This feeling on him was not leaving and the only person he knew who could help him now was Darcy.

Upon seeing him he let out a sigh of relief. "Ohh, Darcy, I am so glad to find you. I need your help. I picked up a Druid ring and this uncomfortable presence came over me and continues to be on me."

"Do you have the ring with you?"

"No, I threw it down in the room where the Sheriff had found it. He and I were searching this room where Percival said he sensed a dark presence. Oh and even more important than this, Percival has disappeared." Then he went on to explain about Percival.

"Edwin, first thing we need to do is rid you of this presence. You have been cursed by Druidry with a spirit of fear."

"Yes, that is true. I don't want to admit to having fear, but it is definitely what I am feeling."

Darcy pondered for a moment what to do next.

"We need to get that ring first before I can do anything about that spirit. Let us go to that room and perhaps I can also discern what was going on there."

Darcy flinched upon entering the room. "There is indeed a dark atmosphere still remaining. Whoever dwelt here had a powerful Druid force. What is coming to me is that Alcana, the powerful Druid priest stayed here. Let me see the ring."

The Sheriff passed it over to Darcy. He studied it closely.

"This is a ring used by Druids to curse specific people. You are quite right in believing it was a trap for you. Where can I get a hammer?"

Edwin ordered one of the guards to get a hammer. Soon he returned and handed it to Darcy.

Darcy without hesitating took the hammer and smashed the ring several times until it was a misshapen piece of battered metal. When he finished, Edwin could feel the fear lifting and in several moments its influence had totally left.

"Whoa, that feels so much better. Now I can focus back on the task at hand. Sheriff, what else have you discovered?"

"Not much except for one key item." He handed over a ring which looked very familiar to Edwin.

"This is Percival's ring. Alcana must have taken him inside in an instant and kidnapped him."

Darcy spoke up, "It certainly is possible. Give me a moment to consider our next step."

After several minutes no ideas had yet come.

"Nothing I would call a great message has come to me. However, I do believe Percival has been taken to Alcana's fortress."

"Oh, not that place," replied Edwin. The thought of the journey and breaking into the fortress again did not appeal to him at all.

Darcy placed his hand on Edwin's shoulder. As he did so an infusion of peace and well-being came on Edwin. All was silent and still.

"Thanks, Darcy, there must have been some remnant influence from that spirit."

"Yes, there was."

"Sheriff, when do you think you can report about what caused the fire and a description of what items were destroyed?"

"I will need another couple of days or so."

"Alright, I guess it's not that crucial to have it before."

As Edwin and Darcy walked away the thought came to Darcy, "The fire was a ruse to get Percival."

He shared this thought with Edwin.

"That makes sense. I know when the Sheriff said another couple of days it didn't seem to matter that much anymore. Now our focus is to organize to rescue Percival. Another damnable delay in our plans to unite Ireland. Our opponents are always wanting to keep us off balance and distracted. We need to find a better way to stay protected and make things happen."

"Yes, Edwin, you are correct in your understanding. We need to not only rescue Percival but also destroy Alcana and his network of evil working against us."

"Yes, that sounds ideal, but how are we going to do that?"

"As you work out the details for the men and supplies we need I will spend time alone pondering how to destroy Alcana and his network."

The two men parted ways.

Edwin went to one of his most trusted officers and together they planned the logistics for the mission before them. They resolved to bring 300 men. This seemed to be the right number as it also included a cushion against the unexpected. The officer was left with the responsibility to put it altogether over the next two or three days.

Now Edwin realized he had to see Greer and Orla and break the news of the upcoming journey. He knew Greer would be brave but she always had misgivings when he left. As well he needed to spend some family time as he had been so caught up with Kingdom business of late he had hardly seen them.

When Edwin stepped into his personal quarters he was greeted with a warm smile and an extended hug. Greer had missed him. As she held him he thought to himself when and how he should share the news of him leaving for a while. "Not now. Tomorrow." When she let go he gave her a long lingering kiss. This led to more kissing and before they knew it only one thing was on their minds.

Later that day as they lay in each other's arms, Greer started to share some of her thoughts.

"Edwin, I am beginning to resent it when you get so wrapped up with Evansing's affairs. Orla and I both need your presence more than ever before. She needs her father to be playing with her and being available to hold and carry her. I can't be both mother and father. Parenting needs both of us to be involved."

Silence.

"Edwin, aren't you going to say anything?"

"Yes, of course. I am trying to think of what to say. Being a father does not come naturally for me. My recollection of my father is limited so what I do remember is almost only bad modeling from my uncle. My normal response to this would have been to say I will talk to Percival about it. But he's not here. I will try my best. I promise you. I do know it is important for Orla that I be involved in her life."

Thinking to himself, "This is going to make going away even more difficult."

The next day Edwin pondered how he was going to manage his family's needs with the need to rescue Percival. He decided today and tomorrow he would spend with his family. Tomorrow he would tell Greer.

In the late afternoon of the next day, Edwin sat with Greer and began to share the plans to leave and rescue Percival.

As he began, Greer's facial features reflected some chagrin but soon it disappeared and she returned to her normal cheerful self. This both mystified and soothed Edwin at the same time.

"Edwin, my lover, I am so grateful you have given Orla and I the gift of your time and attention these past two days. I knew plans would need to be made to rescue Percival. Your leaving tomorrow does not come as a shock. Make sure you come back."

"Yes, my dear, I will come back."

The next day, Edwin and Darcy left for Alcana's castle. They rode at the front of 300 horsemen. The further they rode the more the atmosphere around them seemed to get oppressive, first starting to make them feel a bit sad then it progressively made them feel despairing. Edwin stopped the troop to consider his options. First to confirm all were feeling the same way, he asked how many were feeling despairing. All the hands went up except for one rather cheerful looking individual.

"You, who didn't raise your hand, come here."

"What's your name, soldier?"

"I am Geoffrey, Sir."

"How do you feel?"

"I actually feel quite joyful."

"Why do you think that is?"

"I always start the day off by telling myself something good is going to happen to me today. Then I keep reminding myself of that throughout the day, especially if I sense negative thoughts or emotions trying to get the best of me."

"Have you experienced those today?"

"Yes, Sir, the further we went the more I could feel them and the more I kept telling myself something good is going to happen to me today. That way they never actually overtake me. I keep them at bay and I stay cheerful."

"Hmm, do you think this would work for the rest of us?"

"I don't see why not."

"I would like you to share this with the troop and lead them in saying what you say until we start to feel differently."

Geoffrey then shared how he had kept himself in a good place mentally and emotionally in spite of pressure to be otherwise. Then as directed by Edwin he led the troop in saying out loud, "Something good is going to happen to me today."

This he did for ten minutes straight, leading everyone to keep repeating it over and over again.

Edwin then stopped him and asked his force how many were starting to feel better. Almost half of the soldiers raised their hands. Then he nodded to Geoffrey to resume their journey.

Ten minutes later Edwin had him stop and again he asked how many were feeling better. This time almost all the hands went up.

After an additional ten minutes Edwin decided to resume. He reminded them all to keep encouraging themselves whenever they started feeling oppressed. The remarkable thing was after a while the oppression lifted completely.

Edwin pondered to himself how in some ways he felt this mission seemed impossible. Yet they had successfully rescued Erith and Greer in Alcana's own castle. Then he considered all the other seeming impossible victories and rescues. "What's different about this?"

Up ahead he saw a white eagle flying. He watched it, fascinated by such an unusual sight. Never had he heard of a white eagle, let alone seen one.

"Darcy, what do you think about that white eagle?"

"Well, Edwin, it appears to be wanting to lead us off of our direct course. Have you noticed it keeps going to the south-west of us and then comes back. I don't think this is an unusual eagle simply because of its color. It may be a benevolent spirit divinely sent or a special eagle for our benefit."

"Going south-west makes no sense. It would delay our journey and for what purpose?"

"It may not make sense, but it may well be the wise thing to do."

"How can we know it isn't a Druid trick?"

"Let us stop for a few minutes as I consider what is the source of this eagle."

# Chapter 51

Fifteen minutes later Darcy started to experience a profound peace and assurance that this was indeed a positive sign to be followed.

"Let us follow the bird and see where it leads."

"Very well, Darcy, I will go with that. I have this internal resistance to it though."

"Yes, sometimes the greatest wisdom works against our reason."

The troop continued travelling to the southwest for a couple of hours before the eagle halted its progress. It started to circle around the top of the force then it disappeared.

A sound of shocked surprise lifted up in unison as everyone saw it disappear before their very eyes. They had just witnessed a most amazing phenomenon.

"Now what do we do, Darcy?"

"I'm not sure, but there must be a reason why it led us here."

"Let us wait until we determine what the next move is."

"What if nothing happens?"

"Let's try waiting first and see."

After thirty minutes still nothing had happened.

"Darcy, don't you think we should get back on course and resume our journey."

"No, I think we should wait until we know what the next step is."

Edwin thought to himself, "This does not make sense. What is going on here?"

"I must admit, Darcy, this is starting to stretch me. How long are we going to wait?"

"Edwin, I have tremendous respect for you as a warrior and a leader, however when it comes to matters of the divine you may still need further growth."

Edwin thought to himself, "Me, need further growth? That smacks of impertinence. Doesn't he realize I am Prince Edwin?"

He continued to wrestle with this until a sudden loud noise broke him from his self-reflection.

Over off to the left of the company of men appeared a force of about 200 to 300 men looking rather ragtag and disheveled. One of them had blown a horn calling them into battle formation. Then they charged from about 400 yards away.

Edwin called his men into battle position as well and they started riding toward the attacking force. He picked out a large man twirling an over-sized battle axe. Thinking to himself, "Might as well jump into the deep end." When only 100 yards apart, Edwin put away his sword and took out his bow and an arrow and shot his target in the face. The large man went down with the arrow tip visible at the back of his head.

Edwin cheered, "That felt good."

He then put away his bow and pulled his sword just in time to engage a foe with a bright red cross on his tunic. They slammed their swords together as they rode by each other. Then they turned around. "Ooh, that vibrated my wrist."

This time they stayed alongside each other. They feinted and parried each other for several moments and then the enemy soldier stabbed his sword at Edwin's throat. Everything slowed right down as the sword tip came ever closer. Edwin's sword moved ever so slowly to flick it away. As it looked like this was going to be the end of Edwin a sword from the side came and diverted the enemy sword from its target. It was Geoffrey. He had sensed Edwin needed his help.

Edwin recovered and went on the attack striking his opponent hard. He managed to draw blood when he struck the soldier's left arm nearly severing it. This he followed up with a blow to the top of his foe's helmet. This blow disoriented the man and now Edwin thrust deeply into the enemy's chest.

Hearing a shout of warning, Edwin turned around in time to deflect a blow from another attacker. The man would not be denied as he continued to come at Edwin again and again. By this time Edwin did not feel as fresh as before. The soldier was starting to drain his energy. Edwin slashed his opponent across his tunic drawing blood. This only served to enrage his foe even more as he increased the number and strength of his blows. Edwin managed to knock down the other's sword and then thrust for the man's heart, but he was thwarted as the man got his sword back up. Then Edwin noticed why he was wearying, he had been wounded in his left side and was losing blood. Seeing his leader wounded and starting to flag, one of Edwin's men named Kale came to take over the fight. This allowed Edwin to retreat to a spot some distance away from the battle. He pulled out a bundle of cloth he carried to use as a bandage if needed.

Edwin winced as he first daubed on a thick ointment which helped to slow down the blood flow. Next he placed the makeshift bandage on this wound and started tightening it around his body. As he did so the blood loss appeared to stop almost completely. It didn't stop totally but at least now he wasn't in immediate danger of bleeding to death. He looked around for their surgeon and his assistant. He noticed them about 100 yards away treating a couple of their wounded. He rode over to them, as he did so he determined he could make it even though he started feeling dizzy and weaker still. When he got to the two medical people, he asked the assistant to help him off his horse.

In a moment the surgeon finished tending his patient and had a look at Edwin. He quickly pulled out his needle and thread and commenced stitching the wound after applying some of his poultice of healing herbs. The stitching took about fifteen minutes. Upon its completion, the surgeon called Eamon had the satisfied look of knowing Edwin had been saved. He advised him to remain lying on the ground. This did not bode well with Edwin as he wanted to get back into the fray and he certainly did not like the idea of lying on the field while his men were battling. However, as he laid there he realized it would be foolish for him to endanger his life while in a weakened state.

In the meantime the Evansing troops had gained the upper hand and were pushing the mysterious enemy back and eventually they broke and retreated. Edwin's men chased them briefly and then returned to attend to their wounded.

Edwin had fallen asleep from the exhaustion of losing blood. Darcy woke him up. At first Edwin thought he was dreaming and didn't want to wake up but Darcy persisted.

"Edwin, wake up, you need to get up."

"Oh, what's wrong? Did we win?"

"Yes, we won, but you need to hear what I have to say."

"What is it?"

"One of the prisoners has told us there is a force of almost 3,000 men moving on Evansing Town with the express purpose of destroying it."

"What? Why? Who are they?"

"They are all former Crusaders and one of their leaders got a vision and heard a voice telling him they needed to destroy Evansing."

"Crusaders? Who are they?"

"They are soldiers who went to the Holy Land to deliver it from the hold of the infidels."

"Why would they come to Ireland? Where are they from?"

"Most of them are from England with some from the Continent. Again it was because of a vision and a voice telling them to come to Ireland for their next Crusade."

"Do you think this is Druidry?"

"It certainly is possible. I don't know for sure. I would have to spend some quiet time considering it."

"In the meantime we need to get back to Evansing and help with its defense. We only have about 1,000 men presently under arms around Evansing Town."

"By the way, Edwin, now you know why the eagle led us here. If we hadn't followed it we wouldn't have encountered this force and discovered the impending attack on Evansing."

"Yes, I admit you are right, Darcy. I had serious doubts about the wisdom of diverting our route. It has turned out to be a very wise move."

Altogether they had 18 captives. They selected six who were or at least appeared to be officers. These they took along. They killed the others and left their bodies for the birds circling overhead.

As the troop came in sight of Evansing Town there did not yet appear to be any enemy soldiers. With a sigh of relief they rode into the town's gates.

They were advised the King was extremely ill and bedridden, barely conscious. They were given assurances the King was expected to recover. There was no time to go see him.

First thing Edwin and Darcy did was summon the troops in the capital to key positions of defense. Shortly after that objective was achieved, Edwin spied the Crusaders coming in view.

They were pulling several catapults to bombard their walls.

As well, he noted they had between 300 and 400 archers getting ready to start releasing arrows over the walls.

In addition, they had a huge battering ram with which to bang down their gates.

Edwin had never seen such an assortment of siege equipment before. At first he felt a little bewildered by this impressive array. Then he started telling himself, "Stay calm, Edwin, we can win this."

He turned to Darcy and asked him for his input as to other resources accessible to them.

"Give me a moment, Edwin and I shall see."

Darcy closed his eyes and considered what they could do. After several minutes he trembled at what he had seen in his mind's eye.

"Edwin, this is what I saw. A whole legion of angels coming to help us."

"That is great. We will need every one of them. Now how do we get them to come?"

"You ask them to come."

"I speak to the angels seen by Darcy. I ask you to come and help us now."

They waited for a moment but nothing happened.

"What are they waiting for?"

Darcy waited again. "They want you to be patient. Just because you asked them to come doesn't mean they come immediately. They will show up when it is most opportune to do so."

"Now strikes me as the most opportune time."

"Yes, we always like it now. Keep in mind the spiritual realm knows more than you do. As well their Divine Overseer has plans far exceeding yours. Let's trust they will show up at the best time."

The Crusaders continued to come, their archers positioned themselves to start shooting and their catapults were being placed to start launching large boulders. They had armored the top and sides of the battering ram so as to protect the men carrying it.

Edwin ran down to the gates to survey how well it would resist continual pounding from the battering ram. He commanded several of his troops to go to the blacksmith's shop to see what iron bars might be utilized to provide more support. He also sent several soldiers to the carpenter shops to see who had thick timbers to use as well. After a half hour or so they started returning with iron bars and timbers. The battering ram had already commenced its battering. The gates in place were massive wooden timbers and solidly supported with iron bars. Workers immediately set to reinforce the gates with the gathered bars and timbers. Within an hour they had substantially strengthened the gate. Edwin surveyed the response of the gates to the pounding. He recalled how only a few months earlier he and Erith had discussed building a portcullis and a heavily fortified gate house to further brace the gates. However they considered other matters to be of greater priority.

In the meantime the catapults were smashing against the most vulnerable section of the wall. How did they know there were structural weaknesses in that one specific area? There had been talk of doing something about it but nobody felt it was pressing. After all more important matters needed attending to. Those other matters now didn't seem nearly as important.

Edwin started wondering when their angelic support was going to show up. He didn't like the anxiety he was experiencing. As a warrior he did his best to avoid that feeling.

"Edwin, everything will work out," a voice seemed to speak to him.

Just then an arrow whizzed by his head missing him by less than a foot. It stuck in the ground. Next moment another arrow struck one of the nearby soldiers in the neck. He collapsed moaning in pain and then went silent.

Edwin wanted to go see if he could help him, but he knew he was dead.

He then ran over to where the wall was being smashed. It was obvious that a major breach would occur in less than an hour at the present rate of hammering.

Edwin thought to himself, "What to do?"

Suddenly he recalled seeing two wagons loaded with large stones only about 200 feet  or so from where it needed to be placed. He called to his nearby soldiers to go fetch the wagon. After ten minutes or so the wagons appeared. Edwin instructed them to pile the rocks up against the seriously deteriorating section. After completing the task, he looked with satisfaction at the improvement in the sturdiness of that section of the wall.

"It will help for a while. Hopefully they will run out of boulders to throw at it"

As an additional precaution he ordered one of his men to gather at least another 40 archers to man the nearby sections of the wall. The problem would be situating each of them with arrow slits to shoot through. Some of them would have to shoot over the wall which exposed them to greater risk of being shot.

Darcy showed up with a joyful look on his face.

"Edwin, we are still alive and the walls and gates are still holding."

At first Edwin was taken aback as he had not been feeling so positive about their situation.

"Yes, Darcy, at this moment what you say is true. I am concerned about where we are going to be in an hour or two."

"I know you are, but you have cause to feel good right now. That will fuel your energy and thoughts for what is next. Remember help is on the way."

"I hope you are right. I will try to stay confident."

"It's not like you to struggle with confidence in battle. Something deeper must be going on inside you."

"I am not aware of what that might be. I certainly don't have time for navel gazing right now."

"No, true enough. Keep doing what needs to be done and expect a good outcome."

At that moment the stricken section of the wall started to shake and crumble.

Edwin called to his aide, "Go bring at least 100 troops to defend this section."

Within a half hour the wall had a hole large enough for men five abreast to march through it. The repositioned troops braced themselves for enemy soldiers.

# Chapter 52

When the Crusaders saw the opening in the wall a platoon of 80 men were assigned to start battling their way through it. They of course had to work their way towards it while defending themselves against the archers assigned to defend that section. To counteract the defending archers, the Crusaders' archers launched volley after volley against the defenders thus allowing their platoon to advance under its cover. As well they used their shields to provide protection. Occasionally poorly shot arrows struck their own men. Such were the hazards of such a strategy.

Once they reached the breach, a fierce hand to hand struggle with swords ensued. They experienced the added difficulty of having to overcome defenders with long spears posted in the breach. The narrowness of the opening gave the defenders an advantage, but they were pressed as the initial wave sacrificed themselves in their determination to break through. Soon the bodies of almost 30 attackers had piled around the opening. A dozen of the defenders had died and were also lying at the entrance. Still the Crusaders continued to press until several of them broke through. They were each quickly killed as they were vastly outnumbered. However, it indicated a new momentum was being created by the attackers. The Crusaders sent another platoon to reinforce the first. Within twenty minutes almost ten of them had now entered the Town.

Edwin had returned to the breach in the wall and started engaging one of the enemy. The man was almost six inches taller and somewhat broader in the shoulders than Edwin. He represented a reasonable challenge for Edwin.

"Let's see how well he handles a sword." Edwin rushed at him with a flurry of strokes. His opponent handled himself well. Now Edwin stopped his frenetic approach and walked slowly toward the soldier. This time the Crusader made a mad rush at Edwin. These blows were deftly deflected and turned away. The soldier continued to press but Edwin almost effortlessly turned them aside. Then he sliced high at Edwin's head. The latter ducked and thrust forward with his sword, the Crusader blocked it, but it grazed his side hard enough to draw blood. This gave Edwin greater adrenalin to continue the attack. The other was now on his heels in defensive mode. Another slash by Edwin caught the foe on his sword arm. The Crusader managed to hang onto his sword. Then he did something highly unusual, he grabbed his sword with his left hand and pressed the battle. As they continued on Edwin noted how there seemed little difference in the enemy's ability to fight with his left arm versus his right arm. One of Edwin's men was coming over and about to stab the Crusader in the back, but Edwin waved him away. This man was too noble a fighter to die that way. He would kill this man himself. The man surprised Edwin with a sudden twirl and slash with his sword which almost knocked Edwin's sword out of his hand. Then the man took out his dagger and closed in fending off Edwin's sword while attempting to stab Edwin with the dagger. Edwin pulled out his own dagger and managed to stab the other man in his hand holding the dagger. The dagger dropped and then Edwin stabbed the man in the chest deeply pushing it in as far as it would go. This resulted in the man gasping for air. Edwin left him dying on the ground to turn his attention to the next opponent.

The Crusaders now had about 15 to 20 men inside the wall. Another 50 defenders came to support the breach. The archers on the wall created great difficulty for the attackers to maintain their mass of numbers as dozens were picked off by arrows.

Edwin next took on a pair of attackers, one who appeared to be wounded in his right leg and the other who had an extra large blood red cross. Edwin first swung fiercely at the wounded man pushing him back several steps. He turned to the other in time to deflect the man's sword aimed at his heart. "That was close," he muttered.

This time Edwin replied with a hard slice to the man's right side resulting in a howl of pain and spurting blood. He would have finished him off except he had to contend with the other attacker who now pressed Edwin with another thrust which Edwin set aside. Then he struck the man on his right leg slicing it at the knee. This allowed Edwin to further his attack on the other. The man with the distinctive cross was seriously wounded, but he still had a lot of fight remaining. He was able to fend off the blows raining down on him and even mount a bit of an offensive response. Then exhausted from the loss of blood he stopped and Edwin clipped off his head.

The battle for Evansing continued for the rest of the day. Come nightfall the enemy retreated from the breach in the wall as they had sustained heavy losses with no significant progress in breaking through. They had achieved up to 20 soldiers inside the walls, but because they were vastly outnumbered they never survived long enough to create a beach head.

Darcy and Edwin met at the gate where the defenders had continued to block the Crusaders' attempts to break through. Both men were smeared with blood, dirt and sweat.

"It is good to see you still standing, Edwin. This has been a fierce fight, but we are still here. It is a grand day to give thanks."

"Darcy, I like your style. A part of me feels angry and part of me feels glad."

"Yes, this is one of those times. What are your thoughts about what our next step is?"

"I am sorry to say, but at this moment I have no idea except I need to get some sleep before I collapse. In the meantime I have given orders to continue to man the walls as before. I see no reason to create a new strategy."

That night as Edwin slept he received a very dynamic dream, so clear and real he completely recalled it upon awaking.

He went over to find Darcy who was sleeping by the gate.

"Darcy, wake up. I have a strategy."

His friend woke up with a start, "Whaat? What did you say?"

"I have a strategy. It came to me in a dream."

Darcy smiled. "I knew you were going to get one."

"In the dream Prospero showed up and took me to the enemy's camp so I could hear what the commander was saying to his officers. He told them they needed to take Evansing today and would do so by sending a wagon to the gates packed with something he referred to as gunpowder. He said it would destroy the gates. How it would do that he didn't say, but Prospero gave me a picture. I heard a loud noise and saw smoke appear and pieces of the gates flying all over including high into the air. Then Prospero gave me a pouch of a potion to make me invisible. I drank it and being invisible I penetrated the enemy lines and set their wagon of gunpowder on fire. Then I woke up."

"Do you have the pouch?"

"Yes, it was right beside me."

"Amazing! It appeared in your dream and transferred to the physical."

"Yes, I have never had that happen before. I have used an invisibility wine when Percival and I killed Brydon, a powerful Druid priest. Erith has a recipe for it, but I have never tried it again. Now I have gotten a fresh pouch provided in a most unusual way and I am going to use it."

With that he drank the contents of the pouch. He waited for several moments and then progressively he disappeared from view.

Edwin walked over to where there was a breach and walked around the men guarding the opening. It was a little tricky as he brushed by a couple of them which created a bit of a stir as they wondered what had touched them. Once outside of the walls he had to walk several hundred yards to where the enemy camp was set up just outside of bow shot range.

He spied the wagon he had seen in his dream. It carried several barrels which he thought to himself must contain that substance called gunpowder. Since it was still dark and dawn was at least another hour away there were only a few guards up and around. He considered how to best light the wagon on fire. Nearby was a fire from which he could get a burning stick to start it. But he needed something else to help get it going before the guards noticed and put it out. Then he saw a bale of straw on the other side of the wagon. He carried it over to the wagon, hope against hope that no guard would notice this bale of straw moving seemingly all by itself. Mission accomplished. He then spread the straw around the barrels. Next to get a burning stick to ignite the straw. As he carried the burning stick a shout from one of the guards, "Who goes there?" Edwin quickly threw the stick onto the straw which broke out into flame. He then ran into the nearest guard knocking him down and stabbing him in the throat to shut him up and stop him from putting out the fire. Getting up he knew he needed to put as much distance between himself and the wagon as possible. He had just passed the outer perimeter of the camp when a massive explosion threw Edwin to the ground. He was shaken but was uninjured except for some bruises. Looking back he could see a massive fireball erupting over the camp. He stood up and kept running until he got near the breach in the wall. He then slowed to a walk to catch his breath. Men on the wall and by the breach were all expressing awe and dismay at what they were witnessing in the distance. Then some of them cheered in celebration at the destruction of their enemy. The cheering spread until all the men were celebrating this most fortuitous turn of events. Edwin slipped back through the breach and went looking for Darcy.

He walked toward the gates where Darcy would most likely be. As he did so he noticed how, to himself at least, he could start to faintly see his body. At this point he looked like a ghost. Fortunately no one was around as it still was very early. He needed to get inside a place to let the process of being fully restored be completed. He thought of the room where Percival disappeared. He walked over there and found the door slightly ajar. "Strange," he thought to himself, "it should at least be completely closed."

Opening the door and walking in he felt a strange unease in the atmosphere. He drew his knife prepared for an unwelcome occupant. As he looked around the room he saw a pair of glistening green eyes looking back at him. Then he heard a meow. It was a cat. He had been spooked by a cat. He smiled to himself but then wondered, "Why the unease?"

Suddenly the cat grew in size and leaped onto Edwin. The cat bit and scratched him, Edwin wrapped his arm around the neck of the cat pulled back its head and stabbed deeply into its throat. The cat howled and squirmed, but Edwin did not let go and even strengthened his grip breaking the neck of the cat in the process. The cat went limp.

Getting up and after dusting himself off, Edwin realized he did not now feel any pain or discomfort.

After the adrenaline rush started to subside he could tune into the presence of the room. The unease had disappeared. In the corner he noticed a small lit candle throwing off minimal light but sufficient to examine himself. He now could see that his visibility had totally returned. What shocked him most was that there was no evidence of the attack by the cat. Not even his clothes were torn and no scratches or bites on his body in spite of him experiencing the pain of the violent encounter.

Edwin went over to inspect the cat but it wasn't there. The body had disappeared.

"This is getting very weird," he spoke out loud.

He left the room and resumed his search for Darcy.

Upon finding Darcy he shared everything that had happened.

"You have entered into a new dimension of life, Edwin. I believe you are about to see things you imagined possible as becoming more and more part of your normal existence."

"Well I never imagined this cat experience as possible."

"No, but it does indicate you are starting to relate more and more with the spiritual realm. I am expecting it will be more the good side than the bad side but time will tell. Keep imagining what you want to see and speaking it out to give it legs."

A courier arrived to tell both of them that the enemy camp was still in uproar with many bodies lying on the field. The survivors appeared to be withdrawing.

"I think we should get a troop together to mop up the survivors."

"Yes, I believe you are right."

Edwin ordered a cavalry of 500 men to mount up as quickly as possible.

The gates were opened and then led by Edwin the horse soldiers rode out towards the enemy camp. As they approached it, they encountered the stench of burning flesh. Hundreds of bodies lay around the camp. They were all in awe of the havoc caused by the explosion. None of them of course had ever witnessed such an explosion before. This was to them a brand-new weapon of war. As many horses had also been killed or maimed, most of the enemy were fleeing on foot. The cavalry came charging with swords drawn or in some cases firing arrows at the backs of the terrified mob. The enemy had been completely traumatized by the explosion and had lost all will to fight or be coherent as a force in any way.

Within the hour more than a thousand Crusader soldiers were slain as they fled. The carnage ceased when they observed the remaining enemy soldiers who had gone the furthest were now all set up in positions part way up a hill with a fair amount of protective covering. Being outnumbered, it didn't make sense to pursue them further. Besides, their foe had been substantially eliminated and was unlikely to resume the siege. As well, another thousand Evansing troops would be arriving shortly from the Nerland frontier so now they would be well able to protect themselves. The next concern would be to drive the remaining force out of the Kingdom of Evansing.

After Edwin got back to Evansing Castle, he immediately went to see Greer and Orla.

Greer threw her arms around her husband and held him tight.

"Honey, I am so glad to see you. I tried to stay totally calm, but I have to admit I did feel anxious."

"Yes, it was tense. Fortunately now the immediate danger has passed. How is your father doing?"

"He is still quite ill, but there seems to be some improvement."

"I will go see him and try my gift of healing on him."

# Chapter 53

They both went to the King's quarters. The Royal Physician looked grim and hopeful at the same time. He shared how he was puzzled by the ailment, but he continued to see signs of health returning.

Erith smiled when he saw Edwin and Greer enter his room. Edwin put his hand on the King's chest and said, "Return to good health."

Erith's body jolted slightly and his eyes closed for a moment. The color rapidly came back into his face. His eyes opened and now he looked positively cheerful.

"Something happened. I am starting to feel much better."

After another ten minutes had passed, the King tried to get up and did so with a little assistance from Edwin. He sat at the edge of the bed.

Erith looked at Edwin and smiled. "Bringing you to Evansing was one of the best decisions I have ever made. I heard a few minutes ago that we had successfully fended off an attack from Crusaders. Why would they attack us?"

"Best we can make out is it was an assignment initiated by Druids. When troops return from the Nerland frontier we will go and chase them out of Evansing."

"Yes, that is important. I did have a dream of Percival last night. In it he appeared well although he was sitting in a dungeon. He looked right at me and said, 'Beware of coming the most direct road. There is a better way, a safer way.' Then the dream ended."

"Interesting. On our way to rescue Percival we got led by a white eagle to a different route. It steered us into the Crusaders and we discovered their plan to attack Evansing. I would say your dream should be heeded and we consider other routes. I will get my scouts on to it immediately."

With that Edwin left to find his scouts.

Greer remained to talk to her father.

"Daddy, I am so glad you are doing better. I couldn't bear to lose you now when Orla and I are still so young. I wish we'd had a warmer relationship when I was a child. But I am grateful for the changes I see in you which now makes it so much easier to know you and love you."

Erith was both gratified and disturbed by what he had heard. He was gratified at her calling him "Daddy" for he couldn't recall the last time she addressed him in such an endearing way. He had always thought they had a warm relationship so it came as a new revelation to hear his daughter had considered it otherwise.

"What do you mean, my dear, 'a warmer relationship'?"

"I mean you were not really easy to be with in my early years. I didn't always feel like you valued me as much as you would have if I had been a son. It seemed like you forced yourself to relate to me at times. I think you tried to be a warm father. Often I felt you didn't feel warm towards me."

Erith was silent for a moment as he considered his daughter's words.

"Yes, you are right. I did struggle with wanting a son. I know I did not love you the way you deserved and needed. I am so sorry for wronging you. Would you please forgive me?"

"Yes, Daddy, I do forgive you."

She gave her father a prolonged hug and kissed him on the cheek, her tears mingled with his tears as they both cried.

"My dear, I am so proud of you as my daughter. You are worth ten sons to me."

Edwin found his scouts and gave them their instructions. Then he went to find Darcy.

Finding Darcy, he asked him about the promised angelic support they were supposed to have gotten against the Crusaders.

"Were we victorious?"

"Yes."

"Would you say we won in an unusual way?"

"Certainly it was all of that."

"Sometimes angelic help doesn't seem obvious because we can't see where they are and what they are doing. We just see the results of their involvement."

After a momentary silence, "Yes, I suppose you are right."

"Our next task is to drive the Crusaders out of our kingdom. I would like you to accompany us. We will leave after our troops return from the Nerland border. I think it is important you are along for we need your sensitivity to what is going on in the invisible realm."

"Certainly I will come. What do you want me to do right now?"

"Nothing at this moment until our troops return."

"In that case I want to visit Aoife."

"Yes, of course you do. Enjoy!"

Darcy walked along the path to his beloved's cottage. When he got there he knocked on the door and waited but Aoife did not answer.

"Aoife, it's me, Darcy."

Still no answer. He looked through the window and could see the table and chairs knocked over. He forced the door open and entered. No sign of Aoife. Feeling desperate he walked around the property, but did not see any clues to give him a clear direction as to where she might have gone.

He started running back to where Edwin would be.

"Edwin, I believe someone has taken Aoife. There are signs of a struggle but no evidence as to who took her or in what direction they went."

"Oh, Darcy! That is dreadful news. I will get search parties to start checking out the castle and town. As well I will send out cavalry to ride around the immediate area. Go get the Sheriff and take him to Aoife's cottage to see what he might notice."

Darcy immediately went to see the Sheriff. Fortunately he was available and he and his assistant accompanied Darcy to Aoife's cottage.

After scouting around inside and outside, he shook his head and said, "This is most peculiar. There are no tracks except for yours and they only go in a circle around the cottage other than the path you used to get here. She may have been taken while it was raining early this morning or before so that all tracks were washed away." Something came to him and he returned to the cottage.

He looked up to the ceiling, got on a chair and took a closer look at what appeared to be a hatchway. Someone had opened the ceiling and must have come in, most likely at night. It must be also the exit route as well.

"Druids can elevate themselves, in effect fly for certain distances. They must have flown away with her."

Darcy looked at him amused. "I didn't realize you were so conversant in Druid matters."

"Yes, I know it sounds extraordinary, but how else do you explain no tracks and the hatchway in the ceiling?"

"I believe that is certainly a distinct possibility. Unfortunately that leaves us in a position of not quite knowing what the next step is."

"Darcy, I can check out my spies in the Druid community. They will turn up something."

"Sherriff, you surprise me. Does anyone else know how well connected you are to the Druids?"

"No, I have not shared it with anyone. With Percival around there was no need to share that. He handled the major Kingdom security issues. I used my connections for solving the more mundane matters such as serious crimes.

Mind you, during Percival's extended absence I did check with my connections for Kingdom security, but I veiled my sources. "I just felt it would be safer to keep it to myself. I think Percival knew although we never discussed it. That man has great discernment."

"I will keep it to myself, Sherriff."

"Thank you, Darcy, I appreciate that. I will now get the word out and see what we can find."

The interchange left Darcy feeling more hopeful although he did struggle with feeling the angst of concern over Aoife's fate.

"I renounce all fear and worry about Aoife. I choose to believe she will be rescued safe and sound." That had the desired effect for he knew he could not function well if he was burdened with fear and anxiety.

Darcy then returned to where the troops were mustering for their mission to pursue the Crusaders. The reinforcements had arrived from the Nerland frontier. After a short rest they would all be ready to leave.

Edwin walked up to Darcy and asked him what had happened with the Sheriff.

"We have concluded that it looks like she was taken away by flying Druids."

Edwin looked askance momentarily. "I guess that's possible. I know they can elevate themselves to some extent but I thought it was only briefly."

"The evidence seems to indicate that is what happened, but we're not totally certain."

"I know this is difficult for you to leave with us right now. Would you rather stay behind?"

"Thanks for your consideration, Edwin, I do appreciate it. No, I have released my concern the best I can and I want to come with you."

"That is certainly courageous and selfless of you."

A short time later everyone mounted up and they started their journey to hunt down the remaining Crusaders.

# Chapter 54

The first hour was uneventful. Then an arrow whizzed by Edwin's head almost grazing him.

The troops raised their shields, but nothing further happened. It turned out a lone soldier had been left behind and with that one arrow he lost his courage and ran into the forest. Edwin sent several of his scouts after him for they could hear him running and crunching the branches under his feet.

Once they found him they dragged him back for questioning.

Edwin walked up to the captive, lifted up his chin and smiled.

"What is your name, soldier?"

"My name is Graham."

"Where are you from?"

"A few miles south of London."

"Where is your army going to now?"

"They are heading east to Dublin where they want to catch boats to go back home."

"I am going to keep you as a prisoner for three months. If no attack has occurred within that time I will release you. However, if we are attacked you will forfeit your life immediately. Is your answer the same?"

"That is what I heard. I know nothing else."

"Why would they leave one lone soldier behind?"

"My sergeant didn't like me and decided I was expendable. His excuse was that my sacrifice was necessary so as to assist the rest of the army to get away."

"You are the only one left here at this spot?"

"Yes, sir. That is correct."

"It does seem preposterous that they would expect you to hold up an army by yourself. Perhaps you are right. Your sergeant may have been looking for an excuse to get rid of you."

Edwin and Darcy and several of the other officers conferred some distance away.

"Men, we have two options before us. Believe what this Crusader has told us or continue our chase to make sure they are out of Evansing. Personally I believe we should continue to follow the trail and ensure it is heading east to Dublin."

All the men agreed that the prudent action would be to continue the pursuit.

The troops mounted up and continued their ride. The trail of course was easy to follow. It did appear they were heading east.

Edwin commented to Darcy, "The Crusader army had a good day's ride head start so they may already be outside of the Kingdom of Evansing."

"Yes, I would expect they would be unless they stopped or turned around."

Edwin put up his hand and halted his horse. The troops all halted behind their leader.

"We are placing ourselves in a convenient position for ambush. The terrain near the border is well positioned for such an attack."

He called for the scouts and asked them for an alternative route that would come from behind where any potential Crusaders would likely be positioned.

One of the scouts indicated there was such a trail. It was a fairly circuitous narrow path with lots of cover from a heavily treed forest. It actually slightly crossed the border with Elfereth but only briefly and would come right behind where any attackers could be awaiting.

Edwin gave the order for him to lead the way. The scouts all went first followed by Edwin and Darcy, the other officers, then the rest of the cavalry.

This route took much more patience to ride as it was slow going. After an hour Edwin stopped the party and issued orders to the scouts to ride ahead and see if they saw anything suspicious. An hour and a half later the scouts returned.

The lead scout reported, "Sir, we noted the Crusaders were holed up in heavily protected positions with their archers at the ready. Did not see the positioning of their cavalry."

The news was disappointing for Edwin. He had dearly hoped there would not be a need to fight them further. "Bring me the prisoner."

The prisoner was pushed to his knees.

"Graham, I wished this had finished differently for you, but I am a man of my word."

With that he thrust his sword through the prisoner's heart out through his back.

Edwin mused out loud, "It's interesting you couldn't see the cavalry. Either the cavalry continued on or they are situated where they can rapidly come out of hiding and attack. I suspect it is the latter for it makes no sense to leave ones archers behind simply to delay us when they had already a day's head start."

Addressing the head scout, "Is there a route likely to lead us around the archers and behind their cavalry?"

"I believe so, Sir. I know there is another path behind the one where we came upon the archers. If the horsemen ride slow it shouldn't be so loud as to be heard by the enemy. As they come around behind the archers the scouts can travel ahead and determine where the Crusaders' cavalry lies hidden."

"Very well, that sounds like a reasonable plan. Let's go!"

Evansing's army split up with the cavalry men most adept at archery taking the route to ambush the enemy archers. The other group rode on to where the scouts determined.

It had been resolved that the ambush of the archers would not begin until the scouts had decided where the enemy cavalry men were located.

After a bit over an hour of riding slowly one of the scouts returned with news that the Crusaders' cavalry had hidden in a massive stand of forest but right beside a runway big enough for four horses across to ride through. It was the perfect spot for them to rush a beleaguered force decimated and harassed by the archers.

Evansing cavalry lined up at a spot about 300 yards from the Crusaders' cavalry. Their exit out of their hiding place only allowed for two riders abreast to ride through but once through it was an open field and with their numerical superiority they should win the day. Their signal to attack would be when two flaming arrows were released into the air.

Two scouts rode as quickly as possible back to the men with their bows ready to attack. The signal was given and the Evansing men launched a fusillade of arrows at the Crusaders' archers. Two quick volleys of arrows killed or wounded almost 50 per cent of the enemy. Then their targeted foes took cover and repositioned themselves to be able to return arrows themselves. However, after only a few moments of exchange it was obvious they were vastly outmaneuvered and outnumbered. The enemy began to break ranks and started to flee. The Evansing soldiers pursued them. In the meantime the two flaming arrows were released signaling their cavalry to charge.

Edwin began the charge with himself in the lead. The cavalry they were coming against were in a state of disarray. They had seen the arrows flying and heard their men screaming. This sudden turn of events had come so unexpectedly they were caught unprepared. No plan B had been considered.

The leader of the Crusaders led what measure of battle formation he had left. Edwin targeted him and they clashed together with their swords. The enemy leader was stoutly built with a strong upper body. When he struck Edwin's sword he almost knocked it out of Edwin's hand. This resulted in Edwin changing his tactics to directing his horse behind his opponent. This enabled Edwin to lay a hard blow to the back of the enemy. It seemed to shake up his foe, but he turned around and faced Edwin and attacked with a ferocity seldom seen before by Edwin. The surprising thing for Edwin was all of a sudden he entered a realm of flow which made his ability to fight seemingly effortless. Everything slowed right down and his thinking got very clear. He could see the frustration on the Crusader's face for he was fighting with all his might and made all manner of strategic moves to get past Edwin's defense. All to no avail as Edwin maintained an indomitable wall of protection. Then Edwin thrusted into the man's chest narrowly missing his heart. Nevertheless blood started to spurt from the man's mouth and he groaned loudly as he struggled to stay on his horse. Edwin then delivered a swift blow to the man's neck nearly severing it from his body.

Another enemy horseman came toward Edwin with a lance that clanged against Edwin's quickly raised shield. The blow almost knocked Edwin out of his saddle. Throwing aside the lance he then drew his sword as he approached Edwin. The latter sheathed his sword and picked up his bow and drew an arrow all in one motion and released it into the soldier's heart killing him instantly. Edwin looked around and shot another enemy in the heart. Setting down his bow and pulling his sword he attacked two soldiers engaged in fighting one of his officers. Ambushing them from behind resulted in one being dismounted and the other distracted so that Edwin's fellow officer was able to deliver a deadly blow to the man's head.

At this point the remaining Crusaders began to break and run. The Evansing soldiers pursued them to the Elfereth border and a bit beyond. Many more of the enemy were cut down in the pursuit.

The return trip was most joyous as Evansing celebrated a great victory with few casualties to themselves.

Edwin enjoyed the trip back, but he had difficulty in fully savoring the victory as he started to think about their next mission of freeing Percival. One of his officers noted this and chided Edwin to engage with his men and fully experience the joy of success.

"Sir, the next battle will come, but today we have battled and won. Make the most of why we battled today."

Edwin snapped out of the fog of his thoughts and turned to the officer telling him he was right. With that he started to ride up and down the ranks of men affirming their bravery and skill as warriors with loud cheers.

This time Edwin maintained an attitude of celebration all the way home. When those nagging thoughts threatened he would let out another victory cry.

When Evansing Town came into sight he again started to consider the next mission, rescue Percival and also discover what happened to Aoife.

# Chapter 55

The next morning Edwin woke beside Greer, happy to be able to feel her warmth once more. She was still sleeping. He slipped out of bed so as to not wake her, got dressed and left their quarters. He'd had a rather disturbing dream and needed to resolve how to respond to it. The best person for him to talk to about it would be Darcy. It was still quite early, but he decided he needed to talk to Darcy now even if it woke him up. Besides he knew Darcy would be keen to start the rescue of both Aoife and Percival.

Undoubtedly his heart wanted to pursue Aoife first but was that the most strategic move for the welfare of the

Kingdom? The interesting thing about the dream is it seemed to give a sense of the direction needing to be taken.

The dream had Edwin perched on the top of a very tall tree. A tree so tall he could see all of Ireland from the top it. As he viewed it he could see Percival in Alcana's castle as they had suspected. He looked to be alright although he was kept in a tightly secured cell in the dungeon. Then he saw Aoife in the Kingdom of Tissus, his old antagonists from his by gone life. Where exactly she was he couldn't tell. Percival was northwest of Evansing and Aoife was northeast. As he considered rescuing Percival several barriers arose and a giant whirlwind came scattering Edwin and his men to the four corners of Ireland. When he caught his breath and considered rescuing Aoife first there was a stream flowing carrying Edwin and his men right to where she was.

Edwin knocked on the door of Darcy's home. Almost immediately Darcy opened the door.

"Welcome, Edwin, I have been expecting you."

"Really? But of course you would be. I shouldn't be surprised."

He paused for a moment.

"Did you have a rather interesting dream this past night?"

Darcy replied, "Yes, I did." Then he started to share almost the same dream as Edwin.

"That's the same in all important parts as what I got. What do you make of it?"

Darcy remained silent.

Edwin decided to share what he thought.

"I believe we are meant to rescue Aoife first. It doesn't make sense to me strategically. Percival has greater value to our Kingdom and the uniting of Ireland. However he appears to be safe and great obstacles appear to have been thrown up to the northwest of us. There is something more strategic time wise in rescuing Aoife first. I believe when we do, the hindering obstacles between Percival and us will be removed."

"Yes, I believe you are right. I didn't want to say that because of course my heart is with both Aoife and Percival. Not knowing for sure if I was influenced by my love for Aoife made it difficult for me to want to express what you said."

"This will be an interesting journey through Elfereth. We have not had any close connections with their kingdom other than some trade. Even more interesting will be my facing my old foes, the Tissus. We will need to contact the King of Elfereth and assure him of our peaceful intentions as to his kingdom. This may actually pave the way to incorporate him in our quest to unite Ireland. We will have to eventually. Now might be the opportune time to start creating an alliance. Perhaps he would even want to join us against Tissus. I am sure he would relish an opportunity to strike at Tissus. I will speak to Erith about a letter of introduction to the King of Elfereth. In the meantime I will also get troops and diplomatic representatives together ready to go as early as tomorrow."

The next day at noon the diplomatic mission set off with the letter from Erith to the King of Elfereth. It would take them a full three days to arrive at Elfereth's capital.

In the meantime Darcy had to stay the course in maintaining a hopeful outlook on recovering his soon to be bride. He felt anger towards himself for not ensuring she was protected. Of course that was a groundless self-accusation. He had no way of knowing such an attack would occur behind the castle walls where she would be expected to be totally safe. Nevertheless he castigated himself for not being more aware of that potential. As he thought about it he realized the genius of it as the Druids recognized it would divide his loyalties and the attention of Evansing between Aoife and Percival. As he considered this and the dreams Edwin and he had it dawned on him that what appeared to be an awful dilemma would ultimately turn to their advantage. Before there had been no attention placed on Elfereth and Tissus. Now there could be a shift in focus from trying to resurrect the old alliances to focusing on the creation of new ones.

Darcy went to see Edwin and shared his insights. As he did so, Edwin nodded in agreement.

"Yes, I believe you are right, Darcy. We have tended to resist the next step of developing new allies. Perhaps because it is unfamiliar and required the development of whole new ways of doing things with different people."

"The Elfereth people tend to be different in their outlook than the people we have dealt with. Because I used to be one of them I know that they tend to be more clannish in their ways of thinking. This creates difficulty in expanding their perceptions about a united Ireland. And how we will get Elfereth and Tissus to be peaceable with one another is going to be a most interesting exercise. The Tissus will undoubtedly remember me, my uncle and my father who fought against them. All these factors have inclined us to not bother with them. However if we are truly to have a united Ireland then we must include them."

Late the next week the diplomatic mission returned. The results were mixed. The King of Elfereth had treated them fairly graciously. He seemed rather suspicious about Evansing troops moving freely across his realm even if it was to deal with Tissus. He said he would consider it but must deal with his High Council. We can expect an answer soon, but he didn't define what that meant.

The news for Darcy was bitter. It made him angry. Edwin and Erith were also disappointed because it delayed getting to the objective of rescuing Percival. They both tried to share the pain that Darcy experienced but their capacity for it was minimal. As much as they cared for Darcy he was no Percival. They continued to accord him great privilege and honor for his role in the rescue of Greer and Orla.

The news several days later from Elfereth was not good. Their King said no, he and his subjects would not allow foreign troops to pass through their land even if it was to attack Tissus.

"Father," Edwin addressed Erith in the King's private chambers, "I have been thinking another option is to send a mission to Tissus directly through our neighbor to the east

318

of us, Carford. Their northern border lies on Tissus' southern border. It dawned on me that my history with Tissus has colored my perceptions as to how cooperative they would be. They may be open to an overture from Evansing as they have no history of war with Evansing. My concern about any of them having memories of me may be my imagination."

The King considered for a moment what Edwin had shared. "Yes, you may be correct as to their willingness to cooperate. I must admit I too was influenced by your view of Tissus being totally unreasonable and terrible to deal with."

That very day Erith wrote up letters to the Kings of Carford and Tissus asking for permission to peacefully enter their lands on an important mission to rescue one of Evansing's subjects.

One ambassador was appointed to the Carford mission. For Tissus, one officer fulfilled both ambassador and military commander duties. Each group was accompanied by 30 soldiers. Initially they travelled together but once they entered Carford they stayed several miles apart so as not to raise alarm amongst the Carfordians. At the Carford border both groups received permission to continue on from the regional commander. He seemed more curious than concerned about this unusual occurrence. The commander couldn't recall any official entourage from Evansing before as the two Kingdoms had minimal connection with each other. There was nothing negative between them, but a certain state of ignoring one another existed.

The mission to Tissus was led by a seasoned military commander who also had a skill in diplomacy. His name was Andronicus. His parents picked a Greek name from early Christian writings. The name meant male victor, warrior. It certainly bore out the belief that the name of a person could prophesy their future. Because Andronicus had a strong military commander presence combined with the sensitivities of a diplomat he made the best choice to deal with the warlike Tissus.

The Tissus were renowned for being a difficult Kingdom to deal with. Their history had entailed being oppressed by Elfereth and Carford for centuries. In recent times this oppression had receded. Now there occurred only periodic raids from both sides of their border with Elfereth. Their relations with Carford had become if not overtly friendly at least live and let live.

As Andronicus and his troop came to the Tissus border they were met by a contingent of Tissus Cavalry who patrolled that area.

The Tissus commander barked out a demand to know their business.

"Greetings, Sir, My name is Andronicus and we are a diplomatic mission from the Kingdom of Evansing. Our King Erith has sent us to talk to your king."

"Let me see your documents," demanded the commander.

Andronicus motioned to his assistant to hand over the official communication from Erith.

Upon review of the parchment the officer's face softened slightly. He ordered that half his troop would accompany the Evansing party to the next military post about ten miles down the road. From there another detachment of troops would be assigned to them.

The atmosphere was surprisingly bright and brilliant as they rode deeper into Tissus territory. Quite unexpected given the reputation of the Tissus. At the same time Andronicus noted how the Tissus seemed a fairly morose lot. This seemed inconsistent with the atmosphere. It didn't make sense. How could the atmosphere be so bright and the people so dark?

The young commander of the Tissus detachment decided to ride alongside Andronicus. He had a curiosity about these strangers from Evansing. Unlike his fellow Tissus citizens he saw how they were mainly cheerful, even when the rain and wind picked up.

"Hello, sir, mind if ride with you?"

"No, of course not. I welcome your company. You can call me Andronicus."

"My name is Erin."

"It's a pleasure to make your acquaintance and thank you for your protective presence."

"You are quite welcome. It is interesting how you consider us protecting you as opposed to keeping an eye on you."

"I realize you are doing both. I also know some of your countrymen may not take kindly to a foreign force riding through their land."

"Yes, that's true, we don't get many foreigners coming here. We aren't the friendliest people which leads me to ask you a question, if I may?"

"Certainly, go ahead, Erin."

"As you have probably noticed we tend to be a rather sad melancholic people. But your men have such a cheerfulness about them. I find this most intriguing. What makes you appear to be so contented and even joyful?"

"I would say it is primarily because we have a sense of purpose. In Evansing from the time we are born we have instilled in us that there is a reason why we are alive. Not only to serve ourselves but others as well. We live life with a sense of being interconnected with other people. We need others and they need us."

There was silence as Erin considered what he had just heard.

"To us that is a strange concept. In Tissus we share the same country and yet in many ways we are scrambling to survive with little concern for the good of our fellow countrymen."

"Well, Erin, if our way of doing life appeals to you, then you could be the catalyst for change in your land."

"What do you mean?"

"I mean you could start showing concern for your fellow countrymen in a way that demonstrates care and concern for them and their lives. As you do so, your own state of being will become progressively more and more cheerful. You can't help but be cheerful when you know you are making a positive difference in the lives of others.

And it will come back to you. Not necessarily directly nor from people you help. But life will repay you."

Again Erin was silent as he considered what he had heard. Then a grin appeared on his face which turned into a look of excited anticipation.

"Yes, I can see what you mean. I will do it. I know it won't be easy, but it is my purpose to change Tissus one person at a time. What convinced me of the truth of your words is how our normally drab oppressive atmosphere has turned bright and beautiful in spite of the rain and wind. Your mere presence in our land has shifted things."

Up ahead they could now see the military outpost where they would be handed off to another unit of Tissus cavalry.

At the outpost they were met with suspicion and distrust. The commander looked irritated at the inconvenience of having to escort them to the capital. His name was Killan and his life history had shaped him into a cruel man who lived for self.

Killan had lost his mother at age eight. He had several younger siblings. He then was given responsibility for their upbringing as his father struggled to keep it all together by working in the fields from dawn to dusk. Growing up with little nurture and experiencing a dearth of his own needs being met created a bitterness in Killan which colored his world in a most unfortunate way. To him life had been unkind and he would be unkind back. It had taken from him and he would take back whatever he could. This turned him into a highly ambitious person who at a relatively young age attained the position of commander. It didn't happen because people liked him. It happened because they feared him. Even his superiors knew crossing him could lead to their unfortunate end. On top of this, Killan had a brilliant mind for military command and got results. This could not be denied. He made his superiors look good.

Andronicus and Killan sized each other up in their initial meeting. They both looked at one another warily. Andronicus of course didn't know Killan's history, but he could read people. To him Killan had a certain cruelty which created unease as to their safety. On the other hand

Killan looked at Andronicus as someone rather curious, an outsider who must be watched carefully. These perspectives raised the tensions between not only these two men but also between their troops.

Killan announced they would leave within two hours. In the meantime the Evansing men could purchase food, top up their canteens and take care of their horses' needs.

Once the Evansing men had a chance to meet together away from Tissus' ears, Andronicus shared his concerns.

"Men, it is important we all be alert and have our weapons ready. This Tissus commander is someone who may be a source of harm."

The Evansing men kept to themselves and ensured they always traveled in small groups if they should venture away from the rest of their men.

When the time came to ride everyone was a little bit tense as to what to expect. Initially everything went smoothly. About 12 miles outside of the capital a hail of arrows struck the Tissus soldiers in the vanguard. Several of them were hit and fell from their horses dead or wounded. The rest of the men all dismounted and dove for cover. Several more Tissus soldiers were struck including Killan.

Andronicus ran over to where Killan lay. He pulled him behind a large rock which provided necessary cover. He inspected the wound which was deep into Killan's shoulder. It didn't appear life threatening in and of itself, but Killan was in shock and losing a lot of blood. Andronicus ripped a piece of material from his cloak and applied pressure to the wound. As well he got Killan to slightly sit up so as to raise the wound above his heart. After ten minutes or so Killan seemed to have some measure of recovery. The bleeding had stopped and the initial shock seemed to have subsided slightly.

In the meantime the attackers slipped away. Apparently all they wanted to do was harass and run.

Killan looked into the eyes of Andronicus.

"Why would you help me? I know you didn't trust me and you certainly don't like me. Why would you risk your life for me?"

"You were in need. There was no time to consider whether I liked you or not. After all I don't really know you."

"Thank you for your help."

"There is still the matter of the arrow. We should get you to a surgeon who can do a proper job of removing it."

"We have no surgeons capable of such niceties. They would butcher me and cut off my shoulder in the process. Most likely I would die."

Silence.

"My chances of survival are slim. Would you be willing to try to remove the arrow?"

Andronicus considered the request. He had seen men operated on by surgeons for such wounds. It required a strong stomach and great care to do the least amount of damage. The biggest concern was stirring up the bleeding and causing more shock.

Andronicus called for his aide to come and assist.

Soon not only his aide but also several Tissus soldiers came concerned about what Andronicus was doing with their commander. Killan assured them it was alright and that he had asked Andronicus to remove the arrow.

Andronicus instructed his aide to bring him some strong drink to give Killan for the pain. Also he got a nearby fallen branch for him to bite down on. He then asked that four of the Tissus soldiers each grab an arm and a leg to hold Killan as steady as possible.

When everyone and everything was in place, Andronicus took out his dagger, carefully wiped it off with a cloth soaked with wine and proceeded to dig it in toward the arrow tip. The reaction was strong. The four men had difficulty in keeping him down. Then Killan relaxed and stayed perfectly still. The only sign of pain were his facial contortions and grunting. He had tapped into a personal strength to keep himself still and rise above the pain.

The bleeding began again in earnest. The aide did his best to apply pressure around the wound not directly being cut. Andronicus sighed relief when he got to the arrow tip and started to pry it out. At the same time he had another soldier lightly pull on the end of the arrow. After twenty minutes or so of prying, cutting and pulling, the arrow eased out. The bloody mess then needed to be closed up. Andronicus then proceeded to stitch the wound with needle and thread after applying some wine to disinfect the wound.

Killan appeared to have fallen into a deep sleep. His face was pale but not such that it caused great alarm. He had lost a lot of blood, but Andronicus had seen men survive who had lost more.

"We need to let him rest for a while so we best ensure our attackers don't find us unprepared."

As Andronicus instructed his men the Tissus men also responded even though of course he had no authority over them. There were no Tissus leaders left as they had been killed in the initial assault. Andronicus asked the Tissus if some of them could go and get a wagon and team of horses to carry Killan into the capital.

After an hour or so Killan started to stir. He opened his eyes and looking up at Andronicus' eyes he gave a weak smile. He looked at his shoulder and saw it was still there.

"Thanks. Something told me you could do it."

"You are welcome. I hope you can use it."

"I will use it and I will use it well."

At that time the Tissus soldiers returned with the horse drawn wagon.

Andronicus helped Killan to his feet and into the wagon.

The party of Evansing and Tissus soldiers all resumed their journey.

Three hours later the turrets of the Tissus capital came into view. The scene had a certain forboding sense about it. To Andronicus this seemed consistent with the way Tissus behaved with its neighbors and even how they related amongst themselves.

When the party came to the gates they were met by a stern looking guard who demanded to know the nature of their business.

One of the Tissus soldiers, appointed as an interim leader spoke up.

"We are escorting an Evansing mission come to see the King. We were ambushed some twelve miles from here and are carrying wounded including Killan our post commander."

The guard had heard of Killan and not wanting to stir up anger with him quickly waved them through. They would now soon see the King of Tissus.

# Chapter 56

At the entrance to the King's castle they were met by a royal advisor. He wanted to know the nature of their business. After being informed he appeared to be uncertain as to how to respond. The nature of the request did not fit the normal types of requests. First of all few Kings requested an audience from the King of Tissus. And certainly permission to enter with a foreign army to rescue one of their countrywomen was unheard of. After all why would anyone want to expend so much effort to rescue a woman?

"Is she part of the Evansing royal family?"

"No, she is not, but she is the intended bride of someone very close to our royal family"

After a few moments deliberation the advisor waved them through.

Andronicus waited in the throne room antechamber for almost an hour before being summoned by a servant to follow him.

Andronicus held his letter scroll tightly. This was the moment they all had been waiting for. In the entrance way to the throne room he paused for a brief moment. He noted the appearance of the King. He had a medium build with a sullen look on his face. He was fairly young. No more than 40 years of age.

When within 20 feet of the King, he stopped to bow and introduced himself. The King said nothing in reply. Andronicus handed off the scroll to a nearby servant who after unscrolling it gave it to the King.

After a moment of reading it he handed it back to the servant.

"What assurances can you give me that you wouldn't be up to any mischief while in our kingdom? After all I am well aware of your kingdom's ambitions to gather all Ireland under your control."

"Sire, we have no quarrel with you and our request harbors no intentions of threatening your sovereignty. We simply desire to recover a most valued citizen of our kingdom. As to assurances what would give you the level of comfort you seek?"

"I want your Prince Edwin held hostage by us until your last soldier leaves our territory."

Andronicus paused for a moment. "I don't have authority to agree to that. If we were to agree to it what hostage would you give us in exchange to assure Prince Edwin's safe return?"

The King looked surprised at such an audacious request. "What do you mean? Why would you expect us to give you a hostage? You are the ones requesting permission to enter our land. It could be characterized as an invasion. What nation would allow such an outrageous request?"

"Sire, I have no authority for such a request. I am simply exploring to see how your request can be fulfilled."

"There will be no entertaining counter conditions. I have given you my condition. Meet it and I will grant you access to our lands for 100 soldiers to be on our territory for seven days."

"Yes, Sire, I will send a messenger at once with your request."

Andronicus then bowed low and backed out of the throne room. His face did not reveal his inner thoughts. He did not expect such a request to be granted by King Erith.

The messenger was dispatched within the hour.

When the messenger arrived in Evansing Castle it was after normal hours so he immediately went to the King's personal quarters. He had been instructed that it had the utmost urgency. One of the guards knocked on the door. One of the King's servants opened the door and asked what he wanted.

"A messenger has returned from Andronicus with an urgent message for the King."

The servant closed the door and returned several moments later. He summoned the messenger to follow him. When he entered the room where the King was seated he bowed low and handed Erith the scroll.

Erith unrolled the scroll and read what Andronicus shared about the King of Tissus' request. Curiously the last line above Andronicus' signature was the statement, "We can do better than this."

Meanwhile Andronicus went to visit Killan.

"How is your recovery, Killan?"

"It is coming along better than expected. My doctor tells me you did as well a job as any surgeon he knows. I told you that all we have are butchers. Your men probably don't realize how fortunate they are to have someone like you with your skills."

"It would not be something I would want to do on a regular basis. However given your outcome it is something I would do to save someone's life or even their limb."

"Killan, I wonder if I could ask a favor?"

"Of course you can. If it's in my power I would do whatever you request."

"I have seen your King." He then explained the reason for their mission.

"As a condition of his approval he wants to take our Crown Prince as a hostage until our last soldier has left Tissus. I don't believe my king will authorize such an agreement. Is there any way you could talk to your king and encourage him to consider another option? He has already told me he will not consider a counter offer so my endeavoring to do so through you may not be advisable. What do you think?"

"The King may well consider the help you gave me. He and I do have some relationship as I have gained some renown for my officer leadership. Leave it with me and I will see how best to broach this subject. I will request an audience with him tomorrow if possible. I can do it under the guise of giving a report on your trustworthiness and what has been noted by us during our ride together."

"I appreciate whatever assistance you can give. I look forward to hearing from you."

After Andronicus left, Killan continued to ponder how to best present the report to produce a  favorable impression but without being obvious about it. That would be difficult because he looked at his shoulder and realized the fact that he still had a shoulder and arm and was still alive would not be easy to be merely matter-of-fact about.

The next day Killan went to see the King after receiving news that he would be allowed a fairly brief audience.

The King looked genuinely concerned about the wound suffered by Killan.

"I had heard that you had been wounded and lost some men in a rebel attack. Your shoulder looks well. Tell me how that is possible?"

"I owe this to Andronicus, the Evansing commander. He demonstrated a remarkable skill in extracting the arrow, minimizing damage in the process and then stitching me up. All the while ensuring I didn't bleed to death."

"It's interesting the messenger never mentioned anything about Andronicus. Tell me more."

"When I got wounded Andronicus ran over and dragged me behind a large rock to provide cover. Then he positioned my shoulder above my heart and started to compress around the wound to get the bleeding to stop."

The King was clearly impressed by what he had heard.

"That is so unlike our soldiers," said the King after a momentary reflection.

"I had taken a rather harsh stance with Andronicus when he spoke to me. Even though he did his best to hide his feelings I could tell he was not happy with me demanding their Prince Edwin as a hostage. I wouldn't have been happy with it either. His act of heroism to save you does impact me. What are your thoughts?"

"Sire, I too had a harsh view of Andronicus and the Evansing party. I gave him no natural reason for wanting to help me, if anything quite the opposite. As I have reflected since my wound I recalled the Evansing people all conducted themselves in a way that was professional and respectful. I have no reason to believe that their troops would do anything except what they stated they would do and then leave. They strike me as trustworthy and potentially valuable allies."

The King considered what had been shared without saying anything.

"Thank you, Killan, for your sharing. Would you stake your life on their good behavior?"

Without hesitation Killan replied, "Yes, Sire, I would."

The King looked at him intently. "Leave it with me and I will see what I decide."

Killan left the audience with a sense of mission accomplished. At least he did as well as could be expected. He knew given the fickle nature of the King that anything was possible. He did find it surprising how much the King seemed to be touched by Andronicus' heroic actions.

Back in Evansing, Erith decided not to authorize Edwin being taken as a hostage. He didn't bother telling Edwin for he knew his risk taking nature. He would wait to see what Andronicus' next dispatch indicated.

Two days later the King of Tissus agreed to grant unconditional permission for 100 Evansing troops to cross into Tissus territory and rescue their countrywoman. He increased the time limit to ten days.

A day earlier the messenger returned from Carford indicating their permission as well. The table had now been set. Next was the assembling of the troops near Evansing's border with Carford and readying them for their departure for Tissus. They were already on alert so they were ready to leave early the next morning. Darcy was their commander.

# *Chapter 57*

A ndronicus and his party would await the additional
soldiers and form part of the military force of 100

troops. The Carford mission's 30 men would also enter into Tissus. This left an additional 39 Evansing soldiers to leave from Evansing to make the 100 soldiers authorized.

The two parties, from Evansing and Carford met in Carford and rode from there to the Tissus capital accompanied by two different detachments on the way to the Tissus capital.

In the capital, the troops met and camped in an area set aside for them. Darcy had identified the most likely place where Aoife would be held. It was almost a day's ride from the capital.

The next day the troops moved out before dawn on their way to Kildare Castle. It was known as a center of Druid activity. Its owner was a Tissus noblewoman sympathetic to Druidry. Several high ranking Druid priests were known to stay at her castle under her protection. Even though she was situated in the Kingdom of Tissus she was not subject to its laws as the King and his people feared her spiritual influences.

The force did not encounter any harassment on their way to the castle. One thing they did notice was a peculiar bird sound that followed them along the way. The bird call was unknown to Darcy and Andronicus. Either it was a bird unique to Tissus or it was an indication they were being watched. Most likely it was the latter.

When they could see the castle, they were impressed at its mass and height. Walls 60 feet high and surrounded by a moat. This would definitely require something extraordinary. Of course Darcy came prepared. He already connected with a number of monks and asked them to band together to facilitate strong divine support. At this point Darcy didn't know what that would look like.

The Evansing army stopped and camped behind a small hill a little over a quarter of a mile from the castle. Darcy and Andronicus along with two other officers conferred as to what would be their next step. Darcy shared that it would be best for them to first do a scouting around the castle and its immediate environs to see what could be gleaned for strategic ideas. The other three officers agreed that this was sensible. Two scouting parties were drawn up of 40 men each with 20 staying back at the camp. The two parties would circle in opposite directions and meet one another on the other side of the castle. In less than half an hour the two groups commenced their trek.

Darcy led one and Andronicus led the other. As they rode along they could see activity along the top of the castle walls. They could see the bowmen lined up, but they had made a point of staying just outside their range, a little over 400 yards. A few arrows did fly, but they stopped after a dozen or so dropped harmlessly short.

During their circuit around the castle they could smell fear coming from inside the castle. Not something you would typically sense, but this was detected by almost all the men. They knew the people inside were afraid. It had to be in response to the work of the monks. Their modest number of troops with no special artillery would not normally spark fear for those inside such a well-fortified castle.

Darcy's group was met by a knight in shining armor. Besides being rather unexpected, he had no horse with him. As they came upon him he stood his ground. Darcy rode up to him and dismounted and walked up to the knight.

"How can you help us?"

The knight looked at him with deep penetrating eyes and at first said nothing.

"I know you are here to help us."

"Yes, at the insistence of your friends I have been sent."

Darcy smiled and nodded in response.

"Trust me to help you." With that he disappeared before their eyes.

Darcy wasn't particularly surprised, but of course his men were quite in a state of uproar at what they had witnessed.

They noted how Darcy now had a smile on his face as they resumed their riding. Unlike Darcy they hadn't all clearly understood what the knight had spoken. Even those who had heard it seemed to not quite comprehend it.

Darcy now knew victory was assured even though he had no way of knowing how it would be achieved.

When they returned to the camp the two parties debriefed their thoughts. The realization of the fear of the castle's inhabitants and the knight's assurances gave them all a surge of confidence. They could now expect success even though they hadn't gained insight as to their next step.

That night Darcy was riding a white winged horse over the castle. As he swooped lower to get a closer look he noticed a pool of water just outside the wall behind a large embankment covered with bushes. They couldn't have seen it on their scouting excursion. He whispered to the horse to land. Upon arriving Darcy dismounted and stepped into the pool, he quickly was submerged as it was over his head. After coming back to the surface to grab his breath he dove again. This time he swam toward the wall and discovered an opening. He swam through it and came up the other side into a small room.

Early the next morning Darcy and Andronicus met to consider what they could do in the meantime. Darcy shared his dream and then awaited for how Andronicus would respond.

"Which part of the castle is the pool?"

Darcy stopped and envisioned his dream.

"It was in the northwest corner. Curiously it looks like part of the moat but it actually has land on either side of it. I believe it must be their fresh water supply so they didn't want to foul it with the water from the moat.

"We need to scout it tonight."

That night Darcy and Andronicus led a small party of five men to check out the location of the pool. They had an extra cover of darkness as it was a New Moon. Even so they took great care to camouflage themselves with bushes and darkened faces. As they crawled closer to the castle they could hear the defenders on top of the walls. Not distinctly but enough to know they were there.

Darcy's dream and the landmarks were clear enough that he could lead them to the exact spot of the pool. Upon reaching it he doffed his outerwear and waded in and swam slowly toward the castle wall. Darcy swam until he reached the wall. He came back to the surface to catch his breath. Then he disappeared underwater and felt along the wall. No opening could be found. He came back up and considered what to do next. He decided he needed to go deeper. So down he went to a greater depth. He found it. Running out of air he came back up. Now he was faced with a do or die decision. Should he continue to swim under the wall and trust he would be able to surface in time to get air? He thought of his beloved and decided she was worth the risk.

Taking a deep breath he dove down and went through the opening and when he tried to surface he was blocked by the roof of the tunnel. He kept swimming and feeling along the roof. Darcy did his best to stay calm as he could feel the pressure of needing to breathe again. Then he came to an opening and rapidly ascended. By the time he hit the surface he gasped for air. When he had settled down a bit he looked around and saw a room. He climbed out of the water. Darcy considered how this way of accessing the castle would only be possible for a small number of men. He estimated perhaps 10 to 15 would be up to such a swim. He noticed a door and went over to it. Slowly opening the door he then looked out into what appeared to be a hallway. There was no light so it was difficult to see anything.

Suddenly a light shone only a few feet from where he was standing. He looked at it for it was simply a ball of light suspended in midair.

It started to move down the hallway. Darcy followed it. He came to a door. He tried to open but it was locked. Then the light went through the keyhole. Darcy tried it again. Now the door opened. He went through the doorway and continued to follow the light until he looked around a corner and saw three men standing guard. Darcy stopped and waited. Then he looked to see where the light had gone. As he watched, the light went up to each of the men and they fell over. Darcy came out of hiding and continued to follow the light. This time the light led him up stairs. When he had gotten halfway up he met two guards walking their rounds. They both yelled the alarm and came after him with their swords drawn. Darcy also drew his sword and engaged them fiercely. He quickly dispatched the first one and then had to fend off the second guard by deflecting his overhand blow. This gave Darcy an opening to thrust back at him. But the guard demonstrated great agility in moving out of the way of his sword tip. Then the guard replied with a slash at Darcy's neck. This was avoided by ducking to avoid the blow. Both men backed away from one another to assess their next maneuver. The light jumped into the face of the guard and he went down.

The light continued up the stairs with Darcy following. He came to a door with the guards already down. The light passed through the keyhole and Darcy opened it to find Aoife sleeping on a bed against the far wall. He walked over to her bed and gently rubbed her arm. Her eyes opened and she almost screamed except that Darcy had placed his hand over her mouth and whispered to her that it was he. When she had settled down and had wakened enough to realize it truly was him she gave him an extended hug and started to sob. Next she got up, got dressed and he led her out back the way they came. The light led the way. They continued down the stairs but this time they met three guards coming up to greet them. At first Darcy waited to see what the light would do, but it just hung suspended seemingly waiting for him to do something. So Darcy did something. He launched himself and came against the first guard feet first. This knocked over the guard and collapsed him into the other two guards sending them all sprawling. Darcy relentless in his pursuit then stabbed and slashed until all three guards lay dead or dying.

Taking Aoife's hand, he led her while continuing to follow the light. This time they avoided all other guards and arrived at the little room where Darcy first entered the castle. He looked into Aoife's eyes and asked if she could swim. She said no. This took him by surprise. He hadn't even given it a thought in all the commotion. He looked around for the light. It was gone. Thinking to himself to stay calm; he smiled at Aoife to allay any fears she may have. He considered telling her to hold her breath and he would take her, but he knew that wouldn't work. He barely had made it by himself. He considered the other option of finding and probably battling their way out of the castle. He looked outside the room and there the light reappeared.

He whispered to the light, "Why would you lead me to a dead end?"

"You assumed this was where we would go so I led you where you expected to go?"

When Darcy heard this he was both a little angry at what it said and a little startled at it speaking to him.

As he pondered what he had just heard he realized he had to surrender control of where they were going to the judgment of the light.

"I am wanting and expecting you to get us both safely out of here in the best way."

With that the light started moving in the opposite direction from where they had come. Aoife and he continued to follow the light. This time they stayed on the same floor. They came to another door. The light waited for them. Darcy opened the door. The light went in first and lit up the room. Inside he could see another door, a very heavy door. This door was bolted on the inside with three layers of thick iron bars. The door itself was made of iron. Very unusual for a door to be made of iron. There was no keyhole in this door. Darcy started to draw out the bars of iron. When he had done the last one he and Aoife looked at the door with hopeful anticipation. Darcy pulled the door open and ... there was another door with again three iron bars. This time they had locks on each bar. He looked for the light, but it wasn't there in the room. In its place was a candle shedding sufficient light.

"I thought you said if I was expecting you to get us both out safely the best way, then that is what you would do."

No answer.

Darcy could feel himself getting angry. He then realized this was not the best response. He needed to stay calm for both their sakes. He looked around the room for something that could be used as a tool to remove the locks. They both looked closely which wasn't hard as the room was not large. They found several shields stacked up but they weren't useful for what they needed. Then Aoife looked more closely along one wall where it met the floor. She rubbed her hand along it and behold she found a rod of iron embedded in the floor. She found one of the ends and lifted it up. She was quite a strong woman and so was able to lift the heavy rod.

In the meantime Darcy hadn't noticed what Aoife had discovered. He was distracted by his feelings of anger and yet trying to avoid showing it or expressing it to Aoife.

"Darcy dear, see what I have found."

He turned around to see the rod. He smiled.

"I am glad I brought you along."

She smiled.

He took the rod from her and placed it in the lowest lock. It barely had room for him to slip it through the lock. He then pulled on the rod. Nothing happened. He did it again. Again nothing. This time Aoife added her pulling power. Snap went the lock. They both smiled. Repeating the process for the remaining two locks resulted in both being broken. They both looked at the door with nervous anticipation. Darcy pulled on the door ring and after several pulls it opened. Looking through the doorway they could see outside into the darkness. As they peered into it moreso, they could see the water of the moat just below.

Darcy looked at Aoife and said, "My dear, you are going to have to trust me to pull you along to shore. Don't struggle just relax and let me do the work."

"Alright, I trust you. I will stay calm."

They both slipped into the water and Darcy firmly grabbed her under her arms and swam towards shore. As they started to get up out of the water, two arrows whizzed by their heads. They ran for cover behind nearby trees. More arrows flew but they fell short and wide as the archers couldn't see them in the darkness. They moved silently towards where the Evansing troops were waiting.

The troops had started to think it best to leave soon to avoid being caught within archer range once the dawning light broke. It was with great joy they saw Darcy return with Aoife. They all returned to their main camp, barely returning before the first rays of light.

As the Evansing camp made immediate arrangements to leave they could see the drawbridge come down. This quickened their pace causing them to leave non-essentials behind. The party started leaving just as they saw a cavalry of horsemen coming towards them. The initial strategy was to outrun them. They had a 400 yards head start and so they rode for the Tissus capital. After 30 minutes or so the cavalry had closed to within 300 yards and commenced shooting arrows. Several Evansing troops were struck, three were killed and two others wounded. Up ahead they could see a dense wood. Andronicus and Darcy both agreed they needed to dismount and set up a defense in the trees.

Once there, even better they found a small knoll where they could gain the advantage of higher ground and greater cover. They were now able to return the fire. The pursuing cavalry quickly dismounted to avoid being decimated. The two opposing forces were approximately the same size and now both had lost a number of men. Both had found good cover and were trying to pick each other off. After almost an hour not much had been accomplished as the archers on both sides only succeeded a few times to kill or wound someone. Andronicus and Darcy considered what the next course of action should be. One option was for a force to be sent around to the left where there was a gully and using its extra cover to ambush the enemy on its right flank. As they discussed this it seemed to be the best tactic available to them. There were 32 men selected to move into the ambush position. Within a half hour they were in position to attack and unleashed volleys of arrows on the unsuspecting enemy. Almost 20 of the opposing troops were struck down in a matter of moments. This greatly disrupted their resolve and some of them broke ranks and ran. At the same time the main Evansing force began to release several volleys. This struck down almost a dozen more. The enemy was caught in between two forces, meaning if they were covered from one they were exposed to the other. Finally the enemy started to withdraw, mounted their horses and fled.

The Evansing troops cheered as they saw them go. Then they dealt with treating the wounded and gathering the dead. Within the hour they were on their way, eager to get to the Tissus capital and the protection it afforded.

When they arrived in the capital they were greeted by Killan. The next day he led a contingent of the Tissus cavalry that escorted them all the way to the Carford border.

"Andronicus, it was a pleasure making your acquaintance and I am eternally grateful for your courage in saving my life. As well, you taught me new ways of living life where people matter."

"Killan, I am pleased to have been able to make a difference. Thank you to you and your men for your protection and service to us. And of course thanks again for your mediation with your king."

The Evansing troops then crossed over the border into Carford.

# Chapter 58

In Carford there were dark storm clouds overhead. At first Darcy was concerned about them all getting thoroughly wet. As he considered them more deeply he started to sense something not quite natural about them. The clouds continued to stay with them all the way to the Evansing border. As they crossed it the clouds stayed behind in Carford.

"Now that is indeed strange," thought Darcy.

As he pondered this he started thinking about Percival. Wondered how he was doing. He regretted leaving Percival imprisoned in order to rescue Aoife. Yet he was delighted at the rescue of his beloved. This conflict made the rescue of Aoife bittersweet.

The Evansing men were relieved to be back home. When they arrived in the capital they were warmly greeted by King Erith and Prince Edwin.

"Darcy, it is so good to see you with Aoife. Enjoy reconnecting with one another for a week or so and then we need to plan our rescue of Percival."

"Yes, Sire, it is my most earnest hope to see Percival free."

Several days later a message came with no indication of who the sender was.

It read: If you attempt to rescue Percival, he will be killed as soon as you leave the Kingdom of Evansing.

Erith, Edwin, and Darcy read the message with great alarm. There was silence as everyone considered what they had read.

The King was the first to express his views, "This is indeed a quandary. New considerations must be made as to how we are going to rescue Percival without leaving Evansing."

Edwin and Darcy looked at him quizzically wondering how such a thing could be possible.

"I don't know how such a thing is possible, but I know anything is possible."

# Epilogue

Accompanied by several guards, Edwin and Greer walked down the road from the castle gates toward the middle of Evansing Town.

"Greer, since we resumed the Quest I have experienced some of the strangest and most harrowing times of my life. As I think about what we accomplished, it doesn't appear to be very much."

"You did eliminate the King of Merethath, our sworn enemy, and Nerland has been restored as a faithful ally. I wish the Kingdom of Tara was more resolved, but they and Merethath have new rulers that may be more amenable to be our allies.

"More importantly, Edwin, I have seen powerful changes in you. They have enabled you to be a wonderful father to Orla and you have a sensitivity and warmth with me that wasn't there before."

Edwin stopped and looked closely into her eyes for a moment.

"Thank you for sharing that with me. I feel much encouraged by what you said. It also gives me greater hope that we will determine a way to rescue Percival and then to resume the Quest."

# About the Author

The author, Glen Klassen had the idea of becoming an author after waking up one morning with the following words popping into his head: "The door inched open ever so gingerly." He went to his computer and wrote about the antics of gorillas that had escaped from the Cincinnati Zoo. After this initial short story he continued to write short pieces until the inspiration came for "Evansing - Heart of the Irish Kingdom" and from it "Unlimited - Anything is Possible." Now the sequel to the first Evansing book is here, "Beyond Evansing - Courage of the Irish Kingdom."

Glen has a passion for growing in personal capacity. He has invested much time and effort in the process of personal growth. Consequently it is a subject in which he has gained substantial insight. He enjoys sharing this knowledge and encouraging others to keep expecting anything is possible regardless of current circumstances.

The author is a professional accountant and speaker whilst also pursuing his passion of being an author. He considers the role of mentoring his four grandchildren to be one of his most important roles in life.

www.ingramcontent.com/pod-product-compliance
Lightning Source LLC
Chambersburg PA
CBHW051132030726
47504CB00004B/827